Simone

Bellevue, WA 98008

SimoneReads@comcast.net
www.sjdennis.com

ISBN: 0-6154-4077-0
ISBN-13: 9780615440774

Simone

"...Fathers, Daughters, Love and War."

A Novel by

S. J. Dennis

Dedication

This book is dedicated to the men and women of the world whose lives were touched by the tumult of World War II. A special thanks to Frank Friedman, Norman Friedman, Larry Gourlie and Richard Thomas, my special veterans of the Battle of the Bulge. My characters are fictional but the spirit of these men inspired each word.

Prologue

I thought I knew the men in my life. I thought their feelings were transparent.

I was wrong.

I thought I knew my ex-husband, at least until he came home and announced he was leaving me for little Kimberly.

Above all I thought I knew my widowed father. Retired and living nearby he was my man; my rock. I knew and could depend on him. At age 70 his life had slipped into a predictable routine. Most days I could look at a clock and, with fair precision, guess what he might be doing at that hour. I knew him well.

It turns out I was even wrong about him. I learned that his life, like a puzzle, was made of many pieces. During my 47 years his life and mine have been loosely connected. I knew the general shape of the puzzle and could fill in many pieces. This past year things changed. Together we turned over new and revealing missing pieces that are just now being put in place. His life is far from over, a work in progress.

There have been times I've wanted to freeze his life puzzle, incomplete as it was, preserving images of the past. Now I'm anxious to move on; to see his puzzle and mine fill in. I want to see what further surprises this man, my father, has for me.

This is my father's story; Frank Larson's story. It's a story of love, lost love, war and hope. It's a story about my favorite man.

Anita Chase, August 1995

1

The frigid night air assaulted Lieutenant Frank Larson as he lay hidden in the snow, curled into a fetal ball near the base of a gnarled old tree. The two German soldiers, clad in white, sat smoking just ten feet away; so close the scent of their unwashed bodies drifted toward him along with the pungent smell of their army issue cigarettes. The cloud shrouded moon cast a glow over the constant stream of German soldiers and their dimly lit vehicles rumbling by on the road below the low bank where the soldiers rested. With his dark uniform loosely covered by a green wool army blanket Larson lay rigid, cursing the generals who sent their men to fight a winter war dressed in green, not white.

Beneath the blanket he gripped his unsheathed bayonet in a gloved hand. Fearful of creating a tell-tale cloud with his warm breath in the freezing night air he struggled to moderate his breathing.

Finishing their cigarettes the two soldiers rose and spoke to each other in loud voices to overcome the noise of a nearby armored car. One laughed and slid down the bank to the road, ambling off in the direction of the traffic. The second turned, stepped deeper into the wood and unbuttoned his fly. A cloud of steam rose from the snow as he left his mark on the Belgian forest. As he buttoned his fly he looked toward the lump in the snow that was Frank Larson, Lieutenant, U. S. Army. He reached down, retrieved his rifle and stepped toward Larson with the rifle extended forward ready to poke the mysterious shape on the snow.

Larson launched his foot forward startling the soldier and knocking him to his back. As the German fell Larson flung his blanket aside, rolled toward the fallen enemy and swung his bayonet wildly in the direction of the stunned man. The German gasped as the blade penetrated his chest. Larson, reaching his knees, gripped the handle with both hands, withdrew it and slammed it home a second time as the German's hands flailed empty space. A low groan from the dying man was muffled by Frank's chest, as he rolled onto his victim, pressing him into the bloody snow.

Frank bolted upright, tangled in his blanket. Heart pounding he squinted at the clock on the bedside table. Its red glowing face announced 2:00 a.m. The city streets below were quiet. He freed himself from the blanket, swung his feet to the edge of the bed and rolled upright, trying to force himself back to reality. After a moment he rose and shuffled into the bathroom to relieve himself and splash cold water on his face. Then, grabbing his bathrobe from the back of the door, he wandered into the living room and plopped into his reading chair. He was not ready to risk sleep again.

It was the book, slipping from his lap and thunking to the floor that jolted Frank back to consciousness. He glanced about the room orienting himself. The sun drenched bay, visible through his sliding glass doors at the balcony, announced the arrival of morning. He studied his watch and mumbled, "Damn. Nearly eight o'clock. The best part of the day already wasted."

How many times had he awakened in a living room chair over the years, he thought? Too many. How many times during his forty-three years of marriage to dear Doris had he disturbed her sleep as well as his own with those damn nightmares that were his alone? He couldn't begin to recall. But she had been patient with him. She knew something was going on in his soul but never pressed for answers. It was a part of him she didn't question. Instead, sometime during the night, she would come to the living room, cover him with a blanket and then return to bed.

She was a good woman, God rest her soul.

He pushed his reluctant old body from the chair, gathered his book and glasses, and walked to the kitchen where his daily dose of vitamins and assorted medications awaited. As he approached his seventieth year the collection of pills grew more exhaustive. He'd told his daughter that by the time he was seventy-five he would just be eating pills with no time for food or drink.

A glance at the Phil's Pharmacy wall calendar confirmed the date; July 4, 1994. Even days meant six pills; odd days meant nine. His pill sorting medication marathon was interrupted by the shrill ringing of the nearby wall phone.

"Good morning Frank dear." It was Sharon Webber from down on the eighth floor.

"When you come down could you bring some coffee creamer? We're out and I know you use it."

"No problem. I'm making myself a note right now. Creamer for Webbers. There, it's done. What time do you want me?"

"Ten o'clock is still good. The cinnamon rolls are cooling right now."

"Well, you tell Dave to warm up the backgammon set. I feel lucky today."

"Now Frank, you and Dave need to be sociable. There'll be others here as well."

"Don't tell me this is one of your romantic set ups again," he said with a laugh.

"Shame on you; of course not. They're just two people from my bridge group."

"Don't tell me. They're both widowed and lovely. Am I close?"

"Oh you tease. Perhaps my little coffee would come off better if you and that husband of mine did lock yourselves in his den and played backgammon. I'll see you at ten."

He placed the phone back in its cradle and leaned against the counter, smiling. Good old Sharon. She and Dave were long time friends. Lately she had taken Frank on as a personal challenge. Doris had been gone for five years and Sharon now figured it was time for Frank to renew his social life. In the last six months she had arranged encounters with more than a dozen women, hoping sparks would fly. But he had proven to be damp tinder and, while he had enjoyed the company of several of the silver haired vixens, as he called them, none had produced sparks.

Sharon kept telling him he was a handsome man, for his age. Hell, he didn't see that as much of a compliment given the sorry condition of many of their friends. But, he was trying to stave off the ravages of time, as he called them. He worked out regularly, cycled in the summer and skied in the winter and struggled to keep himself in shape during the spring and fall. He was pleased that his light brown hair, which was scarce on top, was resisting the arrival of silver streaks which were creeping into the brown hair in the sideburns.

So, while several of Sharon's friends had been attracted to him, the feeling was not mutual.

His good friend Sharon just didn't realize the challenge Frank presented to any would-be cupid. Frank was done loving anew. He loved his daughter Anita. He loved his grandchildren. He loved the memory of his wife. He loved his friends, with a different type of love. But he had no interest in complicating the remainder of his life with new loves. He thought of it as practical, rather than callous. And Sharon Webber didn't know what she was up against.

Leon Chauveau eased his immaculate silver BMW to a stop beside his mother's black Volvo. Stepping from his car he was struck by the sultry silence of the place. Surrounded by the Belgian forest, and nearly two kilometers off of the main road, the quiet on a windless day could be overwhelming. With his feet crunching on the gravel drive Leon walked to the rear of the car and retrieved two bags of groceries before making his way down the narrow path to the cabin, or The Lodge as it had been modestly named years before.

Leon had fond childhood memories of time spent in this place. He could recall the simple cabin that existed during his early years. Over time his father had made a series of improvements making the place larger, more comfortable and suited for both summer and winter. But it was still The Lodge to the family.

"Good morning Mother," he said, spotting her tending the small garden below the long porch on the view side of the cabin. "When are you going to give up and let Mother Nature take over?"

"Oh Leon; I thought I heard a strange noise. And you remembered the groceries. Why don't you put the cold things in the refrigerator and I'll be right up to take care of the rest," she called.

Simone Chauveau pushed her tall, trim body to an upright position and brushed the loose soil from the knees of her khaki cotton pants. The sleeves of her untucked plaid flannel shirt were rolled to the elbow revealing long, thin and tanned forearms which disappeared into well used green gardening gloves. Her shoulder length gray hair was drawn back and held in place by small plastic clips and her crisp facial features were shaded by an old, frayed straw hat. She gathered her small tools into a canvas bag and placed it on the porch before climbing the steps.

Leaving her shoes at the door she swept into the cabin, greeting her forty-six year old son with a casual embrace. "You're a dear to pick up the food for me. It saves me a trip to town."

"How long have you been here this time?"

"Just a week."

"Alone!"

"Well, you're here," she said, flashing a smile at Leon while drying her just washed hands on a towel by the sink.

"Oh, you know what I mean. I just worry about…."

"You worry about an old lady like me up here all alone?"

"Now, I didn't say that, Mother. But what if you fell or something; who would know? And, by the way, Francine is concerned too."

"Well, I'm glad you and your sister are thinking about me but, really, I'm fine. If you'll recall I often spent time here alone even when your father was alive."

"Yes, six years ago and you weren't nearly seventy!"

"I'm painfully aware of my age dear. But the phone works, I watch my step and Rolf and Bertha Lentz walk by here on the ridge trail most mornings. Their home isn't really that far away. Besides, I need to come up here. Since I sold the big house and moved into town I feel so confined. Here I can take a good book, climb into that rocker on the porch and look out over the prettiest half of Belgium. At least I can when I don't fall asleep in the chair," she concluded with a wink.

"You're impossible," said Leon, putting the last of the food in the cupboard. "Maybe I'll try that rocker out while I am here. I could use a little rest."

Anita Chase sat tucked in an easy chair, in her comfortable Queen Ann Hill condo, a short distance north of downtown Seattle. It was located in an older brick apartment house that had been updated and converted to condominiums several years before. Many places on the hill had grand views; hers didn't. She had a peek-a-boo view of the city's landmark Space Needle and a great view of the small park across the street but trees and buildings concealed the high priced views of water and distant mountains. She could have afforded a fancier place, with her generous divorce settlement, but she liked the character and warmth of the building and never regretted her decision.

She was oblivious of the time with a coffee cup close by, the morning newspaper in her lap and the cat sprawled over the chair back, paw resting on her shoulder. The 4th of July advertising inserts were tossed in a loose pile at her feet; out of habit she would glance at them later. The sound of arguing birds could be heard through the windows, still open from the day before when the warm summer sun had driven the outside temperature to eighty degrees; a hot day for normally temperate Seattle. The weather map on the back of Section A promised several more days of the same.

She finished a section, tossed it to the floor and took a sip of coffee while looking over the room. She knew she had over-furnished the place. She kept too many things when she sold her house and then added more furniture when her father sold his. She hoped her sons would relieve her of some of the items when they moved to bigger places but, so far, they had shown a preference for cheap furniture that could tolerate a campus environment. So she just thought of the place as cozy rather than crowded.

Anita had her mother's build, shorter and fuller than her lanky father. Some would say she was plump, but in a pleasing sort of way. She had a round face and dark brown hair and, like her mother, she was determined to keep it that color as she grew older no matter what the gray hair gods proclaimed. She could be comfortable in blue jeans or an evening gown and filled them both nicely. She was attractive without the burden of being beautiful.

As she was taking a sip from her cup a gentle knock startled her causing a minor coffee spill on the newspaper. "Seven o'clock! Who could that be at seven o'clock?" she said, speaking to Bandit, whose alert face was focused on the door, whiskers twitching.

Anita's oversized gray sweats hung loose over her body as she rose from the chair and walked toward the door. Running her fingers through her short, sleep crushed hair she vainly tried to improve her appearance before greeting the world or its representative waiting in the hallway. She squinted through the peep hole as she reached for the brass security chain. "Oh shit," she mumbled, recognizing Liz Bowman, her downstairs neighbor.

"G'morning sunshine," chirped Liz as the door swung open.

"Oh Liz, of course; our walk. Come in, come in. I'll just be a minute. Where did the time go? I had no idea it was seven already," she continued, trying to conceal the fact that she had completely forgotten their planned morning walk. "Help yourself to a cup of coffee."

"Take your time. I'm in no hurry. I have no pressing engagements the rest of the day; actually for the rest of the week if you must know the boring truth," she said as she walked toward Bandit, who was eyeing her warily from the back of the chair. Before he could execute his escape plan she swept him up and, with cat wise hands, melted his resolve with an under-chin rub.

"I was going to wear walking shorts but I notice you're in long pants. Do you think it will be cool down by the water?" Anita called from the bedroom.

"Hey kid, it's warm enough for shorts but when you're over sixty with legs like mine you keep them covered in public."

"Oh Liz, don't talk that way," said Anita as she entered the living room clad in a well worn white polo shirt and khaki shorts. "You look great."

Anita knew a little white lie wouldn't hurt. In truth Liz's sparkling personality was concealed in a squat little body that showed all the signs of too much good food and too little exercise. Nearly the same height as Anita, Liz had a dumpling build accented by too short legs that contributed to a slight duck like waddle when she walked.

Anita unplugged the coffee, took a last look around the kitchen and reached for her car keys. "I can drive."

Liz laughed. "Drive! We're supposed to be going for a walk. We can walk to the park in fifteen minutes or so. Drive indeed!"

Anita paused, embarrassed. "Walk, of course, walk. I can do that."

"Good; we'll both be better for it," said Liz, as the two women stepped into the hall. "Drive to the trail; well I never...."

Frank stepped from the elevator, creamer in hand, tapped on the Webber's door and walked right in. "Is this where the party is?" he hailed, hearing voices in the living room.

"Oh Frank," Sharon responded, "I didn't hear you. Come in and meet my friends," she continued, rounding the corner from the living room, coffee cup in hand.

Sharon was an attractive redhead, tall, plump and bursting with energy. The Webbers and Larsons had been neighbors for many years. The families played, barbecued and even vacationed together. The Webbers had two boys, one older and one younger than Anita, and the two mothers always harbored the dream that one would marry her. Instead the kids just grew up best friends, which was OK with Frank.

"Come in, come in," she continued, air kissing his cheek before ushering him into the living room where two matrons, likely aware of Sharon's matchmaking intent, were sitting demurely on the sofa.

"Frank, I'd like you to meet Eli Mardis and Fran Sutfin. Ladies, Frank Larson."

Frank leaned over the coffee table and shook hands with each in turn saying something witty but forgettable and giving everyone a good laugh. Not wanting to take a seat and risk conversational entrapment he was relieved to see Dave come out of the kitchen with a clear glass carafe of coffee.

"Am I glad to see you old buddy. As you can see they had me outnumbered. Now that you're here perhaps I can get the conversation turned to baseball," Dave said.

"Eli here is quite the baseball fan," Sharon offered. "Isn't that right Eli?"

"We had season tickets for years. We never missed a game. Of course that was before..."

"Wow, now that's what I call a fan," said Frank, moving toward the open deck door. "Now I'd like to know why everyone is sitting inside on a beautiful morning like this. It's gonna be a hot one I bet."

From an old infantryman's point of view Frank knew his was a risky move. If either of the women headed toward the deck his escape route would be cut off. But, assessing their round little bodies settled on the sofa, he assumed it would take more than an eligible man to get them to their feet.

Dave followed him on to the deck. "God, you're a master."

"What do you mean?" he asked, setting his cup on the patio table out of sight of the sofa dwellers.

Dave laughed and took a seat. "Every time Sharon tries to introduce you to a new lady you manage to escape. The only question is, how fast can you make your break? Today's might be a record."

"I hope it's not that obvious and I certainly don't want to hurt Sharon's feelings but..."

"Don't worry about it. She views it as a contest. She figures that, one of these days, you're going to walk into a room and be swept off of your feet by one of her friends. She's planning to just wear you down until that happens."

"If it was anyone but your lovely wife I'd have pushed back long ago. Why do women despair so when they see a happy man living alone? I just don't get it," continued Frank.

Suddenly a string of firecrackers exploded somewhere below them causing Frank to flinch, bumping the table and spilling his coffee into its saucer.

"Whoa, you're jumpy. Are you feeling OK Frank?"

Frank rubbed his temples with his fingertips as if driving a headache away. "Yes, yes. Sorry. I guess I'm a little edgy; didn't sleep that well last night.

Dave slipped into the kitchen, returning with the carafe and several napkins to soak up the spill.

Frank sat staring at the empty office building across the street.

"Do you ever think about your flying days? I mean, you caught holy hell over Germany didn't you?"

Dave nodded his head slowly, as if thinking about some past moment of terror.

"Do you ever think about it; dream about it? I mean does any of that old crap ever bother you?"

"Not so much any more. It used to. It used to be real bad. But now, not so much. How about you?"

"Just between you and me?"

Dave nodded.

"Sometimes, not often, but sometimes I get these nightmares that are so real, so vivid that I wake up expecting to see blood on my hands and can almost smell the cordite from the artillery fire. I mean, when's it going to stop?" He paused, staring into space. "Doris put up with it for years, bless her heart. Maybe it's normal, I don't know. But hell, it's been fifty years...."

"I can recall some rough nights, especially right after the war. What helped me was learning that I wasn't the only one going through that stuff."

"Really? How'd you find that out?"

"I went to the twenty-fifth reunion of our bomb group and have been fairly active since. You get that many old fliers together, telling lies, and you'd be surprised how many of them are going through the same stuff as you."

"Really?"

"You can't be the only Army guy who has a tough night from time to time?"

"Don't know," Frank said, sipping his coffee. "I never asked anyone."

"Yoo hoo boys. Cinnamon rolls are on the table and you have to come in to get them," smiled Sharon, leaning out of the patio door.

Frank chuckled to himself. Sharon won this round. He'd tasted her rolls before.

As for the nightmares, maybe he'd ask Emory.

After fifteen minutes of narrow sidewalks, traffic signals and street crossings Liz and Anita reached the waterfront trail in Edward's Park. Separated from the growling traffic by a rolling expanse of verdant lawn the trail led them to waterfront world, far removed from the asphalt and concrete obstacle course they had just negotiated. With the placid bay water lapping at the shoreline bulkhead and the scent of decaying sea life drifting over the trail they joined the flow of cyclists, skaters and walkers heading north in the morning sun. Urbanized Canada geese glared at them from the lawn they claimed as their own, as if resenting the human intrusions.

"How often do you come down here," asked Anita as she tried to match Liz's waddling but rapid stride.

"First time. I've had big aspirations since I moved in last fall but usually find a reason not to come. I just needed you to inspire me."

"Yes, right, like I'm some inspiration. If you hadn't suggested a walk I would still be sitting home. And I'm embarrassed that you moved in last fall and it took us this long to meet."

"Don't feel bad. It took me three months to meet the people across the hall. We just had different schedules. But living below you I am very familiar with your routine, thumping around the unit like you do!"

"Am I really that noisy?" asked Anita.

"Just kidding. You're a fine neighbor," Liz replied looking out over the water. "What's that big black ship out there? I don't recall seeing that before."

"That's where they launch tonight's fireworks. Haven't you ever watched the show?"

"John and I watched it on TV a few times but never down here. I don't like big crowds."

"Hey, a free bench. What say we stop and enjoy the view," Anita said, as she crossed the path and took over the just vacated bench. Settling in she continued, "If you don't mind me asking, what happened to your husband; was it a long illness or something?"

Liz plopped down beside her, reaching for the water bottle in her fanny pack. "No, it was quick; he had a heart attack and that was it. It was unfair in many ways. Unlike me he was the picture of health. There were no signs it was coming. Just one day he was gone and that was that."

"I'm so sorry."

"Yes, well, it happens. How about you? You were married weren't you?"

Anita pursed her lips and nodded. "Married and divorced."

"Sorry. Was it recent?"

"Six years last month," Anita said with a nervous laugh.

"Are you on good terms?"

"No terms really. When the two boys were living with me we had to talk from time to time. Now, with the boys on their own, there's no need to talk which is fine with me. The less I see of him and his little Kimberly the better."

The two women gazed over the water, watching several small black birds diving into the murky water in pursuit of a morning meal.

"You know what?" Anita asked, breaking the brief silence. "You should come to my dad's tonight. He lives on the top floor of that taller grey building over there," she said pointing "You can see the fireworks without fighting the crowd."

Liz seemed to tense, turning to Anita. "Ah, I appreciate the invite but, if you're trying to fix me up with your father then…."

"Oh God, no," Anita replied with a laugh. "I just thought you might enjoy the show and…."

"Well, forgive me then," Liz responded, the tension slipping away. "It's just that so many people think I need a man in my life that I've grown a little wary."

"It's just dinner and fireworks, no romance," laughed Anita. "I insist that you leave my father alone. Besides, he wouldn't be interested. His passion seems to have been buried with my mother. She was his one and only love."

"Now I'm embarrassed. Anyway, I don't want to intrude. He might…"

"It wouldn't be an intrusion. Besides, a new face will liven things up. It's no big deal. I'll let him know and…"

"Is he OK, health-wise I mean?"

"Heavens yes! He's in great shape for a 70 year-old. It just seems he's getting crabbier in his old age. Maybe I nag too much; daughters do that you know," Anita said with a smile.

"Well, I would insist on bringing something."

"The price of admission is a bottle of cheap wine. Now say no more and let's get going. We're supposed to be getting exercise here, aren't we?" said Anita, rising from the bench and joining the flow of southbound walkers with Liz on her heels.

Leon was jolted awake by the slamming of the screen door as Simone stepped onto the wide porch burdened by a tray of fruits, cheeses and a thinly sliced baguette. "Wake up Sleeping Beauty; it is time for lunch."

"I must have dozed off," said Leon, rubbing his eyes and trying to regain his focus.

"If you call sleeping for an hour dozing then yes, you did doze off. I thought you might enjoy a little snack and then go for a short hike with me," she said, pulling up a wooden chair and sitting down. "You must be working too hard."

Leon filled a napkin with apple slices and settled back in the rocker. "Actually I have been burning a candle at both ends as they say. You see, I am in negotiations over a new position. In fact I need to head for Brussels right after breakfast tomorrow. I have a job interview at dinner time."

"A job interview; you're leaving the law firm? I thought you enjoyed your work."

"Oh I do; I really do. But this would be a good opportunity for me and I could use a little change in my life. It's a long shot but very interesting," he said, settling into a chair on the porch near his mother.

"Well, is that all you're going to tell me?"

"For now, yes. I don't want to jinx the interview. Besides, I came up here to get away from thinking about work and Brussels."

"Enough said. Just let me know if anything happens. In the meantime, I'll think positive thoughts for you."

"Say, if this opportunity works out I will be getting rid of my car. Would you have any interest? Yours is starting to look a little ragged."

"Well, you're just full of compliments today. No thanks. Mine is running fine and I'm still not interested in a German car."

"Mother, it's 1994. The war's been over for nearly fifty years."

"I'm very much aware of that but I still don't want your BMX or BMC or whatever it is."

"It's a BMW but, OK, I'll say no more."

Mother and son sat quietly as the sun began to encroach on the narrow porch. Leon finally broke the spell of silence. "What's your earliest recollection of this place?"

"Oh goodness," she said, tipping her head back in a thoughtful pose. "I don't know. I was just a young girl; I do remember that. When I was growing up The Lodge was little more than a one room shack with smoky lanterns for light and a wood stove of sorts for heat and cooking. My Father did some work to make it more comfortable but your father and I made most of the real improvements. The road in was pretty rough until after the war and then we had the driveway cut in so we could drive the last few hundred meters or so."

"Oh, I remember that. We had to carry everything down a narrow path."

"Exactly. It didn't take many trips lugging babies, food and all our gear to convince your father that we needed to be able to drive closer. Then, over time, Jules kept adding things to make it more comfortable."

"Didn't you live up here for a while when you were first married?" Leon asked, savoring his cool beer.

"No, it was right after the war, before I was married. It was my own special place and I loved it. I needed it. But that was a long time ago. A very long time ago.

"Welcome to my humble home," said Frank as he greeted Liz and Anita. Noticing the wine he continued, "You didn't need to bring anything."

"It's nice to meet you Mr. Larson. Anita said the same thing. But please accept this humble bottle as my sole dinner contribution," Liz responded, handing over a bottle tied with red, white and blue ribbons.

"I can do that," he said, accepting the wine. "And call me Frank. Mr. Larson makes me feel older than I am. Now why don't you make yourself at home while I finish in the kitchen?"

"Take in this view," said Anita, leading Liz to the balcony. "I told you it was good but check it out."

The two women stepped onto the deck where the early evening sun was reflecting off of the rippled blue bay below.

Frank glared after them for a moment before returning to the kitchen where he picked up his knife and began slicing tomatoes. The first cut left only a slice of skin, the second a wedge and the third nearly cut his hand. He slammed down the knife and, wiping his hand on a towel, called to Anita.

Leaving Liz alone she stepped from the deck. "What's up?"

"I need to show you something, some papers, back here in the den," he replied, leading the way.

"Is something wrong? You look…."

"Nothing's wrong ," he replied, entering the small room. "I'm fine and I don't need you trying to fix me up with single women. I am…."

"Whoa now. What on earth are you talking about?" she bristled.

"This Liz woman. Don't tell me you're not trying to interest me in….?

"Oh dad," she said, stepping forward, wrapping him in her arms. "You're so funny. Liz is a friend, that's all. Besides, if I was trying to set you up I'd come up with someone your age, not a 62 year old."

"Really, just a friend of yours?"

"Just a friend of mine. Besides, I'm not sure I'd like the idea of you with another lady. You're mom's guy." She released him, took his hand and pulled him toward the door. "Now, let's get back to our guest.

"Well, I'm having enough trouble fending off Sharon Webber's widow patrol. I don't…." He stopped still holding Anita's hand. "Wait a minute. You don't think I could handle a 62 year old? I'm not dead and buried you know."

Laughing, Anita pulled him from the den. "OK, OK, OK. So you can handle a younger woman. But not this younger woman. Liz is just my friend. I'll let Sharon handle the chick parade."

He released her hand and gave a teasing swat to her rear as she headed toward the deck. With his mind at ease the rest of the condiment slicing was more successful and he soon had a plate brimming with tomatoes, onions and lettuce, ready for the burger onslaught.

Understanding Anita's intent, he could look at Liz in a different light. He hadn't heard of this Liz person but was glad Anita seemed to enjoy her company. In his view she needed some new friends, having lost many of the old ones in the divorce. In his view, if anyone needed "fixing up" it was Anita.

"Boy, it's hot out there," said Anita, stepping in from the deck and into the refreshing breeze stirred up by two large fans which were sweeping separate arcs across the expanse of the living room. "Who else is coming? I see you've set for five."

"The Webbers are coming up. Their view is a bit restricted downstairs and, besides, I owe them about ten meals. They're always having me down to dinner."

"It'll be good to see them." Turning to Liz she continued, "The Webbers were our neighbors growing up. They were like a second family to me. You'll enjoy them."

Anita poured two ice teas and then joined Liz sitting on stools across the counter where Frank worked in his white apron with "Le Chef De Barbecue" emblazoned across his chest. "Nice apron Dad."

He smiled and turned to Liz, "A gift from my daughter." He rearranged the tomatoes on the plate and then continued. "Well Liz, are you new to the area?"

"New to Anita's building but not to the area."

"She lost her husband last year Dad. That's when she decided to try in-city living and now she is my downstairs neighbor."

"I'm sorry to hear about your husband. You're too young to have to face that sort of thing."

"And you're too kind," Liz replied, studying Frank over the rim of her glass.

The kitchen discussion was interrupted by the arrival of the Webbers who entered without knocking. Sharon added her garden salad to the menu and Frank was soon smoking up the neighborhood with his secret recipe hamburgers on the outside grill. To the relief of the downwind neighbors the grilling soon concluded and the dinner party gathered at the table.

"I don't know what I'm going to do about your father, Anita," said Sharon as they finished passing the food. "I'm trying to improve his social life and he resists my every effort. Why just today I introduced him to two of my oldest friends and he just couldn't wait to escape with Dave here and engage in man talk, as he calls it."

"Don't listen to her Anita. She's trying to make me her bridge club stud and I'm not up for that sort of thing," he said with a twinkle in his eye.

"Oh Frank!" said Sharon.

"Father!" echoed Anita.

"Dave, tell Anita that's not true," Sharon continued.

"Well, he does have a point there," said Dave, mopping up the wine he spilled while laughing.

Liz looked from face to face not sure who to believe.

"Oh you men! I'm only thinking of you Frank. You're too young and vigorous to live like a monk. No one is trying to seduce you, if that's what you're afraid of. But it wouldn't hurt you to escort someone to a play or concert from time to time," said Sharon. "Don't you agree, Anita?"

"Well I don't know," Anita replied, looking at her smirking father at the end of the table. "I guess I can see dad's point a little. And maybe it's, oh I don't know; maybe it's too soon."

Sharon gave Anita a surprised look. "Too soon? Honey, at our age, nothing is too soon. Times a wasting."

Anita shrugged and took a sip of wine.

"Well, first of all, I think I get out plenty. Second I don't know many monks who would be spending the evening sitting here on my deck, drinking wine with three lovely women. Actually they might be drinking wine but the woman part still applies. And third....I can't think of a third reason, but I will."

"Why don't you give the poor guy a break?" chimed in Dave. "Why just the other day he told me he had three loves; his boat, his daughter and his grandsons. Isn't that right Frank?"

"Yes, but not necessarily in that order."

"David Webber, you're no help at all. But I'll deal with you later," said Sharon with an exasperated laugh. "Now we'd better get the table cleared. We have a fireworks show to watch."

"It was sure nice of you two to help clean up," said Frank, as Liz and Anita finished loading the dishwasher.

"Oh Dad, it's no big deal. Besides, hopefully the traffic has thinned out a little by now. Say, what inspired you to clean your guest room? It looks like a burglar hit the place."

"I meant to tell you. Emory and Lenore Rushing are coming up from Portland for a few days. I invited them to stay here and that gave me the boost I needed to straighten the room out. You remember them don't you?"

"The name. But I'm not sure I'd recognize them if I met them on the street," Anita replied, searching for her car keys. "What's the occasion?"

"Emory is participating in some sort of medical test at University Hospital. He has emphysema real bad. Anyway, he called looking for hotel suggestions and I invited him to stay here. Say, if you're not busy tomorrow, why don't you come by for dinner. I'd like them to see you."

"If I'm not busy; like I have such a full calendar! Sure, I'll come," she said, giving him a light kiss on the cheek.

"It was nice to meet you Frank. Thanks for having me," said Liz, offering her hand.

"My pleasure. Now you take good care of my girl, won't you?" he said with a smile.

Liz and Anita were soon sitting at the garage exit, waiting for a break in the traffic.

"Your dad seems like a great guy," Liz offered.

"Oh he's special," she replied, gunning the car into an opening in the traffic. "I sure wish I could place this Rushing couple. I'm sure I met them. I think he was one of Dad's Army buddies."

"So he's a veteran?"

"World War II."

"What did he do?" asked Liz.

"Dad never talked about the war. He was in the Army. He was in Europe; end of story. We never asked for more and he never offered it. While growing up it was ancient history as far as I was concerned."

"It's not something they talk about," offered Liz. "I really had to work to get anything out of my husband about his Korea experience."

"Actually I don't know much about the pre-Anita Dad. I do know he returned from the war, went to school on the GI Bill and met and married mom. She told me those details.

"What did he do for a living?"

"After college, he went to work for Swenson Homes, a small homebuilder. Mr. Swenson used to brag that hiring dad was the best business decision he ever made. Eventually dad bought him out and took over the company. Through good times and bad that company generated the income that paid my parents bills and allowed us to live well. Yes, I knew about the homebuilding company."

"And you're an only child?"

Anita nodded, turning into her garage. "Maybe I was a disappointment for dad. A son might have joined him in the business and carried on the homebuilding tradition. Growing up he would take me on job-site visits and talk about the glories of building homes. But I never had a desire to build homes. Since mom couldn't have any more children, dad just had to learn to live with a girl."

Anita coasted to a stop in her assigned parking space. "I do remember times when old Army buddies, passing through the Seattle area, would stop to visit for an afternoon or evening. Wives and kids weren't included in the conversation. The men usually sat in the den or on the patio and talked quietly, laughing occasionally. The wives would join mom in the kitchen and talk about their kids, the cost of braces and the new Duncan Hines cake mix. And the kids, if there were any, would be mine to entertain."

"And then they would be gone. I think some sent Christmas cards but, since I couldn't tell college friends from Army friends, I never knew what groups he was keeping in touch with. I suspect that would have been when I met the Rushings. I guess I'll find out tomorrow."

2

"God what a great spot," said Emory Rushing when Frank rejoined him on the deck carrying two glasses of iced tea.

"It's working out OK," he responded, joining Emory at the table.

"So how long you been here?" Emory asked.

"Just over a year; moved in last spring. Probably should have done it sooner but, well you know, it was hard to give up the house and all the stuff Doris and I'd accumulated."

"I know what you mean. Moving up to Portland was a real pain in the ass. Been in San Diego for thirty years. But Lenore wanted to be near the grandchildren and, I suspect, she wanted our boys handy if this damn emphysema keeps dragging me down. Anyway, the way I feel I couldn't have handled the big house much longer anyway."

"Yes, I thought I'd miss the house and yard and all that goes with it. But Anita kept nagging and I suspect she was right. This place is a lot easier for me and I really don't miss all the work you have with a house."

"How'd you pick this place? I mean, a downtown high rise is a big change."

"We have several friends who'd moved here and raved about the location; that made the decision easier."

"The hardest thing for us was disposing of all the stuff we'd accumulated over the years. But we went from 4,300 square feet to about 2,000. Things just had to go."

"Well get this. The guy that had this wanted to sell it furnished. I balked and then finally said, 'what the hell.' So I dumped everything from the old house. In some ways it was easier that way. Anita thought I was nuts but, I guess you just have to do things like that."

The men fell silent, watching the traffic on the bay. Sure, thought Frank, dumping the furniture hadn't been too bad. But leaving the memories behind; now that had been the hard part. He could still recall the last walk through the old house just before the buyers took over. He'd visited Doris' kitchen, her laundry room, her potting shed and all the other places where she'd spent her time and created memories. They'd lived in that house for over thirty years; he'd built it just for her. Anita, who was with him, was moved to tears by the experience.

So he'd disposed of furniture and things they had accumulated over the years. But the memories were with him still. And that seemed right to Frank.

Frank refilled their ice tea glasses then settled back and studied the man he had not seen for years. Emory's desiccated appearance was troubling. The former Emory had a cherubic face and full, well fed features. The Emory sitting at the table was a rail thin shell with leathery smoker's skin hanging beneath his eyes and jowls. But his spirits were still high and he displayed his characteristic exuberance though tethered to a small oxygen tank by a clear plastic hose that curled up from the tank and wound behind his ears before discharging its precious contents into his lungs.

Frank's eyes moved from the life-giving hose to the kitchen where Emory's wife could be seen moving from refrigerator to stove. "Boy that wife of yours has taken over the kitchen. If the dinner is as good as it looks I may ask her to stay full time."

"She does love to cook, though you'd never know it looking at me," said Emory, poking the flat stomach on his gaunt one hundred and thirty pound frame.

The two veterans were still enjoying the deck view when Anita appeared at the open sliding door. "Anita, you snuck up on us. Come on out. Emory, this is my little girl Anita."

Emory push himself to his feet. "Little girl indeed. Why you're a fine looking young lady."

"Oh Dad, I like your friend," said Anita, shaking Emory's hand.

"Oh good gracious," said Lenore, joining them on the deck, "the last time we met you still had braces and were embarrassed that you had to entertain our son while we had dinner with your folks."

"Nice to see you again," Anita said, with a look that suggested she had no recollection of ever having seen them before.

"It's so nice of your father to put us up. It will give the guys a chance to retell old tales and sure beats some old hotel room," Lenore continued.

"When they called I told them the only thing I wanted in return were a couple of home cooked meals while they were here. Well you wouldn't believe the food she brought along. Tonight we're having lasagna and she has a couple of frozen casseroles for other nights. I'm going to be living well," said Frank, giving Lenore a gentle hug. "I'm putting on weight just smelling the garlic bread."

"Speaking of dinner, I'd best get back to it," said Lenore.

Anita soon joined her, leaving the two men laughing on the deck.

"Dad is going to enjoy having some good food for a change. I don't think he pays much attention to what he eats when he's alone," Anita offered, helping herself to a glass of wine from the carton in the refrigerator. "He knows how to do two things; microwave and barbeque. This may be the first time the oven's been hot for months!"

Lenore laughed and continued her search for a serving dish. "Anita, all kidding aside, staying with your father means so much to us. I hope their story telling will get Emory's mind off of his health. He hasn't been doing well lately as you can see. By comparison your father seems to be fit as a fiddle."

"Dad? Oh he's a tough one all right. He's had a few little problems but nothing serious. Do you have any idea how the two of them met. Dad has never said."

"That's no surprise. Most old Army guys are pretty quiet about the war. Emory says the ones that talked the most were furthest from the front. The ones who were in the thick of things tended to clam up. Your dad was in the thick of it."

"Really?"

"Ask'em. Once you get them started you may not get them stopped," she said with a laugh.

"So when did you two meet?" asked Anita, as she served the chocolate sundaes with excess sauce dripping down the sides of the goblets.

"January of '44," Emory responded. "God, Frank. Just think. That was fifty years ago. Well, anyway Anita, it was January of '44 in Wales when we were both assigned to the 28th Division. The Division had been in country since the fall of '43 so we came in as green replacements."

"Tell her about Frank's heroics," offered Lenore.

"I'm sure Anita doesn't want...," began Frank, while he tried to swallow a mouthful of ice cream.

"What heroics?" Anita interrupted.

"Oh that," Emory with a chuckle. "Well, you see, the 28th was a tight knit bunch; they'd been together since 1942 in the States. So along comes a batch of new officers, like Frank and me, and we're not exactly welcomed with open arms. Now, I hadn't met Frank at this point but everyone heard this story...."

"And embellished it," added Frank.

"Yes, right. Well this is the gospel truth. Frank comes in and replaces a well liked Platoon leader who gets promoted or transferred or something. So most troops like to go out of their way to make a young officer's life miserable and Frank's Platoon was no exception. But that all changed a February night in 1944."

"So what happened," asked Anita who is hearing about a side of her dad she had not heard about before.

"Well, you see, that night the Company is engaged in assault training, storming an English beach. As Frank's platoon steps off their boat a popular squad leader, Rocky something, just disappears under the water. I don't know what he stepped into, but weighted down with his equipment he just vanished. So Frank just drops all his sh...err, all his gear and is in the water in a flash. He wrestles this guy out of the depression and drags him to shallow water where others grabbed him and hauled him to dry ground. And there you have it; Frank Larson, instant hero."

"And you were accepted by the old timers after that?" asked Anita turning to Frank.

"It was kind of funny. The guy I pulled out never said anything about the incident but it was like I'd passed a test of some sort. I was now one of them and Rocky and the other squad leaders began to make my life much easier. I guess I'd earned my spurs as they say."

"I hear this story and say to myself that I've got to meet this Larson guy. So I look him up, we hit it off and here we are," concluded Emory with a serious coughing spell.

"Honey, you'd better save your strength for tomorrow," said Lenore, as she began clearing the table. "It's time for you to be in bed."

"Gosh it's getting late," said Anita, following Lenore's lead. "I need to be getting home too."

"Don't worry about the dishes dear," said Lenore. "I've got plenty of time. If I need help I'll enlist Frank here."

And she will too, thought Frank. So much for my uncomplicated bachelor life.

Anita walked from the elevator thinking over the evening's conversation. Emory was a cute old man and Lenore seemed like a dear. Lenore reminded Anita of her own mother, the way she commanded the kitchen. Most intriguing was the glimpse into her father's past. She had never heard that hero story. What else was locked up in his memory waiting to be shared?

Anita tossed her coat on the sofa and the mail on the dining room table. Then, as she swept Bandit from the floor at her feet, she pressed the blinking playback button on her answering machine.

"Hi, Liz here," came the scratchy message. "I picked up a package the mail lady left in the lobby for you. I'll be up until eleven if you want to pick it up. Bye now."

"Well Bandit," Anita said, while opening a pouch of cat food, "I need to see Liz for a minute. This should keep you quiet for a while."

Setting Bandit and food on the floor she gave him one more rub, grabbed her keys and headed downstairs.

"Anita, come on in," greeted Liz, who was clad in long khaki shorts and a loose fitting top. "Your package is on the table there. Can I get you something to drink?"

"If it's not too late for you I could use a cool diet something."

"Coke?"

"Fine. In fact a drop of rum wouldn't be too bad either. Boy, it's a toasty evening."

"Sit near the fan; it helps. How was dinner?"

Anita gave Liz a quick description of the evening. "You know, that story about Dad jumping in the water after some guy is really bothering me. Not the story itself, but it makes me wonder how many other stories I haven't heard; stories I would like to hear."

"Would he talk about his past if you asked?"

"I don't know. I'm not sure I even know the right questions to ask. It's funny isn't it? You know a person your whole life and yet may not actually know him at all."

"I can relate to that. My folks died at about the same time and, except for my aunt, I suddenly found I had lost the key to our family's past. It was very frustrating. How about your mom? Were you close to her?"

"Funny you should ask. Mom and I were real close and I thought I knew her well. But when she died I suddenly became aware of all the gaps that existed in her life story. I wanted to learn about her as a child; where she had traveled; who she had loved; what dreams she'd pursued. I wanted to hear about her parents, her friends, her fears, her passions. I wanted to go through mother's photo albums and learn who those people were, staring back at me. I wanted to ask question after question. And then she was gone; all those memories were gone with her, never to be retrieved."

"It sounds like this Emory is more talkative than Frank. Maybe you can get some stories out of him."

"Maybe," replied Anita, stirring her ice with her finger. "Maybe Emory's visit is a blessing in disguise. There's a lot I don't know about Dad's life, particularly the Army years. There are some big blank spots on his life canvas that need to be painted in. Perhaps Emory can provide the paint. At least that's what I'm thinking now."

"If you want advice from old Liz, or even if you don't, I would suggest you get your little backside over there as often as you can while this Emory fellow is in town and see what you can pry out of them. With my husband I always found it was easier to get him started if one of his old buddies was there to spur him on."

"Was he in the Army?"

"Nope; Marines in Korea. And, let me tell you, it marked him forever."

Anita glance at her watch and jumped to her feet. "Good grief; it's eleven-thirty and I have to work tomorrow. Thanks for the drink and for grabbing the package. And if you don't see me around for a few days you'll know I've launched operation Emory."

"Good luck. I suspect you won't have any trouble wrangling a dinner invitation from Frank."

"No, I suppose not," said Anita, as she headed for the stairway. "The challenge will be wrangling a few stories out of him. But I think it'll be worth the effort."

The sound of the Glenn Miller Orchestra drifted into the kitchen from Frank's oldies station on the living room stereo. "Anita is a lovely girl. And you say she's single?" asked Lenore as she washed the last of the serving pieces.

"Was married; divorced several years ago. Nasty thing it was. If I'd been younger I would've kicked his ass, if you'll excuse the expression, for what he did to Anita. Imagine, after nearly twenty years of marriage he runs off with some bimbo."

Frank finished drying a sauce pan and continued. "Doris always liked the guy; I didn't. He had too much money and too little sense and it all showed in the end. But she got a decent settlement and the two boys have turned out OK so, as divorces go, it could have been worse. Between Doris' cancer and the divorce Anita had to go through two crummy years in a row."

"And so did you, I suspect."

"Yes, so did I," he replied as he watched Lenore wipe down the counters, much as Doris would have done.

She stood back, surveying her work and then, apparently satisfied, hung her apron in the broom closet. "I think I'll check on Emory," she said, slipping from the kitchen.

Frank left his towel in a heap on the counter and wandered out on the deck to look over the sparkling bay.

"May I join you?" Lenore asked moments later as she took a seat on the deck. "My, it's warm tonight."

"Uh uh," muttered Frank as he settled into a deck chair. They sat watching a brightly lit airliner settle into its final approach over the bay. "If you don't mind my asking, how is Emory really doing? He's lost so much weight he looks like a different person to me."

"Not well I fear. Not well at all. Even with the oxygen it keeps getting harder for him to get around. I doubt the doctor will even permit him to go to the reunion and he has his heart set on going."

"What reunion?"

"Your reunion; the 28th Division reunion in Belgium. Aren't you going?"

"Didn't know about it. I haven't kept up with that stuff like Emory has. When is it?"

"This fall. The reunions have been real important to him. We went to Belgium in '69 for the twenty-fifth anniversary of the Battle of the Bulge. That started things. He's been to a number of the Divisions reunions in this country and the both of us went back to Belgium in '84 for the fortieth anniversary celebration. He still keeps in touch with a few guys he's met over the years."

"I was only too happy to get out of my Army greens a long time ago. The less I'm reminded of those days the better."

"But Frank, those trips to Belgium were wonderful. The people were so friendly and grateful for what you boys did. They treated us like royalty. Emory liked that. Maybe the trips helped give him closure; yes, I think that's what they call it, closure."

"Hmmm."

"Maybe you were lucky. Emory has met some guys who had no problems. They just seemed to forget the whole experience and get on with their lives. It really helped him to be around others who were still struggling with the memories of whatever you guys went through over there. Anyway, the doctor is not optimistic about the Belgian trip or his recovery."

Frank stared at the distant shore, just a black strip across the bay. Closure! Now what the hell was closure? It sounded like some sort of psychobabble to him. It would take more than meeting a bunch of other veterans to erase the memory of those terrifying times during the winter of '44.

"Isn't this great; macaroni salad?" said Frank, as he passed the bowl to Anita. "Nothing better on a hot day; cold macaroni salad."

"It looks great. But I suspect poor Lenore had to labor in your hot kitchen to make it so you'd better appreciate it," replied Anita as she dished up a generous helping.

Lenore laughed. "Actually I made it this morning before we went to the hospital so the kitchen was still cool."

"How are the treatments going?" asked Anita, turning to Emory.

"So far it's just been a bunch of people poking me, drawing blood and talking gibberish so I can't understand a thing. I have no idea what they are up to but, what the hey, I'm getting a lot of attention."

Frank surveyed the table scene. It was nice to have company for dinner. Anita was a frequent visitor but it was different having the Rushings actually living there. He'd feared they might disrupt his routine but, so far, no problem. He enjoyed seeing Lenore busy in the kitchen; a kitchen that had not seen the hand of a good cook since he moved in.

The dinner conversation wandered, covering a range of topics from politics to prostate cancer. Eventually a comment about the war slipped into the conversation. Taking advantage of the shift Anita lofted her first get-to-know-her-father-better question toward the two men.

"So Dad, you were eighteen or nineteen when you were drafted. Had you just finished high school?"

"I was eighteen and didn't wait to be drafted. I joined up," replied Frank, with Emory nodding in agreement beside him. "Your two uncles were in the Navy and doing their part. My father pushed the Army for me. He had fond memories of his Army days during World War I. It didn't dawn on me until later that his good days were spent in training camp in the States. His war ended before he ever heard a shot fired in anger. I now suspect that no father who had been in the World War I trenches would recommend the Army to their son."

"So you just walked into a recruiter's office and enlisted?" pressed Anita.

"Actually my three best friends, Reggie, Alex and Steve, joined me at the recruiter's office shortly after graduation in '43. We were proud, our fathers were proud and, I suspect, our mothers were frightened. Mothers are wise."

"Same with me except that I took some ROTC in college first," said Emory. "Of course, I didn't know your father at the time. You have to understand, we thought it was a good war. Our side was good. The other side was evil. It was all black and white; no equivocation. It wasn't like some later wars where it was hard to tell the good guys from the bad."

Frank returned with a carafe of wine and refilled the glasses before continuing. "When we enlisted the four of us planned on fighting the Germans together. But we separated soon after we entered training, assigned to different units. The Army decided I was special and sent me off to Officer Candidate School with the college boys. I didn't realize it was because they went through so many young officers."

"Dad, I've never heard of any of those high school friends. Did you keep track of them later?"

"I never saw Alex or Steve again. Both died in some muddy hole in some muddy field in some far off land. Reggie made it to England in the Supply Corps and was never near the front. I saw him at a high school reunion once and discovered we'd been in different wars. I was in the front and he was in the rear. But enough about that old stuff. Anyone for ice cream?" asked Frank, rising from the table.

"I know I was sure anxious to get into the action," offered Emory, ignoring Frank. "I couldn't wait to complete the training. I wanted to be a good officer. I wanted to lead men. So I tried to learn all the skills of soldiering. I earned my little gold second lieutenant's bars and proudly pinned them to my collar. I didn't know at the time that 2nd lieutenants were interchangeable and expendable. They taught us to lead from the front which, we later learned, was not a healthy place to be. But I was ready to conquer the world when I finished training and boarded a train for New Jersey with a thousand other young men in green for the great adventure that was war in Europe. I remember looking around that rail car and realizing for the first time how young and inexperienced we all were."

Frank returned, distributing four heaping bowls of ice cream. "How many times have you heard these stories, Lenore?" Frank asked.

Lenore smiled without reply.

"Say Frank," Emory continued, "you should come to the Battle of the Bulge reunion this fall. Imagine, the 28th Division returns to the scene of our glorious victory fifty years ago."

Frank continued to savor the ice cream without responding. A victory for the 28th, he thought? On the first day of that battle one Regiment was obliterated and the other two decimated. That is considered a victory? In the end the good guys won but much of the 28th Division simply did not exist, crushed under the weight of the German armor.

"We talking about the same battle Emory? As I recall we got our butts kicked good and hard by those krauts. And I don't recall anything glorious about it. In fact, glory was in short supply that winter in Belgium."

"Oh you know what I mean. Our Army kicked their Army back across their old Siegfried line didn't we?" Emory asked, ending the question with a coughing spell.

"Suppose so. I suppose so," said Frank, with his eyes drifting toward the orange sunset light, streaming through the patio door.

The sound of the baseball game on the living room TV seeped into the kitchen where Lenore and Anita were busy with the dinner dishes. Anita had thrown Frank out of the kitchen so he could spend time with Emory and watch his precious game. Besides, she thought, it gave her some time to speak with Lenore.

"Tell me about your work. Your father says you work in a law office. Are you a lawyer?

"No; just a lowly paralegal in the estate planning group," Anita offered with a laugh.

"That must be interesting work."

"Not very exciting stuff but I enjoy it and it pays the bills.

"And you've been divorced for about six years?"

"I see Dad's been talking. Yes, six years this month."

"Are you seeing anyone special or still playing the field," Lenore said with a laugh.

"I've dated some; nothing serious. I've also been hit on by some of the old married lawyers at work, who shall go unnamed. Those guys I avoid; I'm not planning on breaking up someone else's marriage like little Kimberly did mine. I guess I'm saving myself for something special."

"You'll be a fine catch for someone."

"Don't be too sure about that. It's not easy for a 47 year old woman to get into the dating thing. Besides men my age seem to be trading down for the trophies, like my ex did, not up for the marriage veterans."

"That's their loss. I think marriage veterans, as you call us, have a lot to offer."

Anita laughed as she put the last plates into the dishwasher. "Well, I seem to keep busy. I don't know where the time goes."

At least that was her standard answer to these questions which came all too often from well meaning friends. She had kept busy when the boys were home. But the youngest, Chad, left for college two years ago and the empty nester thing wasn't setting well with her. The nest was too empty. "You need to get out more," Frank would insist when they were together. "You're a fine looking girl. You can't just hide in your house all day or hang around with me. Besides, all my friends are too old for a young filly like you. I thought women these days could ask men out. Why don't you ask someone out?"

"Oh dad, you don't understand," she would reply.

So she had an empty nest and had nearly convinced herself she was fine with it.

"This is good enough," Anita said, surveying the kitchen. "Let's check on that game."

With a confidant air, Simone Chauveau strode across the Bastogne town square acknowledging familiar faces with a nod and a smile as she passed. And many of the faces were familiar. Simone had been born in, raised her family in and buried her late husband in this picturesque Belgian town. She moved and looked much younger than her 68 years with her long silver hair pressed back by the afternoon breeze. Her long legs carried her swiftly toward the tourist information center, at the edge of the square, where she was to meet her daughter, Francine. The late afternoon sun cast a long shadow as she walked into the center.

"Hi mother," said Francine from a desk behind the counter. "Let me wrap up a couple of things and then we can slip over to Anton's for a glass of wine. I need one."

Francine shared her mother's height and trim build. People often said they shared a smile and eyes but Simone wasn't too sure about that. But Francine's fair complexion and sandy blond hair contrasted with the dark complexion and brown, nearly black, hair of her siblings and her parents, before gray set in. Now, at 48, Francine's brown hair was showing her first touches of gray, much as her mother's had done at the same age. Unlike her mother Francine kept her hair trimmed at collar length in an easy to care for manner.

Mother and daughter conversed in French, their preferred language, though both were fluent in German and English. Simone's father, a secondary school teacher, had encouraged a love of languages and she had passed on the skill to her children. Francine managed the tourism office part time and ran a travel agency as her primary business.

"Any special tours on the schedule."

"Strong Tours, from New York, have a couple bus loads of veterans scheduled for tomorrow. We've put some packets together for them but we're not involved with the tour. There sure has been a swarm of American veterans this season and more are on the way.

"Well dear, it is the fiftieth anniversary of the battle. It may be the last trip of any kind for many of these gentlemen. They are getting up in years." said Simone as she straightened up a stack of brochures on the counter. "Now why don't you lock up and let's have that drink you promised me."

Simone and Francine, mother and daughter, entered Anton's and settled at a small table overlooking the square where parked cars competed for space with the centerpiece of the square, a well preserved fifty year old Sherman Tank, now a battlefield memorial. Anton's had the look of an exclusive old men's club with its dark wood paneling covered, in places, by library shelves crowded with musty books which were more for decoration than for reading. Men and women of all ages occupied the sturdy wooden tables scattered about the place.

The two women had always been close. Francine was the first born, which may have accounted for the special bond they shared. She was the only child still living near her mother so Simone saw Francine and her family more than the others. Her sister Sylvie lived near brother Leon in Brussels, two hours away by car. Francine had been welcome help when Simone's husband, Jules, had died suddenly back in 1988.

"Is your handsome husband going to make it home for the weekend?" Simone asked.

"Charles plans to. He's going to drive up as soon as his Paris meetings are finished." Francine paused before changing the subject. "What you said about this being the fiftieth anniversary of the war is interesting. I hadn't thought of it in those terms. I do enjoy working with the veterans groups. And I am always impressed by the volunteer support we receive from people in town, particularly the older ones."

Simone ran her finger around the rim of her glass while gazing at the street scene. "It's the older ones that remember what it was like;

they appreciate the sacrifice made by those young soldiers fighting a long way from home. Yes, they remember; I just hope someone remembers when my generation passes on."

"I guess that is my job," said Francine, following her mother's gaze to the square. "Is that why you have been so involved with the memorial committees for all these years? It seems you moved straight from raising three kids to raising memorials."

"I suppose. I always had a passion to preserve the memory of those young men but with you kids off, I finally had time to pursue it. Plus the mayor at the time, a family friend, tapped me for several committee and fund raising efforts. It just grew from there. But now I'm happy to pass the baton."

The conversation was interrupted by the arrival of three elderly men, each wearing a baseball cap that identified them as army veterans. One, with a cane, was talking loudly to the leader, who wore large hearing aids behind each ear. After much high volume deliberation they selected a table some distance from Simone's and settled in to continue their reminiscing.

"What was it like back then; with the Germans and Americans marching through here I mean. You allude to the time but have never talked much about it."

"No, I haven't, have I. Well there are some good memories but mostly there are visions I would like to bury. I suppose I have been good at burying both."

"What do you remember about the German invasion in 1940? You would have been what...thirteen or fourteen?"

Simone clasped her hands around the narrow stem of her glass and paused before answering. "Fourteen. It's funny in a way. There was a war and the Germans rolled through the town but there was no fighting. Our army was further west sitting in their forts. So we knew we were at war but didn't see a big change. The trucks and tanks and soldiers passing through were scary and we were told to stay inside. I did that gladly.

"It was sad when we heard our army had surrendered and worse when we heard the French had collapsed too. No one expected that. But the news dribbled in. We had a wireless but no TV or cable news or any of that other instant news. No, it just dribbled in and was all bad. Later we had German administrators issuing mandates of one sort or other. Rationing came soon after. Food and fuel became scarce. Medical supplies too. Everything we had taken for granted became precious. I do remember that."

Francine studied her mother. She had rarely been able to induce her mother to talk. This was good, but she didn't want to push too hard for fear of shutting her down. She ordered a second wine for the two of them and, without speaking, waited for her mother to continue.

"It was awful when they came to take our young men for their army. At first they came for men eighteen to twenty-five. Later they took them younger and older. Sad to say some of the boys were glad to go. At times I fear some Belgians are more German than Belgian, particularly in the border towns to the east. So some went willingly to the German war machine and some just went, resigned to God's will."

"Is that what happened to father?"

"Yes, I didn't know him then but he was twenty-four and had just finished medical school. They were of course glad to have him to patch up their troops. But he was not alone. My cousin Mark, from Wiltz, and my friend Jan Reuss were both taken. The Germans touched everyone. Can you imagine a town without young men? That is how it was."

She stopped, her face reflecting the sadness of the memories. "Here I am rambling on about sad times past. But things are good now; we should focus on the present and future."

"No mother, do go on. When did they leave? When did the Americans come? Was there fighting?"

She gave Francine a slight smile. "Oh I remember when the Germans left. It was October or November of '44. They didn't look like the super race we had seen in 1940. I was living with my Aunt Anne in Wiltz at the time. No, they were a scared beaten lot that passed through town. We tried to stay away from them, out of sight. There was fear in their emaciated faces. Strangely I remember feeling sorry for those young men. Can you imagine? After all they had done to us I felt sorry for the beaten young boys that were dragging through our town."

Simone paused, studying her glass. "Well anyway," Simone continued, "the German departure left a void. And a few days later the Americans filled it as their troops came rumbling into town in a race to the German border. There was no fighting as the Germans were all hiding in their border forts; their west wall. So the Americans just arrived, some passed on and some settled in."

"The veterans are so nice now. What were they like then?"

"It's funny, thinking about it, but they were somehow more casual than the Germans. They walked with a confident swagger like they owned the place. But they were courteous and treated us well. I was working at the town clinic and met several of the medical officers. They gave me the same food they were eating which was a big improvement for us. It came in little waxed cardboard boxes and was supposed to be very nutritious. I would take the tinned meats home and put them in our soup. They weren't too bad. And for the first time in years the clinic had medical supplies, compliments of the U. S. Army. They began using our clinic as their infirmary mixing in with the civilian patients. That must have been early November for I recall the days were short and the weather cold and damp."

"Four men moved into our upstairs room so I moved down to the first floor and shared a room with Aunt Anne. They were only there a few weeks. Then they moved out and another group moved in. We didn't see much of them. They did something at the headquarters the Americans set up in town. But they shared our kitchen and kept us supplied with the best food we had seen for several years. I'm sure it was nothing fancy but, after all those years with so little..."

When Simone paused Francine noticed tears welling up in her eyes. She reached across the small table and took Simone's hands in hers. "You ok mom?"

"Yes, I'm fine dear. Just fine. Forgive me darling. That was a defining time in my life. Friends made; friends lost; lives changed forever....But I'm fine now. How did we ever get onto that dreary topic? On a nice summer day we should be talking about good things.

Francine glanced at her watch. Simone was right. It was time to go. "Thanks for telling me a little about that time. I really want to know how it was."

"OK dear. Perhaps we can talk later. For now we both need to run. Thanks for the drink."

Anita bustled between her kitchen and dining room putting the last touches on the table setting. Having her dad and the Rushings to dinner on a work night was probably a bad idea from the start. But Liz had been a dear, volunteering to help, and the finished dinner was looking pretty good.

"Anything I can do to help?" asked Lenore. "I'm afraid Emory has cornered poor Liz. He's explaining the differences between the Army and the Marines."

"She'll hold her own. Say, while we're alone, I wanted to ask how Emory's treatment is going."

Lenore leaned against the counter, shaking her head. "It's only our second week. This Friday they are supposed to give us an update. I'm keeping my fingers crossed but...."

"Well then, so am I," Anita replied, pausing to embrace Lenore. "Now, let's call the others to dinner."

The dinner conversation drifted over a wide range of topics before striking one that seemed to prick Frank like a sharpened bayonet. "Say Anita, did Frank ever tell you about the time he got stuck behind German lines?"

"Really?" Anita responded looking at her father.

"That's ancient history," declared Frank, glaring at Emory.

With Frank's eyes rolling skyward Emory continued. "Huh, I didn't think he would tell you, the old scoundrel. Well, I wasn't with him, mind you, but some of the story is recounted in the Unit History. As I understand it, during the first confusing days of the Battle of the Bulge Frank, like a lot of other guys, ends up behind German lines. But no surrender for Frank. Instead he ends up moving in with a Belgium family in a place called Wiltz. So while your dad is sitting all cozy in some cellar with a warm bed and warm food my Company gets pushed way the hell and gone to the north and ends up under the command of that pompous Brit, General Montgomery; old 'Monty.'

"Really Dad; did you get left behind the Germans lines?" asked Anita.

"As a matter of fact I did, and it wasn't quite as cozy as Emory would have you believe."

"What was it like; I mean what did you do?"

"It's a long story dear; too long to start on now."

"Well, I want to hear it too," interrupted Emory. "You see Anita, by the time Frank rejoined the unit from his vacation in the cellar I'd lost a piece of my backside and was sitting in a hospital in England. I didn't see him for years after that. Actually I just assumed he bought it during those first days."

Frank smiled but offered no details.

"Dad, you're impossible. I'll just have to get you liquored up some night and squeeze the story out of you."

"Oh Anita, that reminds me," Emory continued. "The 28th Division is having a fiftieth reunion in Belgium this October and I'm trying to get Frank to join me. Maybe you'll have some luck persuading him to attend."

"Dad, you ought to go. You could do with a vacation."

He smiled and shook his head.

"You've got to come to the next one Frank," Emory encouraged as Liz brought in the angel food cake with a warm berry sauce. "Besides it's the fiftieth and should be a barn burner. Anita, give me your address and I'll send you a copy of the trip brochure. Then you can work on him. We need guys like Frank. The group is getting smaller every year. We need some fresh blood."

"I've never been much on reunions," replied Frank. "It's just a bunch of old men like us telling war stories. What could be the fun in that?"

"Oh come on now you old curmudgeon. You would take a different line if you could see the memorials they've built to commemorate the battle. And the cemetery in Luxembourg City will take your breath away. I can't think of that place without a lump in my throat and a tear in my eye. Besides, you need to do it for the guys that are there; for the ones that never made it home.

"Why don't you consider it dad?" Anita chimed in.

"Why don't you come too?" said Emory, turning to her. "Several of the guys have brought their adult children to recent reunions. Frankly I think the kids have had as much fun as the dads. Remember Captain Burmister, Frank? He took his daughter to the fortieth and everyone thought it was his trophy wife. They both had fun with that. You could come as a trophy wife Anita. People would really envy old Frank here."

"I'm just not sure I could, what with the expense, my work and all," she said, flustered that the pitch had been turned on her.

Later that evening, sitting in bed with a book on her lap and small glass of Contreaux in her hand Anita reflected on Emory's suggestion. If she wanted to get to know her father a trip to Europe would be a wonderful opportunity. She understood that. But then there was her job. She had responsibilities. She just couldn't run off on a trip. Or could she?

3

Frank gave Lenore Rushing a farewell hug in the driveway of her Portland townhouse. "Thanks for lunch and you take good care of that old malingerer."

Lenore forced a smile, and with tears welling in her eyes, turned to embrace Anita. "Thanks so much for coming all the way down here. It meant so much to Emory. As for the lunch, I'm afraid it wasn't one of my best performances. Anita, you're a dear to keep your father company."

"Oh Lenore. You know it's not a bad drive and in this big old car…," she said, patting the roof of Frank's Lincoln. "It's like riding on a sofa. Besides, Emory is my favorite story teller. We would've come last weekend but didn't want to tangle with the Labor Day traffic."

"I'm just glad you came and so is Emory. I'll let you know if anything changes, if you know what I mean."

Frank knew only too well what she meant. The experimental treatments at the University of Washington, which were terminated after only a two week trial, had done little to stem Emory's insidious decline. And a recent respiratory infection had further weakened him. After a short hospital stay Emory had returned to his home to recuperate under Lenore's watchful eye. During Frank and Anita's day long visit he had barely stirred from his living room lounge chair.

Lenore stood alone in her driveway, waving resolutely, as they coasted toward the entrance of the townhouse complex. "She's quite a lady, isn't she Dad?" said Anita as she buckled her seatbelt and settled into the big leather seat. "I wish she didn't live so far away. I might consider adopting her."

Frank smiled as he merged into the flow of traffic heading toward the Columbia River and, three hours further north, Seattle. "Sounds like her boys have been helping her out and she seems quite close to the one daughter-in-law."

"Well, you'd better be nice to me because I'm all you've got," she said, turning, leaning against the door.

He chuckled but didn't respond

They drove silently up the green fringed freeway corridor where the trees were beginning to show the first signs of fall color. A sunny fall day in Washington is hard to beat, Frank thought. It was definitely football weather. Football fan Emory wouldn't be attending any games but at least he could pass the long days in front of the TV. That would be good for him. His reverie was interrupted by Anita.

"Dad, may I ask you something?"

"Fire away."

"Well, before this summer you maybe saw Emory a half a dozen times since the war. Perhaps you exchanged cards at Christmas but he was hardly what you'd call one of your close friends. But since July; well I don't know how to describe it. There's something, a bond perhaps, which seems to have blossomed between you two. Don't get me wrong, it's wonderful. But I can't recall any other person who has touched you quite like him."

"Hmmm," said Frank, stroking his chin with a free hand.

Ah, Anita, he thought. You pose a question that has me perplexed as well. Why is Emory different? Is it because he reminds me of a time, long since past, when I saw bravery, terror, anger, love, compassion and lived through a kaleidoscope of never to be repeated experiences that would mark me for all time? Is Emory special because we were, as Shakespeare said, part of a band of brothers, bound for all time by the experiences we shared; experiences that can never be duplicated nor adequately described?

"I mean," she continued, "how many other guys from your Army days do you keep up with?"

"Most of them are dead."

"Oh Dad! It must be more than that."

That truly was an issue, Frank thought. She just doesn't understand how hard it is to lose those who are close to you. For him they came in two waves. During the war he lost friends every day in combat.

He lost friends that were far too young to die. Now he lost friends because they were just growing old. Either way was hard.

"But that's a factor. If you think about it, a lot of our friends have passed away. When you have fewer friends to think about you can think about each one a little more," he continued, with a smile.

Anita pondered his response for a moment while Frank eased around a logging truck which was leaving a trail of bark strips in its wake. Changing the subject, she continued. "You should go to that reunion."

"The reunion; the reunion in Belgium?"

"Of course the one in Belgium. It would be good for you and it would mean the world to Emory."

Frank shook his head from side to side. "It wouldn't matter two hoots to Emory."

"Dad, he's been promoting it since July. Didn't you hear him today? 'You've got to go for me Frank.' What kind of a signal do you need? He had tears in his eyes when he was talking about missing it. It was like he has finally faced the reality that he's not going to be in condition to travel any time soon. Don't you see, it would mean a great deal to him if you went; kind of like a surrogate Emory."

"Now why would I want to do any such thing? It would just be a bunch of old guys that I wouldn't know telling tales about a time I would rather forget. What's the joy in that? And besides, it's only a month away. There's no way I could get organized for a trip to Europe in a month. I have too many obligations."

"I have a good idea what your calendar looks like. If it's a football game you're worried about I can see that your tickets don't go to waste," she said, nudging his shoulder with her hand. "It would be good for you. You haven't traveled since Mom died. You need to get out. Think of it as going for Emory. And there must be some good memories from your Army days. I can't believe that everyone you knew has passed away.

"Anyway, it's too far to go alone. I'd likely spend a week talking to myself and come back a nut case."

Go to Belgium? Frank had resolved long ago not to go to Belgium. The cost, timing and memories of that time all rallied against the idea. It would mean lowering his guard and exposing himself to memories he had long suppressed. Could any good come from such a trip? Yes, Emory would appreciate it. That was clear. And what had Anita said, "There must be some good memories from your Army days." If she only knew. But even those were in the past. What good would there be in stirring them up again, fifty years later.

"Last Memorial Day I heard this lady on NPR talking about how soldiers repress their memories of war and how stressful that can be. Of course she was talking about Vietnam but I'm wondering if…."

"Anita dear. I don't need to be analyzed by some lefty from NPR. I'm doing just fine, thank you very much. I appreciate your concern but you don't need to worry about me."

Anita studied her father as he drove. His hands clenched and then relaxed on the steering wheel. It appeared that some comment was striking home; he was in deep contemplation.

"I think you're just being stubborn. I know a great travel agent. She could make all the arrangements in no time and…."

"Will you just let it go?" asked a frustrated Frank. "I'm not going, Emory or no Emory. Maybe you should think about your own travel plans. You haven't left the state for years. Maybe you should go. The break would do you good."

"Oh Dad, you're making no sense. Why would I go? You're the veteran."

"You should go because….well just because. You think it's such a great idea for me. You're young and could surely travel better than me. You might even meet a guy. If you're not careful you're going to end up as a spinster for life."

Anita flushed with anger. "That is a mean thing to say and it's not true. I'm doing fine. You're the one that seems to be afraid to live a little. I'm only thinking of what's best for you."

"Well, maybe you should spend some time thinking about what's best for Anita; that's all I'm saying."

She glared at him while he looked down the highway, concealing all emotion. "Fine," she said finally. "You just stay home and miss the opportunity. You know mother would have said the same thing I'm saying. Just think about that. But stay home; it makes no difference to me."

She sorted through his CD collection, selected one she could tolerate and slipped it into the player.

Good, thought Frank. No more talking.

The next morning, well before sunrise, Frank sat on his balcony studying the city lights that fringed the now still harbor. Wrapped in a purple and gold stadium blanket he hoped the chilled morning air would help calm the tossing turmoil of the bedroom. Another damned nightmare; when would they let him go?

At first, years ago, most of them were first run events. But then he slipped into reruns like tonights. Some were clear and vivid; recognizable names, faces and incidents played and replayed over the years. Others were hazy composites; a mélange of frightful scenes with no beginning or end and no apparent purpose but to drive him from his bed in a panting sweat. A few, a very few, were actually welcome dreams; scenes recalling good times set on a stage of war.

Tonight it was a nightmare; a hazy composite nightmare. There was a burning tank. There were artillery shells exploding and men screaming and there was nothing he could do to stop the carnage; nothing at all.

Now, as he sat alone in the cool morning air, he tried to assemble the nightmare fragments into a rational whole. He had gone to war unprepared for the horror of artillery. War wasn't supposed to be like that. The war Frank had trained for was more personal. He'd spent hours at the rifle range learning to hit neat targets that stood still across a dirt field. Inhale, aim, fire, do it again. He was good at that. He was rated a marksman. But the Germans didn't stand across fields. Everyone played by different rules.

Frank closed his eyes in a vain attempt to sleep but memories conspired to keep him alert. He remembered going to war thinking it was all about people shooting other people; kind of a gunfight at OK Corral kind of fight. But it was usually more impersonal than that. Artillery killed more people than bullets. If you were in the wrong place you died. If not, you lived a little longer. The men in his nightmare tank were in the wrong place. Frank was in the right place more often than not. The war had been a game of chance.

As the first morning ferry eased into sight below, Frank pushed his chilled body from the chair and retreated to his kitchen to brew a morning pot of coffee. While waiting for it to burble through the filter into the pot he returned to the closed patio door where he could stand and enjoy the view without the morning chill.

"Why don't you go to Belgium?" Anita had asked. Why indeed? Wouldn't it just stir up those old memories even more? But he hadn't been there for fifty years and the memories were as pervasive as ever. Could it be that his strategy of avoiding the place was one hundred and eighty degrees wrong? Could it be that by trying to evade the memories he had instead perpetuated them? That's nuts, he thought, shaking his head.

Then there was Emory. "Go for Emory," she had implored. He could do that but what difference would it actually make. How could his presence in Belgium make up for Emory's absence?

And then there were his obligations. He did have some obligations. He couldn't just up and leave the country on a moments notice. And if he was gone Anita would really be alone.

His reverie was interrupted by the silence of the now resting coffee maker. Coffee would be good; it would clear his mind, he thought, as he shuffled toward the kitchen. And he needed a clear mind. He was confused.

"Come on in; it's unlocked," Anita hailed in response to the knock at her door.

"Whoa, something smells good. I'm a lucky person to have you as a neighbor," said Liz, setting a large bottle of wine on the counter.

"Hey, you weren't supposed to bring anything. It's your birthday after all." Reacting to the sound of the phone she continued, "Grab that for me, would you."

Liz picked up the phone and chatted with the caller for a few moments before handing the phone to Anita. "It's your father," she said.

Anita pushed a pan off the burner and turned off the exhaust fan. "Hi Dad. What's up?"

"Is this a good time? I don't want to interrupt dinner."

"No this is fine."

"Well, I've been thinking about our conversation in the car yesterday. As long as you don't say 'I told you so' I have a proposition for you."

Anita walked to the kitchen table and eased into a chair. "I'm listening."

"I'll go to Belgium...."

"Really!"

"...if you'll come along."

"What?"

"That's the deal. I'll go if you go. You can go as my daughter; my trophy wife; whatever. But you're the one that thinks it's such a good idea so you can come and sit through all the boring speeches surrounded by doddering old veterans. You've been asking a lot of questions about the war. Now you can see the ground I walked on first hand. What do you think?"

"Well I...I couldn't....I mean there's my work and other commitments...I just can't drop everything on such short notice and run to Europe. And there's the cost. I just can't. But you don't need me. You would do just fine."

"I'll cover the cost. If I can drop everything to go I don't know why you can't. You haven't taken a vacation since you started at that place. Surely you can pull a week or two off."

"But Dad, it's different; don't you see."

"No, I guess I don't. But it was just an idea. You go, I go. You stay, I stay. Think about it. I'll let you go now. I know you have company. Wish her happy birthday for me."

"Dad, no wait. That's not fair don't you see…." She realized she was talking into a dead line. He'd hung up on her.

"What a scoundrel," she exclaimed.

"This side of the conversation was interesting. What's up?" asked Liz as she joined Anita at the table with two glasses of wine.

Anita took advantage of Liz's receptive ear to explain the recent phone call set against the perspective of yesterdays conversation in the car. Liz listened patiently, rising only once to refill Anita's glass which had been emptied in gulps between words. "So can you believe the gall of that man?" she concluded.

"So why don't you go?" Liz responded after allowing the last words to settle in the room. "You said you wanted to learn more about your father; who he is, what he'd done. What a golden opportunity. You'd be one on one with him for over a week while visiting places he hasn't seen for fifty years. You could learn more in one week than you'd have learned in years just picking his brain a little at a time."

"Hey, whose side are you on?" replied Anita, with a hurt expression.

"I'm not choosing sides and, if you prefer, I'll just keep my mouth shut and we can have a nice dinner as planned," Liz said, rising from the table.

"No, you're right. Sit down and tell me what you think. I promise that even if I don't agree with you I'll still serve you dinner. Now sit and talk," she said, patting the table at Liz's place.

"Will you forgive me if I go over the line?"

"It depends how far over you go. I'm ready," she said, raising her glass. "Now give me your sound opinion."

"OK. As I see it there are two perspectives; your father's and yours. From his, this trip would be good for him and he now says he'll go. It would be a shame if he missed it because of you. Now it may be a dirty trick to place the burden on you but he has. In reality he might not want to travel alone. But whether that's a trick or not, if you don't go, he doesn't go."

"I'm with you so far," said Anita, swirling her wine around the glass. "Now from my perspective."

"Now I am on thin ice, but here goes. I've only known you a few months and have really enjoyed it. You're younger and active and an inspiration for me. But you're a neat lady without much of a life. I don't know what you were like when you were married but besides your father and me you're not very social now. You, my dear, seem to be in a rut! You go to work. You go to your Whidbey cabin, often by yourself and you don't do much else. Now, maybe that's fine but you'll never know unless you get out of that rut and look around. If you come back and decide to climb back into the rut, so be it. But I'm not sure you know what life is like outside of the narrow world you've constructed for yourself. This trip could just be the chance for you to see the world above the rut."

Anita stared at Liz without responding.

"Will I need someone to taste my food before I eat it?" Liz asked.

After a pause Anita responded with a chuckle, "Oh, of course not. I wouldn't know how to dispose of the body if I poisoned you here. So you think I'm in a rut?"

"What do you think?"

"I don't know. I haven't thought about it that way I guess. Perhaps I've gotten a little boring."

"Your word, not mine," said Liz, reaching for the placemats. "Now why don't we eat and talk at the same time. It smells too good to go to waste."

Anita and Liz enjoyed a relaxed meal with the conversation moving in new directions. But as it did Anita couldn't help but ponder Liz's observations. Am I in a rut, she asked herself. Things certainly did change after the divorce. When the boys were still living at home life revolved around them, taking her further from a life of her own. They were gone but her pattern was set. Maybe she was in a rut. But how could a trip to Belgium help that.

Now, as for helping her get closer to her father's past, that was a different story. But there was still the job, the house plants, the plans to paint the second bedroom....all those things would be upset.

After carving up the small birthday cake Anita had made the two friends said their farewells leaving Anita alone to ponder the day's discussion.

Oh, she reflected, why is life so complicated?

Anita aimlessly shuffled files across her desk for the sixth time. Her day at the office was beginning to drag. She had arrived early hoping work would take her mind off Frank's challenge. It hadn't worked. Her mind kept wandering from the Last Will and Testament of Orlan Smith, which was her assignment for the morning. At ten o'clock she walked down to the building coffee shop to purchase a cup of coffee, avoiding the firm's lunchroom where the coffee was free. She needed to think.

Coffee finished she crushed the paper cup while riding the elevator back to her floor. Reaching her cubicle she began dialing the phone before sitting down.

"Dad, Anita. You'd better get your passport out of the safety deposit box. We're going to Belgium."

4

Frank Larson squirmed in his seat, seeking a comfortable position for his seventy year old, six foot frame. Thank God we're in Business Class, he thought. He wasn't sure how a person could survive a nine hour flight to Europe crammed in those tiny seats in the rear of the plane. He was staring across Anita to the freezing white nothingness of clouds outside the window, numbed by the constant whirr and hum of aircraft noises.

She closed her book and turned to her father. "How are you doing dad? Only six more hours to go," she said with a smile, gripping his arm on the armrest they shared.

"Oh I'm fine. Just staring. You know how I hate long flights."

"Do you have a book?"

"I have one tucked in somewhere. I'll get it later. I was just thinking about the last time I was on this flight. It was probably in '87 or '88. Your mother and I came over with the ski club. She really enjoyed those trips. Not sure where we went that time; Italy I think."

"It had to be '87, because Eric and I were still married and you stopped in Venice after skiing. Mom bought me that wine carafe with 'Eric and Anita Chase' inscribed in gold on the bottom."

"Oh yes, that purple thing. Well I bet that was one thing you and Eric didn't have to fight about when you divided things up."

"You're right about that! I don't think his little Kimberly would have appreciated having reminders of me around their cozy love nest."

Frank smiled and settled deeper into the leather seat.

"Dad, you and mom went skiing in Europe several times. Why didn't you ever take a few days and visit places you were in during the war? You saw lots of France and Belgium. I should think it would be fun to retrace your footsteps across the continent."

He thought about the question for a moment. "Guess we just never had the time. Always had work waiting for me, you know..."

"Didn't have the time or didn't take the time?"

He looked at her with a knowing smile. 'Maybe a little of both. Yes, maybe a little of both."

"Why?"

"You sound like a precocious two year old with the why, why, why..."

"I haven't been two for forty-five years and you can't blow me off with a two-year-old's answer."

He smiled. "Why don't you give me one of those super sleeping pills you've been touting? I need to get some sleep."

"I guess that just ended our conversation."

"We'll have plenty of time to talk. Our journey has just begun."

A cool October wind whipped across the Bastogne town square as Simone approached the tourist information office. She burst through the door startling Francine, working at her desk behind the counter.

"Good morning Mother. What brings you out so early?"

"Good morning dear. I wanted to get your opinion on a birthday gift for your hard-to-please daughter. Then I can return the others. Tell me what you think," she said, laying three sweaters on the counter.

"Go with the red. Definitely the red."

"Oh good. That was my first choice as well."

As Simone gathered up the sweaters her eyes fell on a stack of folders sitting behind the counter. Picking up a packet emblazoned with a red keystone shaped symbol she asked, "Is the 28th Division reunion this weekend?"

"Yes. The program starts tomorrow; early check-in is here." Seeing the packet in Simone's hand she continued, "How did you know it was the 28th? Did you recognize their logo?"

"Don't forget I worked a few reunions in my time."

"Well, in the last few days I've learned a little about the 28th. According to one veteran the Division came from Pennsylvania, which is called the Keystone State in America. Hence the symbol. Apparently the Germans called them the bloody bucket brigade because they thought the red keystone looked like a bucket."

"Yes, that's true. I had heard that before, the bloody bucket brigade. How disgusting. By the way, do you have the list of the attendees from the 28th?" said Simone as she loosened her trench coat and silk scarf.

"Do you know someone in it?" Francine asked as she laid the list on the counter.

"Mmmm, not really. But they were in Wiltz for several weeks before the Germans came across and I might recognize a name or two." Simone opened the roster and ran her finger down the list of names until she reached one that caused her to stop and gasp, gripping the edge of the counter with her free hand. Francine didn't notice Simone's initial reaction. But when she turned she was surprised to see her mother frozen, as if she had seen an apparition.

"Mother, what is it? Are you ok?"

Recovering, she shook her head as if snapping out of a trance. "No, I mean yes, I'm fine. It's just seeing all these names and knowing these young boys are now old men it's just, I don't know. But I'm fine, really I am."

"Here, have some water. You frightened me. I guess you worked too many reunions."

Yes, she thought, perhaps I did. Perhaps I did.

Anita returned to her seat in the dimly lit cabin, careful not to disturb her sleeping father. She covered his shoulders with a blanket and then leaned against the chilled window, studying her seatmate.

It is going to be different traveling with Dad, she thought. They had never traveled like this, just the two of them. She wondered how it would be to share a room with her father, suspecting it would take some adjustment for both of them.

There was something comforting about a predictable travel routine. After eighteen years of marriage and traveling with husband Eric, they had their routine down pat. He packed some things and she packed others. For example, she was responsible for the hair dryer and any medications. He handled the camera, film and maps. Each packed their own clothes. And they knew how to share a bathroom. He showered first, because he was fast. She went second and could linger. They traveled well together. At least she thought so. Maybe she annoyed him then too. She'd never know and, at this point, didn't care. She smiled wondering if his little Kimberly always capped the toothpaste. That was one of his hot buttons!

Her reverie was disturbed by the morning snack service. She leaned over and jostled her father. "Dad, wake up. We're going to be landing in a few minutes."

Frank eased forward while fumbling for his glasses in his shirt pocket. He found them, slipped them on and then studied the colored map being projected on the screen at the front of the cabin. "We've made quite of bit of progress. How long was I asleep?"

"I'm not sure. I was out too.

"It always takes me a few days to adjust to the time change," he said, slipping his watch off his wrist. "That is the only good thing about coming over by ship. You at least get a chance to adjust your body clock to the time change."

"When did you and mom ever come by ship?"

"Oh, we didn't. We always flew. But the Army was good enough to send me by ship. It took nine days, not nine hours."

"Wasn't that dangerous? I thought the Germans sank a lot of ships trying to get to England."

"Yes it was dangerous. But we were a part of a big group of ships, a convoy, protected by scores of little Navy ships that darted around our bigger slower ones, day and night. We had submarine alerts several times but we never saw anything and I don't think any ships in our convoy were sunk."

"Like, did you have your own cabin during the voyage or what?"

He smiled, chuckled to himself, and shook his head. "Oh, I had a cabin all right. You see, we were on an ocean liner, the San Paulo, which had been converted to transport troops. For the junior officers they took cabins made for two, added two bunks and assigned eight men. We took turns sleeping. It was the same for the enlisted men but they all shared these big bunk areas that had been constructed in the ballroom and other large open spaces. The bunks were stacked from the deck to the overhead and there wasn't enough room to sit up in bed. My God they were jammed in.

"That must have been quite an experience."

"Oh, it was my dear. It surely was."

"So, what was it like, arriving in England I mean?"

"It's funny how impressions stay with you. The sky was gray, like the one out there," he said, nodding toward the small cabin window. "Everything seemed gray; the sky; the buildings; the people we passed on the way out of town. England had the look of a tired country after four years of war.

The conversation was interrupted as the cabin crew busied themselves collecting the cans, cups and bottles that had accumulated over the long flight. The plane continued its pre-landing maneuvers bumping and rattling through the angry looking low clouds. Soon the plane, flaps extended, dropped below the gray overcast to reveal the white capped surface of the Copenhagen Harbor and the featureless landscape of northern Denmark. Within minutes they thumped down on the airport tarmac and taxied to the waiting gate.

The two hour lay-over provided them with just enough time for a strong cup of coffee and a calorie packed, delectable Danish pastry. Then, after racing down the long concourse, they boarded their connecting flight to Brussels. They were moving closer to the past.

With Anita behind the wheel Frank navigated them from the airport onto the highway to Bastogne. Free of the big city congestion Anita settled back, turned their rental car east and picked up speed. A two hour drive from Brussels faced them and she wanted to get there as soon as possible. Frank, who felt he was perfectly capable of doing the driving, had yielded the driving chore to Anita at her insistence.

Still tired from the flights he relaxed in the compact seat of their little Passat. Funny how things change with time, he thought. Here he was riding in a German made car to a reunion celebrating the defeat of Germany.

As Frank closed his eyes he thought about the woman sitting beside him. She was the son he'd never had. Growing up he tried to spoil her so neither she or her mother would notice. But Doris knew what he was doing. He tried to groom her to take over his company but failed miserably. He had two strikes against the idea. Doris didn't like it and Anita had no interest.

So he'd compensated in other ways. He taught her to ski and she was a hell of a skier. He taught her to run their boat and she proved to be a master helmsman. He'd encouraged her to attend University of Washington, just to keep her in town. She resisted at first, just because teen age girls were genetically wired to resist parent's suggestions, but she went and had a good experience.

He opened his eyes and studied his driver. When you have a single child you only get one chance, he thought. All in all I think Doris and I did right by our girl.

Scudding gray clouds kept the sun at bay except for intermittent splashes of light as the highway rolled out before them. The countryside, with its array of fall colors, concealed all signs of the many armies that had crossed it over the centuries.

"Do you recognize anything?"

"What?" he responded, recovering from his daydream.

"Do you recognize anything from when you were here?"

"No honey, I don't think I was ever here before," he replied, looking around the passing scene. "As I recall we came into Belgium from the south, through Luxembourg. But I probably wouldn't recognize anything there either. You have to remember that we moved around in the back of trucks, often at night, and spent as much of that time as possible sleeping. So I'm afraid I'm not much of a tour guide."

"I hadn't thought of that. I am so used to traveling by car. So you don't recall any sights you saw back then?"

He pondered the question for a moment, studying the truck beside them. "It's funny. I do have a few recollections but they are more like mental snapshots than moving pictures. Pretty mundane stuff. I do remember Paris though."

"You were in Paris?"

"Yes, for a parade of all things. Have you ever seen that picture of U. S. soldiers marching down the Champs-Elysees with the Arch d'Trumph in the background?"

"Maybe."

"Well, that was us. We didn't know it at the time but there was a concern the communists might rise up and take over the city. So in addition to French troops they wanted a show of American force when the Germans surrendered. We were close by so the 28th was picked to provide the show."

"What an honor!"

"We weren't sure what it was at the time. One day we are chasing Germans. The next we are on parade in our full field gear and the day after we were chasing Germans again. Oh sure, there were some hugs, kisses and flowers but no one could stop and enjoy the sights or the ambiance of the fabled city. So we were famous for just a day."

"You and mom visited there didn't you?"

"We stayed after one of our ski trips and spent a week in Paris. It was a wonderful time. Now I remember those days much more fondly than I recall my first visit."

"But dad, I'm still a bit surprised you don't have a better idea where you were when you were over here. I'm surprised you didn't keep a map or diary or something. You're so good with directions."

"If you saw how we lived you would see how difficult it would have been to maintain either. It was even tough to find a time and place to write letters. You see, our war was about one hundred yards wide. We were told who was in front, behind and on either side of us. We had to trust those on either side to protect our asses and we protected theirs. And if things got out of hand we expected our reserves to come forward to assist. We focused on what was happening in our little patch of the war. When we were done with that patch we would move to another, dig another hole and learn who we faced. So for us the war was a series of hills and foxholes and assaults and an occasional move to the rear to refit and relax. But France, Belgium and Luxembourg looked all the same to us and we were always chasing the krauts."

"You should have asked for a refund. Sounds like whoever booked your tour did a lousy job. I can't imagine going to Paris and not visiting the Louvre," she offered with a laugh.

He smiled and nodded. "So right. I can tell you there were many occasions we questioned who was leading our 'tour' as you say."

"So you were in one fight after another?"

"It seemed like it. After the Normandy breakout in August it was skedaddle time for the Germans. They were heading for home. Oh, you had to stay on your toes. They would hold a crossroads from time to time, just to make our life interesting, but for the most part they were on the run. So we just rolled from nameless village to nameless village until one day we found ourselves in Belgium. Hell, we were sure we'd be home by Christmas at the rate we were going."

"I guess if you had made it home by Christmas we wouldn't be on this trip would we?"

"And a lot of men that died that December would be alive today. A lot of men would be alive..."

As they approached Bastogne Frank resumed his navigation responsibilities and carefully studied his Michelin map. The small print was a challenge, but with his reading glasses he was able to maintain the correct course. The map made it clear why the small town had been so important to the Germans that December long ago. Seven roads led in and out of Bastogne. It was truly a crossroads. As he studied the map he chuckled to himself.

"What's so funny?" Anita asked, detecting his mirth.

"Oh, I was just thinking of a story that came out of the siege of Bastogne. You see, just after the 101st Airborne Division arrived the Germans cut off the last open road. Now the 101st was a bunch of battle hardened paratroopers who had a well earned reputation as a tough unit. As the story goes one guy calls to his buddy, 'Hey, I hear the Germans have us surrounded, the poor bastards.'"

Anita smiled, not fully appreciating the humor.

"You see, those guys were trained to jump behind the enemy lines. If they weren't surrounded they just didn't feel comfortable. Though I wonder how they felt a week later when they were freezing their butts off. Oh well."

"Just get me into town now. We can do more history lesson later."

After a few missed turns and one stop for directions Anita pulled the little Passat into the car park behind the Cavaness Inn. It was a modern looking building that offered little in the way of exterior charm. But the lobby was clean and neat and the front desk staff patient and efficient. The clerk seemed particularly impressed with Anita's command of the French language and engaged in a prolonged discussion with her while Frank stood by as useless as baggage.

Looking around the lobby he noticed a group of older men, some wearing Veterans of Foreign Wars hats and other signs that they were likely here for the same purpose as Frank. He was struck by how old some of them looked. One kept a grip on his aluminum walker, even as he sat down. Several were accompanied by equally old looking women who were definitely not their daughters.

Their modern room, with its bright blue carpet and beige linens looked like any small town hotel in American. With its two double beds, small desk and compact refrigerator it would be more than adequate, thought Frank, easing his long body onto the bed nearest the bathroom.

"What do you want to do dad?"

"Nothing at all. Maybe we could just eat dinner here. I saw a dining room in back. Then I'd like to go to bed early. I'm exhausted."

"Suits me, though I want to stay awake as long as I can. My body adjusts to the time change quicker that way. In the meantime I want to run up to the Tourist Information Center. The desk clerk said it's open for another half hour and it's not far. So you settle in and I'll go for a quick walk."

Anita slipped on her green Gore-Tex parka and was soon hurrying along the narrow walk on her way to the town square and the TI office. Traffic was thick around the square but she made her way across and was soon perusing books and brochures in the glass walled office.

"May I help you find anything," a woman's voice asked in French from behind the counter.

Anita turned and responded in the same language.

"You are American?"

"Yes I am. I'm here with my father for a military reunion."

"Your father was in the 28th Division?"

"Yes he was. How did you know that?"

"I am involved in all the reunions. They are a big thing around here you know. By the way," she said rising and walking around the counter, "my name is Francine Hardenne."

"Anita Chase and I am very pleased to meet you; and pleased that you can understand my mediocre French."

"On the contrary. Your French is quite good, with an English accent of course; but good none the less. Not many Americans we see speak any French. No, yours is quite good."

The two women visited for some time, discussing the town, its history, places to visit and their respective professions. At times they slipped into English, for Anita's sake, for her French vocabulary was both rusty and limited. Soon it was time to close up the TI and they parted, both expressing the hope to meet again at the reunion over the next few days.

Anita retraced her route back to the hotel proud of her first real French language encounter with a local resident. Until that time she'd few opportunities to polish her rusty French skills. When she returned to the room she found Frank dozing on the bed where she'd left him.

Rousing him, she related her experience at the TI office and then escorted the still drowsy man to dinner. It proved to be a quick and quiet affair. Both were tired. Both were pleased to be at their destination after hours of travel. And both were looking forward to exploring their new surroundings on the following day.

Simone arrived home in the fading light. She had walked the eight long blocks from the town center rather than drive. She preferred to walk, when the weather permitted. She loved the fresh air and exercise and dreaded trying to park in the congested little town. She lived alone on a quiet residential street, in what Americans would call a townhouse. Her corner unit had windows on three sides with a good view of one of the many small city parks. Like so much of the town, her home was built after the war.

Francine had questioned Simone's decision to move into town from the spacious farmhouse in the country where she had lived since shortly after she and Julian were married. But the house and grounds demanded more of her time than she wanted to give and the silence in every room was more than she chose to bear on her own. Her new home had been updated by previous owners and, with its three bedrooms, large main floor areas and full cellar; it was more than adequate for her needs.

Delighted to see Leon's car parked in front, Simone picked up her tempo as she neared her front step. Entering the unlocked front door she found Leon sitting in his father's old leather wing backed chair near the unlit fireplace with a yellow tablet on his lap and his briefcase open on the ottoman.

"Leon darling, it's so good to see you," she said as she crossed the room and leaned down to kiss each cheek. "Why didn't you light the fire? It's chilly in here."

"Oh, I didn't notice. I got caught up in finishing a document I had been turning over in my mind on the drive over. I didn't want to forget anything before I put my thoughts down. As I get older my memory gets more unreliable," he said with a smile.

"Forty-six is not old," she quipped, leaning down to light the gas log in the fireplace. "I'm the old one. You certainly have a few good years left in you unless you break your neck on one of your climbs. Would you like a quick drink before we go to dinner? Francine is going to join us and she can't be far behind."

"A glass of red if you please. That will give me a minute to finish my last good thought for the day."

She returned to the entryway, hung her coat on a hook near the door. Shortly she was back with three glasses, a bottle of red wine and a basket of sliced fresh bread on a small silver tray. Leon slipped his work into his briefcase to clear a space for the tray. She poured for both of them and then settled into a small brocade chair opposite his.

"You look just like your father in that chair," she said, sipping her wine. "That was always his favorite."

"I'm glad you kept it when you moved. It's nice to have a bit of the old house here when I visit. Even though father was never in this house I still think I can smell his pipe."

"I suspect you can. That chair alone likely absorbed enough tobacco smoke to maintain the smell well into the next century. But I always said that if smoking a pipe was the worst vice your father had I could accept that. Plus he always seemed so relaxed when he was in that chair with a good book and his pipe.

"Miss him still?" he said, reaching for a piece of bread.

She pursed her lips in contemplation. "You don't live with a man for over forty years and not miss him I suppose. I miss the presence of him the most; the memory is still there. How about you?"

"Yes I do. I used to call him and tell him things I was doing, projects I was working on, that sort of thing. He was always a good listener. I wonder what he would think of me moving to America."

"I'm not sure what I think about it. I'm going to miss not having you just two hours away. You've been the man in my life for the past six years and have been such a help since Jules passed away. I will miss you more than you will know."

"Francine and Charles are close by. Besides, you always liked her best," he said with a gleam in his eye.

"Oh you devil; don't talk like that. I've always loved all three of you. I've been very fortunate to have such a wonderful family. By the way, how are the kids?"

"Saw Jon yesterday. He has moved into his room on campus and is ready to start classes. I will tell you, it makes me feel old to have a son in college. And as for Elle; her mother has made it so hard for me to spend time with her that I feel like I have lost my daughter. So my leaving the country shouldn't be a problem for them. In any case, I suspect I will be traveling back here nearly every month for some meeting or other so I can stay in touch."

"I feel like I have lost my granddaughter too. Jon calls once in a while but I never hear from Elle, even when I send her a gift. But divorce is never conducive to maintaining good family relationships. Now," she said leaning forward, "count me as an old snoopy mother but are you seeing anyone or are you still married to your beloved mountains?"

Leon smiled at her reference to his passion for hiking and climbing the mountains of Europe. "The mountains are still my first love dear mother. They can be fickle and turn on you but they are always there when I need them as an escape. My work offers the complexity I need in my life. I don't need a woman to add confusion and uncertainty to my existence."

"Spoken like an insensitive man! I won't try to debate you but I do think a good woman offers more than confusion and uncertainty in a relationship. Men can be quite unreliable too you know."

The banter was interrupted by the arrival of Francine who burst through the front door, flinging her purse and coat on a table. "Leon, Leon, my favorite brother, you look so comfortable," she said, while moving to his chair and kissing him gently on the forehead. "How was the trip over?"

"Routine. Too many trucks and too many ill mannered German drivers but, other than that, routine."

"You two look so cozy by the fire; I hope I'm not interrupting anything..."

"I was just asking mother why she always liked you best," he said, watching for Simone's response.

"Leon, you know that's not true."

"Ignore him mother. He's been saying that for years hoping you will do something special for him to assuage the guilt you shouldn't have. I'm going to make some tea. Does anyone else want a cup," she said, moving into the nearby kitchen.

"I have some wine here," offered Simone.

"I'm saving myself for dinner if Leon's buying. Besides, I'm a bit chilled."

Francine soon joined the others by the fire with a fresh pot of tea on a small tray in her hands.

"Leon, Charles and I have a wonderful idea for you."

"Will this cost me money?"

"No silly, now listen. Charles needs to be in Luxembourg Monday at a trade show for his winery clients. He has a suite set aside near the hall and I'm going to join him. We thought it would be special if you came along. We could visit and just have a final family time before you leave the country. We've always had such a good time in the city we thought it would be a grand send off."

"After visiting this weekend I thought we would have had enough of each other"

"Well, you see, that is a problem. Charles has to go down early and insure things are set up properly and I have some work to do this weekend."

"So you couldn't even take time off for your favorite brother?"

Francine smiled and shrugged.

"Luxembourg? It would be fun to go down. I'll tell you what. Let me see if I can rearrange a few things on my schedule and it might work. No promises but I will try."

"Did that invitation include me?" said Simone, with a look of mock indignation.

Caught off guard, Francine recovered. "I didn't think you would be interested but, of course, you could join us."

"No, I was just toying with you. After this weekend I will need a rest. You young people can have more fun when you are not looking after grandma."

"What's keeping you girls so busy this weekend?" Leon asked.

"Its one of the U. S Army reunions; the 28th Division. There are activities scheduled for Friday night, Saturday and Sunday," replied Francine.

"The 28th Division? I know I have heard reference to them. Why does the name stand out? Were they the ones here in Bastogne or something?"

"I don't know what you may have heard but they were the ones in Wiltz just before the December fighting," offered Simone.

"That's it," said Leon. "Cousin Mark said they lived with you at Aunt Anne's. Was it a guy from the 28th that you hid from the Germans?"

"As a matter of fact it was."

"Mother, I've heard Mark's story too but I've never heard it from you. Mark said you hid a soldier from the Germans for nearly a month. Wasn't that a dangerous thing to do?"

"Well, first of all, your cousin Mark exaggerates. The young man was with us for less than four weeks. And, yes, I suppose it was dangerous when you think back on it. But what could we do; turn him over to the Germans after he risked his life for us? Many people were much braver than us but we did what we could and I'm pleased to say we were able to turn a much healthier man back to the Americans when they returned."

Leon pressed his questioning like a good lawyer. "Did you ever hear from him or stay in touch in anyway?"

Simone stared into the fire, hesitating before responding. "Once. He returned once near the end of the war. He brought food and was very generous with us. Food was still very hard to come by in those days you must remember. But the U. S. Army must have been the best fed army in the world for they seemed to have an abundance of good food and he had managed to get his hands on quite a supply. Things like sugar, flour and coffee were prized. Even the soldiers' field rations tasted good to us.

"And you never heard from him, or any of the others, again.

"No," she said pausing, "never again."

"Wouldn't that be amazing if he were here this weekend?" offered Francine. "I'll bet I could get the newspaper to do a feature on such a reunion. They are always looking for special ties to the veterans groups."

"Don't get your hopes up dear. You said there were less than two hundred veterans returning with the Division. Thousands served in those units during the war. So I wouldn't call any reporters yet. Now, I don't know about you young people but I have a need to dine on a regular basis and I believe one of you offered to buy dinner so I suggest we find a place to eat before this old woman falls asleep from too much wine."

"I'll second that," said Leon, "and I'll buy. Maybe if we give mother another glass of wine we can hear more tales of the past that she is always so reluctant to speak of."

5

Anita spotted Frank as she stepped from the elevator, reading alone on a lobby sofa near an unlit fireplace. She came up behind and kissed him on the top of the head. "Good morning young fellow. How are you doing this morning?"

"Much better, thank you. I hope I didn't wake you when I left the room."

Anita took a seat on the heavy wooden coffee table, facing her father. "I don't think a fire drill would have awakened me. I was having a little trouble about one o'clock so I took one of my magic pills and I don't recall a thing after that. How long have you been up?"

"What time is it now?"

"A little after eight."

"I guess I came down around seven so it hasn't been that long. I helped myself to some coffee in the dining room so I am fired up and raring to go. How about breakfast?"

The dining room was bustling and the clatter and clink of silverware and dishes mingled with the hushed conversations of the guests. There was a mix of business people, dressed in professional attire, and tourists or veterans, dressed more casually and, generally, looking much older. Before picking up their plates Frank and Anita surveyed the entire buffet laid out on the long sideboard near the kitchen. The smell of fresh cooked bacon and potatoes competed with the coffee and hot chocolate for dominance. Bright colored fruits and preserves gave the buffet a holiday look. With a plan in mind, they made their way through the buffet adding dribs and dabs of the fruits, breads and hot entrées until their plates were embarrassingly full. Frank, leading the way, found a vacant table for two near a window looking out over the car park.

"God, I can't do this everyday. I'll leave the country looking like a blimp," Anita said, as she broke her soft boiled egg over a piece of tepid toast. "I bet this is a far cry from Army rations?"

He finished a small apple pastry before replying. "This is better; yes, this is definitely better. But you know, we learned to appreciate what we had when we had it. Say you have cold rations for a few days. Then you appreciate a hot meal even if it's only hot mush and coffee. After a day or two of hot mush and coffee you start longing for bacon and eggs, which we rarely had. It seemed like any menu could be good when compared with something worse."

The server arrived with a pot of coffee and pitcher of warm milk for the table, leaving as silently as she had arrived.

"I never thought of it that way, having missed so few meals in my life," she said with a laugh while pinching the bulge at her belt line. "I probably could afford to go on short rations from time to time."

"Oh you look just fine. Some smart man is going to figure that out one of these days and then I'll never see you again.

She reached across the table and squeezed his hand. "That's why I love you so much; you're my one man fan club. Now what would you like to do today?"

"How about a tour of the area? I was talking to that old gentleman over there," he said, nodding toward the couple seated in the center of the room, "and he said there was a bus to the big museum leaving about two. I told the fella at the front desk and he said he would make the arrangements."

"Good for you. I thought I'd have to talk you into getting out of the hotel."

"I didn't want you to start nagging," he replied with a smile. "How about you? Do you want to come on the bus?"

"Let's wing it. This morning I want to get unpacked and straighten out my things. I may just wander the town, look in the shops and that sort of thing. Besides, you probably want to spend some time without your den mother at your side."

"Not a problem. I told that guy over there you were my wife and he has spent the entire meal looking at me with envy and at you with lust."

Anita shook her head in disbelief, ignoring her father's remarks.

"Will you take my book back to the room when you go? I think I need some fresh air," he said, slipping on his jacket.

"Can you remember the name of the hotel, in case you get lost?"

"That comment doesn't deserve a response," he said with an offended look. "Now, if you will excuse me...."

Frank walked toward the lobby head high, like a proud infantryman. But before leaving he paused, returned to the front desk and picked up a business card which he tucked into his wallet. Then, with renewed confidence, he departed the hotel

---

Don't get lost dad! That daughter of mine is a character, thought Frank. I haven't lost my sense of direction yet. That will come in time I suppose but for now, I'm still sharp as a tack. Well, almost as sharp as a tack. But no matter.

The air was crisp when he left the hotel but the sky was blue and the sun felt warm as he walked on the sunny side of the narrow street. As he reached the end of the block he was surprised to see an American Sherman tank perched in the middle of the town square climbing a slight grade on its slab of monument granite. For a moment he stood, admiring the green steel shape sitting as if frozen in time.

Frank could recall the comforting rumble of a Sherman approaching their positions at the front. Sometimes the sound also drew enemy artillery fire, which was not so good, but generally the stodgy Shermans gave them a sense of security they didn't get in a shallow foxhole. He crossed the narrow street and walked around the monument at a reverent pace. As he rounded the front he stopped, his gaze fixed on a neat, baseball size hole in the side. He stepped closer, fingers tracing the outline of the rusty wound. That hole meant a German shell had gone neatly through the armor and, once inside, transformed the tank from a weapon into a coffin.

God that must have been awful for those boys, thought Frank. I wonder if their parents had any idea of how they died.

He backed away, as if he couldn't take his eyes off the cold steel of that once formidable weapon. A few feet away he found a bench, warmed by the sun. He sat down, tucked his hands in his coat pockets, and let his mind wander back; many years back. How many lives were changed by that one small hole in the tank, he wondered; how many lives were shattered forever?

Left alone in the dining room Anita ordered a second pot of coffee and removed a pen and several postcards from her purse. Poised to write, her eyes surveyed the room filled with tables for two or four or six. It is just like home, she thought. The world is set up for couples. Oh sure, business people travel alone and stay in hotel rooms alone; at least most of the time. But the vacation crowd seemed to be a couples crowd. That was certainly true of the dining room.

This was not a new thought for Anita. It first occurred to her shortly after her separation. All their friends had been couples. They usually invited couples over when they entertained. The single people Anita knew, usually the product of a divorce, just didn't fit in as well. Now, as a single woman, she was viewing the world from the other side. When she was included it often created uncomfortable situations. Table seating arrangements were awkward. Football tickets seemed to come in pairs; same for concert tickets. Oh sure, single people could buy single tickets but she had come from a couples world and most of the people she and Eric socialized with were couples. So she often felt like a freak at invite time.

She addressed a postcard to her oldest son and then paused again, her mind still spinning on the couples merry-go-round.

All their friends had been friends as couples. With the divorce those old friends had to drop them both or chose up sides. Some dropped and some chose. But with his little Kimberly, Eric was still a couple so he quickly resumed a semblance of a social life. She hadn't.

At first it had been OK. She'd been consumed as a care giver during her mother's illness. And she was responsible for raising two high school aged boys. Yes, she'd managed to stay very busy. But with her mother gone and the boys off to college time was growing heavier on her hands.

Maybe Liz was right; she was in a rut. Work was her only serious outside the family activity. Thank God for that. She wasn't sure what she would have done if Frank hadn't pulled a few strings at the firm that handled his company's legal work. But, pressured to hire her or not, no one could argue that she didn't carry her own load at the firm. And, unlike the younger paralegals, she was not likely to get pregnant or run off to get married. The firm could count on old Anita; old reliable Anita.

During a visit Liz asked her a question that had been troubling her since. "Do you want to remarry?" Her answer at the time was no; an emphatic no! But her heart wasn't so sure. She certainly didn't want to fall into another Eric lifestyle trap. She liked her job. She liked her independence. And the selection of fifty something men was as appealing as prunes. She realized she wasn't a pin-up candidate herself but....

She was beginning to make some single friends, like Liz. True they were mostly female friends but that seemed easier; no sexual tension to disrupt the conversation. Men were hard to meet. She worked with many men but she didn't want to mix work and play. In any case, she wasn't sure she liked lawyers. They had too much ego for her blood. Not all of them of course but she felt it was a fair generalization.

Well, she thought, putting her unfinished postcards back in her purse, I'm not going to resolve my social conundrum sitting here in Belgium. For the next week I can forget all that and just remember I'm here for Dad. I can worry about Anita when I return home. I'll just have to be careful I don't eat so much that no one recognizes me when I return.

With a smile on her face she walked toward the elevator, ready to start her first full day in Belgium.

Anita walked along the main shopping street, gazing in shop windows as she went. Stubby little delivery trucks rumbled up and down the street, interrupting the steady hum of cars. She wasn't looking for anything in particular. She'd already decided that the clothing styles were so conservative that she was not likely to find anything of interest. But she was genetically wired to shop and shop she was going to do. Besides, it was a beautiful day, she was on the sunny side of the street, it killed time and it gave her a chance to get the lay of the land, as her father liked to say.

As she paused to study the newspapers on display in front of a tobacco shop she was surprised to hear, "Anita?"

Turning she saw the woman from the TI, standing just a few feet away.

"Anita! I thought I recognized that green coat. Are you enjoying our little town?" asked Francine.

"Oh, good morning. I was surprised to hear my name. I'm not well known in this town. Not yet anyway," she offered with a laugh.

"Well I am sure you are well known in your own town, isn't that true?"

"Not true. Not true at all. But I'm enjoying Bastogne. I find the shop keepers friendly and very tolerant when I abuse your native tongue."

"Nonsense. You are an ambassador for our language! Say, I'm on my way for a morning coffee," she said over the roar of a passing truck. "Why don't you come along? I would love the company. My brother is planning to join me but he is notoriously late."

"Well, I have a pretty full schedule but..."

"Really? I wouldn't want to interfere with..."

"No Francine. I'm absolutely free and would love to join you for coffee. Show me the way."

The mixed aroma of coffee and fresh bread greeted the two women when they entered the bustling shop. Francine seemed to know everyone there and introduced Anita to several people as they made their way to the counter to examine the bakery choices. But both women resisted the temptation, each claiming to be watching their weight, and retreated to a window table that gave them a good view of the town square. A waitress soon discovered them, gave the table a cursory swipe with a damp cloth and took Anita's coffee order. Francine just ordered the "usual."

In the relaxed atmosphere of the small shop the two women shared stories about their respective families, their jobs and prospects for the weather during the coming weekend. They spoke in French, drifting to English only when necessary.

The conversation was interrupted from time to time as newcomers greeted Francine with a friendly wave. "Say, I don't want to impose on your holiday but I have an idea," said Francine as they finished their coffee.

"Oh, Oh! I don't like the sound of that."

"No, No! It's just that you said your schedule is open and I was wondering if you might assist me with check-in at the reception tomorrow at the school. You see, one of my normal volunteers is out of town and the other one doesn't speak very good English. You speak English and French and would be such a help. Besides, you will find these Army gentlemen are most delightful. You wouldn't believe what flirts they are, even with their wives standing beside them; and with them all over seventy. Can you imagine? You might really enjoy it. I don't want to impose but, think about it."

"I don't need to think about it. That's a wonderful idea. It will get me out of my dad's hair for a while and I'd enjoy it. Maybe I'll meet a rich widower who will carry me away to his private island somewhere. Just tell me where and when and I'll be there."

Francine hesitated for a moment, as if unsure about the rich widower remark, then smiled and passed on the time and place information.

As they were finishing their coffee Leon walked into the shop with a celebrity air, waving to Francine and shaking hands with an older gentleman sitting just inside the door. When he arrived at the counter the little lady behind greeted him like a lost son and leaned forward so he could kiss each cheek. Finally, with a complimentary pastry in one hand, he approached Francine's table.

"Sorry I'm late sister dear but I got hung up on the phone. May I join you two ladies?"

"You're always late and of course you can join us," she replied, moving her purse and calendar to the window sill.

"Anita, this is the unreliable brother I was telling you about. Leon, meet Anita Chase, from America."

He greeted her in English and she replied in French.

"Ah, a French speaking American. How delightful. What brings you to our little village? You are too young to be a veteran."

"No, but my father's not. I've come to an Army reunion with my dad. I'm his official date," she replied, catching a whiff of his musky smelling cologne.

"And your husband chose not to come?"

"There is no husband so there was no choosing. No, it's just dad and me. But I think he is hoping to pass me off as his wife to the other veterans. He believes that would impress them."

Leon gave a hearty laugh. "I like your father though I have never met him. Yes, your presence will spark the envy of the entire unit; the 28th correct?"

"I'm impressed that you know the Division number."

He smiled and took a seat next to Francine just as his coffee arrived.

"Leon works for Microsoft and is moving to America in a few weeks. Where is it you are moving Leon?"

"Redmond. Redmond Washington," he replied stirring a packet of sugar into his small cup of coffee.

"You've got to be kidding. I live in Seattle. What a small world."

"Is that close to Redmond?" inquired Francine.

"Dear sister. They are one in the same. You fly to the Seattle airport to get to Redmond. They are part of one large city cluster." Turning to Anita he continued. "I have been to the main campus several times. I often stay in downtown Seattle. I enjoy your city very much. You will have to tell me all the places to go and things to do."

"What do you do? I mean are you a programmer, marketing person or what?" Anita asked.

"I'm actually a lawyer; an international patent lawyer. I was with the law firm Microsoft used in Brussels but now they have hired me to work inside, doing much the same kind of work I did before. I'm looking forward to the change."

"That will be quite an experience for your family. Do you have children in school?"

"Yes, but they are older and will not be going. And I suspect I will be back and forth a lot so I can still see my dear sister on a regular basis."

"Listen to him," Francine said, "he talks like a lawyer and a salesman. I never know what to believe. Leon, Anita has been gracious enough to agree to help me at the reception tomorrow at the school. Isn't that wonderful?"

"Well, you two have fun. I'm going for a long hike. I need exercise more than I need patriotic speeches. But I'll be home for mother's big dinner. Is your husband going to make it?"

"No, and I haven't broken the news to mother. Some problem has come up in Luxembourg and he had to go there directly from Paris to straighten the mess out. She will be disappointed but.... say, have you decided if you are going to come down to Luxembourg with me on Sunday night?"

"I plan to, unless something comes up."

"Well, see that nothing comes up brother dear. Charles will be most disappointed if he misses you. Now, I must get back to work. I'll see you in the morning Anita. And I'll see you at my house for dinner tonight, right Leon?"

"Yes, don't worry. I will be there."

Francine scurried out of the shop leaving Anita and Leon at the table.

"Well, I should really round up my father and figure out what we are going to do today. It was nice to meet you Leon. And I would be happy to show you around the Seattle area when you settle in." Anita said, rising and offering her hand.

"The pleasure was all mine. Do you have a card or something so I can get a hold of you for my tour?"

Standing, she fumbled in her purse for a moment, retrieving a business card. "You can call me at my office. It's no problem."

Examining the card he asked, "Are you a lawyer?"

"No, just a paralegal working with a bunch of lawyers."

"Ah, now that must be very interesting," he replied revealing a wide, warm smile. "Well Miss Anita Chase, goodbye then, until Seattle."

They shook hands in a formal manner and then parted, heading in opposite directions. Leon took a few steps before turning to gaze at Anita as she wandered away studying shop windows as she passed.

Frank joined the flow of tourists ambling from the bus to the Musee de la Bataille des Ardennes. After lunch at the hotel Anita had chosen to lie down; a headache or something. He didn't mind. She needed her time alone. Reaching the museum entrance he was pleased to learn that veterans were admitted for free. That was a nice touch, he thought.

The walk through the exhibits was a memory mover for Frank, reminding him of how little he actually knew of the massive battle. He'd been but a small thread on the battle's grand tapestry.

The grainy black and white photos of civilians, caught in the tumult of war, brought back memories of his time with a family in the nearby village of Wiltz. When the 28th arrived there, following their thrashing in the nearby Hurtgen Forest, Frank and two others had moved in with a family named Gelsi. They shared the house with the owner, a stroke victim who had difficulty walking, her son and a niece who was caring for the aunt. The son lived in the cellar and the niece shared the main floor with the aunt in what at one time had been the parlor. Frank's men took over the second floor, replacing soldiers from another unit that had recently departed. Everyone shared the kitchen area in the rear of the house.

The aunt was a feisty, guarded woman who kept an eye on the girl and her son. Four years of war had left her reluctant to trust anyone in a uniform. The son had been conscripted by the German Army and was home recovering from wounds he received on the eastern front. Frank was never sure if he'd deserted or was home legitimately but there was no doubt he hated the Germans with a passion.

The niece was the surprise. When Frank arrived he guessed the tall and skinny girl was about 15 years old. Turned out she was nearly 20, suffering from years of too much work, too little sleep and poor war time food. But in the month Frank shared their home, supplying all the food, she changed dramatically and, in his eyes, turned from a girl into a woman. She and Frank, under the watchful eye of the aunt, spent many hours in the kitchen, preparing meals, eating and just talking about the kinds of things young people speak of.

The girl helped the aunt in the morning and then was gone the rest of the day, working at the town clinic. That went on seven days a week. Frank was busy as well, making frequent trips to the quiet front lines east of town, to deliver intelligence reports and to remind himself what a cushy job he had in the rear. But in the evenings he and the niece would talk; she spoke wonderful English. They could talk like he couldn't talk to anyone in his unit. He heard about her family, her brother, her schooling, life under the Germans; they just talked. For Frank she was such a pleasant reminder of values and people worth fighting for.

The son, Mark, joined in the conversations when he was home. He shared his experiences in the German army, a topic Frank found most fascinating. Frank introduced Mark to the division intelligence officer who found him useful as an interpreter when a captured German was brought in. He was paid in rations, which were more useful than money at that time. But the intelligence officer soon learned it was never a good idea to leave him alone with a prisoner. He didn't like the Germans and was not afraid to express his feelings in corporal ways.

After one week Frank's roommates were reassigned, leaving him alone in the house with the family. He didn't announce the spare beds at Division Headquarters. He didn't want to share his new family. The son moved from the cellar back to his own second floor room and the little housekeeping arrangement went on unabated into the month of December. While Frank was living there he could almost forget there was a war going on. He was soon to be reminded....

God that was a long time ago, thought Frank, as he climbed back on the bus burdened by the weight of long suppressed memories. I wonder what ever happened to those fine people.

The roar of the bus, as it eased forward, brought him back to reality.

"Today sure worked out well," Frank observed as the waiter brought their coffee and cleared away the last of the dinner dishes. "Do you think you'll be up for a full day tomorrow?"

"Oh, I think so. I was probably just fighting a little jet lag. It was fun seeing Francine again and meeting her brother. It gave me a chance to practice my French. I'll have to introduce you to her at the reception. Did I tell you she asked me to come early to help with the check-in and set up?"

"Really? Well that's nice. I can relax without you looking over my shoulder," he said with a smile. "How will I get there if you take the car?"

"I'm going to walk. You may want to as well. It's only a short distance from here. I can give you directions. I walked by it this afternoon just to see if it was walkable. Come early and maybe you'll see some guys you know. I hope so."

Frank studied his steaming cup. "It's funny. I've thought a little about that. I'm not sure I want to see them again. As it is I have them frozen in my mind the way they were 50 years ago; young, optimistic, with their whole life ahead of them. At least the ones that survived. Strangely I'm not sure I want to change that image. I don't know what I gain by doing so."

"I think I know what you mean dad. A few years ago I ran into my favorite teacher from high school. She was the neatest lady and I had nothing but fond memories of her. When I saw her she was in a wheelchair at the mall. She'd suffered a stroke and couldn't get around on her own. Now that image has replaced the other one and I'm not sure that's good. Now I know people grow old and there's nothing wrong with that. But if someone is not really a part of your current life and doesn't need to be, what advantage is there in updating the image if the update is not as good as the original?"

He studied his daughter as she spoke. "That is exactly what I am talking about. Why update the image? Well put. But I'll go tomorrow and if I recognize anyone, so be it. But I doubt that will be a problem. For now, I'm beat. The time change is catching up with me. I think I'll head up to the room."

"I won't be far behind. I may sit in the bar and listen to the piano for a few minutes. Don't wait for me."

Anita was glad she'd taken a few extra minutes to unwind in the bar. A comfortable extension of the hotel lobby it lacked the "meat market" atmosphere that characterized the trendy Seattle bars. Most of the customers appeared to be hotel guests and no one seemed to be trolling, which was fine with her. The bartender was generous with her brandy and not too talkative; that was also good since she felt more like sitting than talking. And the piano player is doing a nice job filling the room with music without overpowering the space.

It had been a nice day, totally unplanned. That is so unlike me, she thought. I normally like to have my day laid out in advance. Yet I started today just wandering around town, ended up meeting Francine and Leon for coffee and then just lazed the rest of the day away. Maybe there was something to be said for being more spontaneous; less planned!

She had thoroughly enjoyed Francine and Leon and was touched by the kindness they'd shown her, a complete stranger. She wondered how people would treat them in Seattle if the roles were reversed. Bastogne was a small town, and that did make a difference. But she suspected that part of it spoke to who they were and how they were raised. Perhaps she would meet their mother tomorrow.

She was looking forward to working with Francine. It would be fun though it could present a bit of a linguistic challenge for her. And she hoped to see Leon again. She'd enjoyed their brief time together. He said he would call when he arrived in Seattle. Showing him around her hometown would certainly be different; if he called, which he probably wouldn't.

Back to reality Ms. Chase, she thought. For now you need to get some sleep and remember you are here for dad. Your life can get restarted when you return to Seattle. So it is off this bar stool and up to the room. Tomorrow would be arriving too soon.

6

Anita and Frank sat beside a window in the nearly empty dining room, leisurely finishing their breakfast. The gray skies visible over the nearby buildings promised another cool day.

"I can't believe we both slept in," Anita said, scraping the crumbs on the tablecloth into a neat pile. "We must be adjusting to the time change; now we're sleeping too much instead of too little."

Frank smiled and poured himself more coffee.

"I need to run along now dad. I promised Francine I'd be there early. What do you think you'll do the rest of the morning?" she asked.

"Oh, I'll probably go up and get my book and read a little in the lobby. That big chair near the fireplace seems to have my name on it and the light is good for reading."

"Well, don't be late. I know you like to arrive places at the last minute. Your coat and slacks are on the same hanger. I hit them with my little travel steamer yesterday and they should be fine. Your white shirt looked good too," she said as she finished her coffee. "I'll bet you'll be surprised today. I can't believe that in a group of nearly two hundred men there won't a friend or at least someone you knew. And I don't think you've changed that much from that old Army picture you showed me. Your hair has changed some but I bet they'll recognize you," she said, pausing to kiss him on the forehead. "I'll see you there."

After retrieving his book from the room Frank settled into the comfortable lobby chair. But instead of reading, his eyes drifted to the low flame of the gas log in the fireplace. It was funny he thought; Anita seemed to believe his army days had been like some summer camp. But how could anyone understand if they hadn't been there?

No, it wasn't like the summer camps she attended growing up or those Austrian ski tours that she and Eric joined. Soldiers didn't come back with good memories and photo albums. It wasn't like that at all.

He gazed around the lobby at the strangers, veterans like him, that passed through. It wasn't that he hadn't made friends in the service. He'd made a number of close friends during training. By the time they left England for France they'd been together for five months. They drilled, trained, drank and just generally hung together. But by December, just six months later, he'd become a veteran among strangers. His buddy Westover was dead. Rushing was in the rear, wounded. Most of the original men in his Platoon were either casualties or assigned to other Companies.

The replacements came like pawns in a grand game. Some of them lasted a day; some a week. Those with six months under their belts knew they didn't have much more time. They could do the math. The statistics were all against them.

The persistent flame of the fireplace left Frank in a state of animated reflection. Thinking back he could recall giving up worrying about his physical survival. He might live or he might die but the process was so random he couldn't change the odds. But he did learn to protect his emotions. It was hard to lose a friend. He never learned how to do that painlessly. So he quickly learned the best way to avoid the pain was to keep his distance. He shut down his emotions and did his job. He knew his troops thought he was cold and impersonal. But his job was to follow orders and keep as many of them alive as possible. He could do that with men who respected him. They didn't need to be his friends

Would he see anyone he knew today? Not likely and he was sure Anita wouldn't know why.

"Well, you girls seem to have things under control"

Anita looked up to see an elegant older woman standing across the table from Francine.

"Oh, mother. I didn't see you come in. The initial rush has past and I was just trying to get the remaining packets back in some order. Anita, come here. You must meet my mother. Mother, this is Anita Chase, the American I was telling you about."

"It's a pleasure to meet you Mrs....?" Anita began in French, reaching over the table to take Simone's outstretched hand.

"It's Simone, Anita. Please call me Simone.

"Well, it's a pleasure to meet you Simone. Francine tells me you used to be quite involved in these reunions."

"True. And now I'm quite pleased to be uninvolved. As you can see they can be a great deal of work. And in any case it is time for the younger people to get involved."

"Don't let her fool you Anita. Mother is still involved behind the scenes. For example, it's through her connections that we are able to use the school facilities like this for such a small fee. No one in the school administration would dare to say no to Simone Chauveau, community leader and daughter of the highly respected educator, Henri Challon. She may not be working the registration tables but her mark is on these reunions."

"Ignore my daughter Anita. These are the remarks of a headstrong woman who thinks flattery will keep me involved in the reunions."

"By the way mother, its looks like Charles will not be coming to dinner tonight. He is stuck in Luxembourg. He sends his regrets and said to tell you that you're still his favorite mother-in-law."

"Oh that husband of yours. He works too hard. Well, that means it will just be you and Leon." She paused, turning to Anita. "Say would you care to join us for dinner? I would enjoy talking to you and learning more about your family, where you live and what you think of our small town and country."

"Why, I'd love to but I couldn't abandon my father."

"How inconsiderate of me. Of course your father is included in the invitation. I always enjoy talking to the veterans."

"That is very kind of you" said Anita. "I'll check with him when he arrives and let you know. But I don't think he had any plans. He's been letting me pretty much set the schedule."

"How is your father; in good health I hope?"

"Oh he's a rock; at least for a seventy year old. He had a tough time when mom died but he's bounced back and is healthy as a horse. I wish he'd show up. I'd love for you to meet him."

The conversation was interrupted by the arrival of a van load of veterans. As Francine and Anita searched for their packets and directed them to their seating area Simone slipped away and made her way into the main hall. After greeting the mayor and other local dignitaries she took a seat on the side where she could see the veterans and the door through which they entered.

Frank stood in front of the mirror carefully tying his red, white and blue necktie picked just for the trip. It was the first new tie he'd purchased in many years. When he'd sold his business he threatened to burn his necktie collection and forever live with an open collar. But Doris would have nothing to do with such foolishness. He needed to look presentable, she would say. As usual, she'd been right. At least he'd been able to cut back the number of times he had to wear one, so he felt he'd won a partial victory.

But today he didn't mind the tie. He'd always worn a tie at funerals out of respect for the departed. Today he wore one as a show of respect for his fallen comrades and for Emory.

So I want to look good and, I might say, I do, he thought. Compared with some of the broken down old codgers I've seen in town I look good: damned good.

Before departing he carefully pinned his miniature combat infantry medal on his lapel. It had never before been out of its case.

It was a five minute walk down the old streets of Bastogne to the secondary school. Most of the buildings looked "post war." He tried, without success, to figure which buildings might have survived the German attack fifty years ago. He was sure that some had but, despite his experience as a builder, he couldn't pick them out.

A steady stream of people was approaching the school building when he arrived. Most were dressed in their Sunday best for the occasion. However the younger ones, and there were some younger attendees, tended to be dressed more casually; some in jeans and souvenir tee shirts. And some of the veterans were dressed in shiny nylon jackets, purchased at a previous division reunion, adorned with the red keystone symbol of the division and their name in spiral embroidery.

He found Anita busy at the registration table. She paused long enough to point out Francine, who was working nearby and to find his name tag in the veterans pile in the middle of the table.

"Where have you been? The program's going to start in just a few minutes. Did you fall asleep or something," she said with a nagging twinkle.

He ignored her and walked into the main room, taking a seat on the low stage in the veterans' area. The other attendees were assigned to folding chairs on the main floor. As he anticipated no one looked familiar. He introduced himself to the men on either side, one from Iowa and the other from Texas, and contented himself with small talk while waiting for the program to begin.

The national anthems of Belgium and the United States brought everyone to their feet and tears to a few patriotic eyes. The mayor was followed by a current U. S. Army general who wasn't born when the battle for Bastogne raged. It was during the general's remarks that he saw her.

She was seated on an aisle near the front. There was something regal about her, accentuated by the light from the nearby window. Were his eyes playing tricks? The mouth; the eyes; they looked so familiar. The hair was silver with streaks of dark, swept back and held in place by small clips on each side. She could have been a queen at her court. Her dress or blouse, he couldn't tell which, was partially covered by a gold scarf that draped around her shoulders.

After fifty years, could it be her? He didn't know. He certainly didn't want to look like an old fool rushing up to some stranger and asking her if she could, just perhaps could be Simone Challon. The woman's face was fuller. But the Simone he had known had endured five years of war and poor food. No, her face should be fuller, he thought. But the eyes, the eyes were so Simone…

Suddenly their eyes met and he was sure, absolutely sure that he detected a sense of surprise; of recognition. Or was he so sure? After all, he knew he had changed too. He was no longer the skinny boy she had known. He wasn't even sure he would recognize himself after all the years but yet, he had a sense that she'd seen him; had seen something in him. He had an urge to run from the stage; run to this woman that looked like Simone; run to her and touch her. Instead he sat, transfixed, wishing his eyesight was better; clearer.

His reverie was interrupted by the dimming of the lights as a commemorative video began; projected on a screen, accompanied by marshal music. Attendants walked down the side aisle and pulled heavy drapes across the windows, making the dark complete.

He strained in the dim light of the video screen to make out the woman from his past but the audience had become a blur in the hazy darkness. When the video was over and the lights came up she was gone. Had she ever been there? Was this just the hallucinations of an aging man? No, he was sure someone had been there. But was it her?

He had no idea what the video had been about. His every thought had become hazy from the time he saw her, and he was certain he saw her, until he was standing by Anita after the program. Frank had left the stage and was standing by the woman's empty chair when Anita came up. She was chattering about the program and he didn't know what all. He was only beginning to refocus.

Whatever his state of mind it was effectively masked from Anita. She'd thoroughly enjoyed the program and was having a wonderful time. She shared some of the wise remarks she'd heard from flirting veterans during check-in and told him of the dinner invitation.

Back in the room he concluded that he must have agreed with the dinner idea as Anita was quite excited about the idea of going. But now he was having second thoughts. "They're your friends Anita. They don't need me. I'll just grab a bite downstairs."

"Nonsense. Francine's mother was quite clear with the invitation. We were both invited. Besides, I think you'll enjoy her brother Leon. He's the one that's moving to Seattle. So it won't be all girl talk as you say.

That argument seemed to win him over and he agreed to go as long as they didn't stay long.

"They said the dinner was casual but I don't know what that means in Belgium. What do you think of this skirt and blouse together dad," she inquired holding them up on their hangers.

"Hmmm, fine," he replied.

"You men are all alike. You didn't even look. Oh well; it will have to do," she said, heading to the bathroom and leaving him alone.

He lay back on the bed, mind wandering. How would he find Simone? There is only one more formal event scheduled for tomorrow, a wreath laying ceremony at the big memorial east of town. She might be there. But what if she wasn't? What if she didn't want to be found? If she saw him and then ran off, didn't that mean she didn't want to be found? Maybe she didn't recognize him. Maybe she left for some other reason.

He tossed the alternatives around, reached no conclusion and finally resorted to his favorite escape; he would sleep on it. First they would endure a dinner with Francine and her family. They would all jabber in French and he would do his best to nod and look interested. And then he would return to their room, lie down and decide what, if anything, he should do about looking for Simone Challon.

7

Father and daughter walked carefully along the dimly lit sidewalk, on their way to the dinner engagement with Anita's new friends. Feeling a need for exercise they had decided to walk, soon learning that the street lights, which were just in the process of coming on, were not as frequent in the residential areas as they had been closer to their hotel. In places it was difficult to see and the sidewalk narrowed forcing them to walk single file dodging an occasional puddle. In time they reached the correct street and were standing in front of a neat looking townhouse that matched the description provided by Francine.

As they approached the step Frank paused and turned to Anita. "Now remember; I don't want to stay too late. I can find my way back to the hotel, so if I decide to leave you can stay if you like. I'm not sure how much chatter I can handle."

"Oh dad, you'll have a good time if you'll just relax. They're wonderful people. Don't be such a putz!"

Anita turned, stepped on to the porch and rang the bell. Sounds of laughter emanated from somewhere inside and, in a moment, a shadow passed the sidelight and the door swung open to a warm greeting from Francine.

"Come in, come in," she said in English, for Frank's benefit. Francine hugged Anita and, more formally, shook Frank's hand. "I'm so glad you could come."

Leon, who had been seated by the fire, rose to greet the guests just as a third person entered the living room from the back of the house. "My brother Leon," Francine continued, "and this is my mother Simone Chauveau. Mother, this is Frank Larson."

Simone and Frank, eyes meeting, froze like characters in a tableau. Then, after what seemed like an eternity to Anita, Frank, almost trance like with his eyes fixed on Simone, eased forward taking her down stretched hands in his. Almost in almost a whisper, Anita heard him say, "Simone Challon?"

The others stared in silent disbelief as the scene played out in slow motion before them. Anita glanced at Francine, as if hoping for some explanation, but Francine's perplexed expression offered no relief. Then, with a movement so graceful it appeared to have been choreographed, Frank wrapped his arms around Simone as she buried her head in his chest. Time seemed suspended as they stood together, swaying slightly while their children stood close by trying to understand the scene before them.

Relaxing his embrace, Frank stepped back, leaving his hands resting on Simone's shoulders. Anita stared in wide-eyed disbelief as her conservative father used his thumbs to lightly brush away the tears that were streaming down her cheeks.

Then he turned toward the others and said in a breaking whisper, "This is the woman that saved my life. This is the woman in Wiltz that took me in and saved my life."

The majestic Simone, only a head shorter than Frank, was now standing beside him, wiping her eyes with the white towel that had been tied apron-like around her waist.

"I can't believe it," said Frank, staring at Simone. "I just can't believe it; after all these years."

Leon was the first to recover his tongue. "This is amazing. Why just the other day Mother was telling us about taking in a wounded soldier and hiding him from the Germans. And now we meet him. How wonderful," he said, surprising Frank with a hug before moving to embrace his mother.

Francine and Anita just stood spellbound watching their parents. It had all happened so fast!

Following Frank and Anita's dramatic arrival everyone retired to the kitchen, where Simone tried to continue with dinner preparation. But, whether it was the pressure of performing her kitchen magic before an audience or the emotion of Frank's arrival, she seemed unable to concentrate on the task at hand. Finally Francine poured her a glass of wine and sat her on a stool between Leon and Frank, where she could supervise the final steps and Francine could perform the actual work without tripping over her wandering mother. Anita, recovering from her initial surprise, volunteered for her own assignments helping Francine.

"I feel so awkward, being tossed out of my own kitchen," Simone said as she sat down.

"You shouldn't worry Mother," said Leon. "You trained Francine; she should be able to handle the pressure."

Francine gave Leon a "thanks brother" look and went about her work with practiced efficiency. The pork roast, covered with onions and herbs, was pulled from the oven and set aside to cool before slicing. Roast potatoes and mixed vegetables made up the rest of the main course, assisted by a fresh green salad and bread.

Normally the food would have captured Frank's full attention but his eyes never seemed to leave the Simone, sitting at his left hand.

Later, at dinner, the conversation twisted and turned over a wide array of topics but always returned to the parents. The three children, overflowing with questions, found Frank and Simone short of words.

How did you meet?

What was it like?

What did you think of Americans?

Were you afraid?

In response to Leon's persistent questioning they finally spoke of their first meeting when Frank and his men moved into their second floor rooms.

"But then the Germans came back in December and Frank just disappeared," Simone explained. "He just disappeared that first day of the battle. One day he was there and the next he was gone. The way the Germans seemed to bowl over everything in their path I really feared the worst; death or capture. I just didn't know."

"How long were you in the dark about his fate?" asked Francine.

"About two weeks; two long weeks," she said, looking Frank's direction.

He broke from his trance and continued the story, mentioning a Jeep accident and a nighttime return to Wiltz. "So they find me in the alley behind the Gelsi house, drag me inside and save my life, just like that."

"I don't know that we actually saved your life. You looked pretty bad, half frozen and disheveled, but I suspect you could have figured some way to survive."

"Oh sure," he said with a smile, "at one of those nice resorts the Germans kept for their prisoners. No thanks. I much preferred your cellar."

But all the information extracted from them during dinner took a supreme effort on Leon's part. Both Simone and Frank seemed reluctant to talk about the war or anything else. So they answered questions but volunteered very little.

Dinner over, the dark wooden dining room table was a cluttered collage of glasses, dishes, silverware and an array of serving platters, most nearly empty. All five diners appeared exhausted either from the weight of the food consumed or the intensity of the conversations.

When Francine could no longer stand looking at the mess on the table, she stood and began collecting the dishes. "Say, I have an idea Mother. Why don't you and Frank move into the living room by the fire and Leon and I can clean up. Then we can all have dessert in there with you."

"I'd be happy to help," said Anita, as she stood with a platter in each hand.

"She can have my place," quipped Leon.

"Nice try brother. You can load the dishwasher.

"Really, I can handle the kitchen," protested Simone.

"Mother, you have company and you have lots of catching up to do. Now off with you. I'll start the dessert when we have the kitchen cleaned up. Coffee will be ready in a few minutes.

Pushed along by her willful daughter, Simone soon found herself seated by the fire with Frank nearby in Jule's old leather chair. Two fragrant cups of coffee were soon delivered by Francine, placed in steamy splendor on the small table between them.

Alone again Frank stared at Simone while she stared into the fire. "I can't believe I'm sitting across from you. I really can't," he said, shaking his head. "Of all the people and places in this country and this world where you might be, I find myself at dinner with Simone Challon, or I guess I should say Simone Chauveau, after all these years. What is this, karma or something?"

She sat demurely, with her hands folded in her lap. "It is strange isn't it?" she said in English. Most of the conversation at dinner had been in English, for his benefit. "But, I must confess, I had seen your name on an attendance list so I thought you might be in town. But I didn't expect you to be Anita's father and be at my home for dinner." She turned toward him, "But I'm very glad you're here."

They sat for a few moments with the silence broken only by the hiss of the gas fire and the muffled chatter of the young people in the kitchen.

"Did you see me at the program today?"

Yes, she nodded.

"Why did you run away? I was certain that was you and yet, when the lights came on, you were gone. Do I look that bad?" he said with a smile.

She gave him an embarrassed smile in return. "I don't know. I just wanted to run for some reason. At some level I was afraid that the image of Frank Larson, which I have carried for fifty years, would be shattered by the reality of you now. And worse, I was worried about what might happen to your image of me, if you still had one at all. That sounds silly of course but that was on my mind. Don't you have a saying, leave well enough alone?"

He studied her over the rim of his small cup. "That's funny. That's one of the reasons I've avoided the reunions in the past. First I didn't think I'd see anyone I recognized and, if I did, I might not like what I saw. So I kept their old images in my mind and let it go at that. I mean, you look around that hall today and you see some very rickety old codgers doddering along. And I suspect they say the same thing about me."

"That's not true Frank. You look like you have taken good care of yourself. But is this really your first reunion?"

"Yes, this is the first one," he replied, setting the coffee down and settling back in his chair.

"Why did you choose to come this time?"

Simone listened intently as Frank told her the story of Emory Rushing and of Anita's insistence that he attend.

"Anita seems like a fine daughter. How long has she been divorced?"

"Five or six years. Time flies. It was about the same time as my wife, Doris, was diagnosed with cancer. Between that and the divorce Anita had a couple of tough years."

She watched him closely as he spoke, radiating sympathy with her eyes. "I'm sure you did as well. Losing a loved one is never easy. At least my Jules didn't suffer. He died quite suddenly of a weak heart. He was seventy at the time and lived a full life so we were thankful for that."

"But it was still a loss."

"Yes, of course it was a loss. He was a good man. Francine and her husband were a great help and Leon was here almost every weekend. It seems we are both blessed with good children."

They slipped again into silence, staring into the fire, each lost in their own thoughts. Finally she turned to Frank and said, "Forgive me for being such a vacillating woman. To be honest, for years I have wanted to see you just one more time. The 28th Division has been here several times before and I hoped you might come. It was silly I know for I was a married woman and I would have only been satisfying some curiosity. And then, today I see you and I run away. I guess I still don't understand myself."

Frank watched as her voice tailed off. He then leaned forward, reaching for her hand just as the door to the kitchen swung open and the three 'children' burst into the room, laughing gaily and speaking in rapid fire French.

"Leon, quit picking on Anita," said Francine with a laugh. "She is our guest and I don't want to provoke an international incident.

"Me; she was the one that started the discussion," replied Leon. Switching to English he went on, "Have you two gotten reacquainted? I still can't believe the coincidence."

Anita took a seat on the arm of Frank's chair and placed a light hand on his shoulder. "I do believe your mother has grown more attractive over the years, Leon. She truly has. Why she was just a skinny little thing when I first met her," said Frank.

Simone blushed while the others laughed. "Your father was my meal ticket, Anita. I figured if I was nice to him he would keep bringing us food, as dreadful as some of his food was."

"I bet our food was better than the Germans," said Frank.

"Well, I didn't have to put Germans up in my house, thank heaven. They never stayed around Wiltz very long. I will say I thought the Americans were cuter. Sloppier in their dress and manners but cuter."

The three children exchanged a surprised look, impressed by the relaxed demeanor of the parents.

"I had the feeling that your aunt didn't trust me or any of the others that stayed at the house."

"Would you trust your niece in a house full of Army men with guns and no inhibitions? No, you're right. She wanted to keep an eye on me at all times. But I really think she grew to trust you. And after you came back and were hiding in the cellar, she figured you were too weak to be a threat," said Simone, smiling.

"Now I am offended," said Frank. "In those days I always thought of myself as a threat. I just didn't know how to be threatening."

The light banter continued while they finished their coffee beside the welcoming fire. Finally, with the clock on the mantel showing ten o'clock and Frank threatening to tell a poor joke that she'd heard many times before, Anita rose saying, "Well Dad, we'd better leave before the dinner wine causes you to say something you'll regret later. We don't want to wear out our welcome with these fine people. Up with you now."

"I need to leave as well," said Francine. "Let me drop you by the hotel. It's right on my way."

"Why don't you two go on ahead? I can walk back?" said Frank. "I'm not feeling too tired."

Anita smiled and rolled her eyes. "Come on dad. We have a big day tomorrow." Turning to the others she continued, "I'm his resident nag."

"What is nag?" asked Leon with an innocent air.

They all shared a laugh as Anita explained the meaning and coaxed her father from the chair. "And Francine, we'd love to accept your offer of a ride."

There was no handshaking as the group of new friends gathered at the front door. Instead it seemed to Anita that everyone was kissing everyone in a departure cheek kissing frenzy.

With reluctance Frank climbed into Francine's Volvo for the ride back to the hotel. It had been a busy day.

The sounds of muffled cocktail lounge conversations wafted across the empty lobby as Frank and Anita entered their hotel.

"Gosh, I'm so keyed up I don't think I could get to sleep," said Frank with an uncharacteristic boyish enthusiasm. "Would you like to stop for a nightcap? You can be my trophy date!"

Taking his hand in hers she said, "I'd be glad to be your trophy date. I'm flattered by the offer. Why don't you order me a glass of their house wine while I hit the ladies room? I'll be just a minute."

Frank picked an isolated table near the door and far from the piano which was filling the room with lazy sounds. Waiting to place an order his mind wandered over the delightful evening and to Simone Challon. How many times had her image crossed his mind over the years, he wondered? And now, to see her again; to think about what they had meant to each other. He'd often thought of her in the years following the war. But life had moved on and the memory, like an old photograph, had grown hazy with time. Tonight brought his past back into focus.

Anita joined him at the table, settling into the padded red booth. "This is a good idea," she said. "I'm not sure I could have gone to sleep either. I have too many questions to ask about tonight; about Simone. Maybe I can get you liquored up and get some answers."

He smiled while stirring the ice in his brandy with the swizzle stick.

"Aren't they wonderful people? I feel like I've know Francine forever."

"You two do seem like old friends. Francine reminds me of someone; I can't quite place who. Oh well, maybe it'll come to my old mind after a good night's sleep," he concluded with a chuckle.

"OK, now I'm curious." Anita said, leaning across the small table. "You skimmed over a lot of details at their house; details I want to hear about. Like, what was it like when you first met her? Were you the conqueror or something?"

"Not really. At least I didn't feel like one. I do remember feeling sorry for those people, having to live under the Germans for years. Like I said, when we moved into their house she was just a skinny teenager. I probably lusted after her a bit just because she was a girl and I was a boy. But I behaved; my mother would have been proud of me. We used to sit in the small kitchen after dinner and talk. Her aunt would go to sleep early and her cousin worked odd hours with the intelligence guys. So it was often just the two of us, a couple of old wooden chairs and a warm stove.

"She would tell me about life in Belgium before the war. She told me about coming to Wiltz to help her aunt, leaving her family in Bastogne. She was older than she looked, nineteen, and well schooled. She tried to teach me a few French and German words but I'm afraid I was a poor student. I don't think we ever saw each other outside of the house. That seems strange now that I think about it. But she spent long hours in the clinic, the weather was cold and damp and it grew dark very early. Her schedule plus my nearly daily trips to the front with replacements limited our encounters to that warm kitchen."

"Were you lovers?" boldly asked Anita.

"Now what kind of question is that?" he responded with a hurt expression. "We were a couple of scared kids. I just enjoyed being able to speak to someone my age that wasn't wearing a green uniform. That's all."

Anita grinned, "I just had to ask. So what happened? You mentioned a jeep accident or something..."

"Yes, that pleasant escape from the horrors of war was short lived. It ended for good on December 16th, 1944, a dreary, cold and foggy day. We'd experienced cold weather and snow for several days and, with Christmas approaching, a holiday atmosphere had settled over the little town. That morning began with the rumble of artillery somewhere to the east. The fog and hilly country combined to make it difficult to tell what was going on. I wasn't aware of any plans for us to attack and, if it wasn't us, it could only mean one thing. I grabbed my gear and walked up the hill toward Regimental Headquarters. I didn't think of saying goodbye to anyone. I didn't plan on being gone long."

He paused, hailed the waitress and ordered a second drink. Anita sat, waiting for him to continue. When he didn't she prompted him with, "So you arrived at headquarters..."

"'Larson, get your ass in here,' was my greeting upon arrival. 'We need someone to go forward and see what the hell is going on up there. We're getting conflicting reports and I need some confirmations on the ground so I can sort things out. Sounds like the krauts are up to something. Get your jeep and pick up Major Lux, from intelligence. He can accompany you. Now move it.'

"It seemed like a reasonable request. I'd been back and forth on that road dozens of times. I knew the route as well as anyone. I ran down the hill, retrieved my jeep from its hiding place in the shed behind the aunt's house and was soon on my way back to headquarters to find Lux. He was waiting at the building entrance. I can still picture him wrapped in his wool overcoat with a forty-five holstered across his chest.

"It was chaos in the streets of town, with trucks and jeeps grinding up and down the road. We wound through them and found the road east from Wiltz surprisingly quiet; free of traffic. The fog forced me to drive slowly, always moving toward the sound of big guns. As we made our way down the last hill toward the Company command post it happened. I say 'it' because I don't know what. It could have been a mine or a shell but, whatever it was, it created a terrific explosion and the next thing I recall is lying in deep snow, at the base of a tree, hearing German voices nearby. Falling snow now added to the fog, further cutting visibility. In hindsight, I guess that was good for me.'

He paused, as if talking was a struggle. Anita shared his silence.

"My first instinct was to get up and do something but I found that my right leg wasn't working. I slumped back into the tree well and scraped the snow off of my leg discovering a nice, saucer sized, piece of metal stuck in my thigh. Though it was a shallow cut, that leg bothers me to this day."

"I've often wondered about that red mark on your leg. You've never said..." Anita said with a hint of discovery.

"Anyway, I was able to remove the metal shard, apply sulfa powder and bind up my wound. I was pleased with myself for doing that without fainting as you know I'm a wimp when it comes to the sight of blood, especially my own."

She shook her head in acknowledgment and gave his arm a supportive squeeze.

"I thought of giving myself a shot of morphine but wasn't sure I could do it or if it would fog my thinking. I think the numbing cold must have eased the pain.

"I figured later the jeep had careened off the road and down a low embankment, coming to rest against a tree. Later, when I crawled to the jeep, I found Major Lux, very dead. His wool coat, watch, wallet, boots and pistol were all missing. The Germans hadn't overlooked anything of value or warmth. I'm just lucky they didn't see me. I wasn't that far away.

"From the sounds of vehicles and voices, on the road above, I assumed the Germans were heading west. How far west I didn't know. I also didn't know what had happened to our 110th Regiment that was supposed to insure the Germans didn't end up on the road heading west. Something was wrong; terribly wrong. I couldn't grasp how wrong. But then it took our Generals several days to figure it out too and they were in a better position to know than I was, cloaked in fog, sitting in that snow bank below the road."

He emptied his glass before continuing. "I hoped falling snow would cover my tracks as I crawled back to my tree well. I knew I was near our lines so I figured that I would try to make my way there later. At the time I had no idea of the trouble I was in. God that was a long time ago. But enough of the bad memories," he concluded.

He stopped speaking but his mind moved forward. Today I was reintroduced to Simone, he thought. She was the one bright and shining memory that I carried home from Europe. And today's image was every bit as good as the old one. Different but every bit as good....

"Dad, maybe we should head up. But I do want to hear the rest of the story."

He smiled, slipped easily from the booth and followed Anita to the elevator.

8

"Good morning Lieutenant Larson," Anita chirped as she joined him at the breakfast table. She was clad in a forest green sweater, a black wool skirt and knee high leather boots.

Frank lowered his "Financial Times" and peered at her over his reading glasses. "I gave up on you. I thought you were never going to come out of that bathroom so I came on down. There's coffee in this pitcher."

"Great. I need a cup," she said while pouring.

"You look quite dressed up for standing in the cold laying a wreath. And your hair is different too, isn't it."

"You noticed. I'm impressed. I just put it back a little on the sides. Not much of a change really."

"Well, if I was twenty years younger I'd be chasing you around the dining room," he said as he raised his paper and continued his reading.

"Aren't you the spry one this morning. You must have had a good night's sleep. I know I did. I slept like a rock.

"I noticed. You beat me to lights out."

Frank lowered his paper and watched Anita as she made a pass through the buffet line, returning with a bowl of fruit covered with yogurt and slice of heavy local bread.

"That won't carry you to lunch," offered Frank, glancing up at her return.

"I have to watch my girlish figure dad. I am determined not to return to Seattle looking like a blimp. Anyway, I love their bread."

"What surprise do you have in store for us today? Have you made any other new friends in this town?"

"It's a good thing I made a few friends or you might not have seen Simone," she said, sipping her coffee. "Wasn't last night just fabulous? I mean, imagine, you meeting a woman you haven't seen for fifty years. Maybe I'll get you on one of the local talk shows when we get home. I mean, this is really something. And Simone is such a lovely lady, isn't she?"

"Mmmm; suppose so," he replied, looking into the distance. "Yes, she is a nice looking woman. And it's funny; I recognized her at the program yesterday. There's just something about her that hasn't changed. She says that's true for me too but I have trouble believing that."

At that moment they were interrupted by the clerk from the front desk. "Excuse me, but are you Mrs. Chase; Anita Chase?"

Anita nodded.

"There is a call for you, Mrs. Chase. You may take it on the phone by the fireplace."

"You're getting calls now?" asked Frank with a hint of surprise.

"Must be Francine. She said she might call. I won't be a minute," she replied as she pushed back from the table and made her way to the lobby.

In a few minutes she returned with a happy but puzzled look on her face.

"Well, what have you and Francine cooked up for today?"

"Ah, well, we actually have cooked something up, as you say, but only if it is ok with you."

"OK. Spill it. You have that 'I have something to ask' look. You know, the one you used when you wanted to borrow our good car when you were in high school. This should be good," he said, folding his newspaper and laying it to one side. "You have my full attention, young lady."

She paused, assembling her thoughts into a plausible form. "Well, here's the deal. You may have heard Francine and Leon talking about going to Luxembourg City tonight to meet her husband at some trade show."

Frank was silent.

"Well, anyway, they are; are going to Luxembourg City I mean. They say it is a beautiful city and there are lots of things to do and it is near the Moselle Valley, a wine growing area and..."

"And they've invited you along."

'But only if it's ok with you. They understand that we're here together and they, I mean I, would understand if you preferred that I stay here and do some touring with you; but they extended the invitation in case I had an interest. Leon said his mother would love to show you around for a couple of days and it would give you two a chance to catch up. But if you don't think it's a good idea just say so."

"Now what makes you think that Simone would want to spend several days with a worn out GI?"

"Leon asked her and she thought it would be a delightful idea. At least that's what he said. He said she suggested a drive to Wiltz to see her cousin; the one that lived with her and helped rescue you. She had some other ideas as well and seemed OK with the idea." Anita paused, biting her lip and twisting her napkin into a knot. "Oh, I'm sorry dad. Now I feel so manipulative. I shouldn't go and leave you here. We came together and need to stay together. I'll just tell them I've decided not to go. I'm sure they'll understand. Yes, that's really the right thing to do. And we can still see Simone and the cousin."

Frank laughed at her discomfort and leaned across the table, grasping her left hand. "You'll do no such thing. Hey, I'm an adult. I don't need to be entertained. I'll be just fine. I like the idea of going to Wiltz with Simone. That's a wonderful idea. Will we still make the same flight home?"

"Francine can make all the arrangements. She runs a tour company you know. Anyway, she said she can rebook us from Luxembourg City, rather than from Brussels. The Copenhagen flight is the same. Even if there is a charge it will only be a small one and Luxembourg City is a little closer than Brussels so we don't have as far to drive."

Anita's words gushed as if from a prepared speech. Frank was amused by her obvious discomfort.

"I'm impressed. You haven't overlooked anything. So, do it. It sounds like a grand idea and you should go. I'll be fine. It'll be nice not having to share a hotel room for a few nights. I can toss my clothes around and be as messy as I want. So go; it will be good for both of us. I just hope Simone doesn't get tired of me."

Anita smiled, unknotted her napkin and pushed back from the table. "I need to pack then. I won't be coming back here." She gave Frank a hug from behind as she left for the room, whispering in his ear as she did so, "I love you dad. You're the greatest."

Then she was gone with a bounce to her step.

The low clouds continued to block the sun as they pulled into the parking lot near the museum and memorial. The pavement and grass glistened with the fall dew and the dampness drove the cold to the very bone. Leon was waiting near the entrance to the museum and waved as they drove past. By the time they came rolling to a stop he'd covered nearly fifty yards of pavement and was ready to help them from the car like a hotel doorman. He opened Anita's door first.

"Anita and Frank, it is so good to see you," he said as he traded cheeks with Anita. "Mother and Francine are saving you seats. Let me show you the way."

Frank trailed behind, surprised to see Anita take Leon's arm as they walked across the lot toward the seating area. Frank smiled as he listened to their laugh filled and animated conversation. He couldn't understand a word of it.

Looking ahead he spotted Simone sitting on an aisle next to her daughter. They rose as Frank approached. "Here are your seats Mr. Veteran," said Francine. "The rest of us are supposed to stand."

"You sit back down Simone. No sense in you standing."

"But the seats are for the veterans and their families. I really should stand with Leon."

"You are my family today. Anita is young and healthy. She can stand. Besides, I understand she's joining your family for a trip to Luxembourg and you're stuck with me for a few days so she can start standing with them now. Can you imagine…her abandoning her poor old father in a strange country?"

Simone gave Anita a concerned look.

"Ignore him," Anita said with a sparkling smile. "He's trying to make us feel bad. When I told him he could spend time with you he couldn't wait for me to pack and head out of town. I'd be careful with him Simone. I have no idea what he has in mind for the next few days."

Simone blushed and shook her head as if not quite knowing what to believe.

Simone and Frank stood side by side on the front porch, watching Francine and the others pull away, on the way to Luxembourg. "May I offer you something warm; tea or coffee? It's chilly just standing out here," she offered.

"If it's not any trouble. I don't want to become a pest and lose my tour guide for the next couple of days."

She offered him a confused smile. "I am never too sure if you are serious or not. Of course you won't lose me as a tour guide, as you call it. You're not really worried are you?"

"No of course not," he replied, opening the heavy front door and following her into the warm house. "I guess my quirky sense of humor may not translate very well. You may have to try Anita's approach. She says she ignores about half of what I say and that leaves her with plenty to work with."

"I'll remember that. Anita must know you very well. But if I seem a little confused from time to time please forgive me."

She led the way into the kitchen while he examined the home with a builder's eye. It was modern with a Scandinavian flavor; clean lines and natural woods. It showed little sign of the dinner party that had been produced the night before.

They agreed on coffee and she soon was pouring steaming water into her French press. She placed it on a silver tray with the cups, coffee service and a plate of shortbread cookies she'd produced from the cupboard near the stove. When all was in order she carried the tray into the dining room followed by Frank.

Before taking his seat Frank paused to examine a collection of family pictures on the wall behind the buffet. "Is that Jules?" he inquired, pointing to a photo of two people posed on a ski slope.

"Yes it is. And that is me buried in that ridiculous fluffy hat. You can barely see my face peeking out. It was taken in Zermatt many years ago."

"He was a fit and handsome man."

"Yes he was. He was sort of a thin Leon. Leon has many of his features but eats more and better and it shows."

"Now be kind to those of us who carry a little reserve weight around the waist. You never know when it will come in handy."

"That's what Leon says. I actually thought Jules was too thin but he never agreed. He never put on weight after he came back from the Russian front. I don't know if it was physical or mental but he never seemed to gain."

"What was he doing in Russia?"

"He was conscripted by the Germans and that is where they sent him. He didn't talk much about it but I understand they endured terrible hardships. He always felt his shoulder wound saved his life because he was sent to a hospital in Denmark. He said it was better to be a wounded German soldier than a healthy Russian prisoner. The Russians would not have cared what country he was from if he was caught wearing a German uniform."

"Did you know him before the war?"

"No. He grew up on a farm west of here and was eight years older. We met after the war when I went to work in the clinic here in Bastogne. He had been released from the hospital at the end of the war and moved to Bastogne to set up a practice at the town clinic. It took over a year to fully recover from his wound. It did a great deal of damage to the bone and muscle of his left arm. That arm was never very strong but he didn't let it slow him down."

"Love at first sight?"

"I don't get your meaning," she replied, confused.

"Did you have a long courtship?"

"Oh, I see. Did we fall in love when we first met? I'm not sure I would describe it that way. We were both war weary young people and we were good for each other. Maybe we needed each other. Most of our town had been destroyed; many friends were gone. It wasn't the same place after the war. Our world was changed and it was comforting to have someone like Jules to lean on as we tried to construct a new life out of the ruins. I guess love just happened because we were together so much. Do you understand?"

"It must have been a most difficult time."

She nodded while swirling her cream into the coffee. "How was it with your wife; Doris isn't it?"

"Yes, Doris. We just hit it off I guess," he said, studying a cookie. "I'd known her in high school but lost contact when I went in the Army. But a friend of a friend knew where she was working so I gave her a call when I returned just to catch up on old times. Six months later she is Mrs. Frank Larson. Anita came along the next year and life just seemed to take a course of its own."

"Children do that to one's life. What struck me though is how quickly they pass through your life and you find yourself alone. One day they are born and the next they are graduating from school. I always thought I would be devoting most of my life to child rearing and yet, in twenty years I was done and they were on their own."

Frank thought about her remark for a moment before replying. "Funny. I've had the same thoughts. Seems like we spend the first quarter of our life growing up and going to school. Then the next is consumed with marriage and children. Finally the last half is without children. So basically the kids are around only about one quarter of your life, unless you have a whole string of them."

"A string of them?"

"That means lots of them. If you have lots of kids they consume more of your life. Of course, we just had one so she was in and out of our care quickly."

They sat silently for a few moments, lost in their own thoughts.

"When did you get involved with the reunions?" he asked.

"Interesting question. Actually I first became involved in 1969 when we were organizing the 25th anniversary events. My involvement really grew from then on. But I have always enjoyed the work. Maybe I like old soldiers," she offered with a laugh.

He finished the last of his coffee and placed the cup back on its fragile saucer. "If I told you I was just a lonely soldier in town looking for some female companionship would you join me for dinner?"

She laughed softly. "Aunt Anne always warned me about lonely soldiers. Anyway, you don't need to take me to dinner. I don't want to monopolize your time. I'm sure there are people you want to see."

"The only person I know in this town is you and it just so happens that you're also the only person in town that I want to see. But if you'd like a quiet evening without guests, I'd understand. But if you would like to share a dinner with me I'd be honored. It's the least I can do after the wonderful spread you laid out last evening. And you'll need to pick the place. I'm a stranger in these parts," he added with a western twang that was lost on Simone.

She tilted her head and studied the man sitting at her table, as if trying to decipher him. Then, leaning forward and taking his hands in hers she said, "Of course I will have dinner with you. Why don't you pick me up at seven? If you can trust me to choose, I will make some calls for reservations. All the restaurants are not open on Sunday but I'm sure I can find something."

Comfortable in each other's company Frank and Simone cleared the table and deposited the dishes in the kitchen. Then, politely but firmly, she shooed him out of the kitchen and the house. When he was gone she turned and leaned against the heavy front door. Staring into space she shook her head resisted a slight smile and then headed upstairs to her room.

A party atmosphere prevailed in the car as the happy trio careened down the highway to Luxembourg City. The fast moving conversation left Anita struggling to keep up with their rapid fire French. After a time Leon turned his attention to Anita, peppering her with questions about Washington State, her current and his future home. Surprised to learn that the state was home to a growing and respected wine industry Leon exacted a promise that Anita would lead him on a tour of the best regional wineries when he arrived at his new home.

"You had better be careful with Leon, Anita," cautioned Francine. "He forgets you have a life of your own to live in Seattle. He will try to monopolize your time if you don't keep him in line."

"I doubt that," she said with a laugh. "He'll soon fall for one of those Microsoft millionaire women and will forget we ever exchanged phone numbers."

"Good idea," said Leon. "If I found a rich woman I could buy a villa in Switzerland and forget about international law and all of that nonsense. I like your idea Anita. I will have to look for a rich woman at Microsoft. But aren't they all computer nerd type people?"

"Oh, I'm sure you can find someone in marketing or something. Marketing people are supposed to be more fun than programmers," she said with a laugh.

It grew quiet in the car as the three watched the colored fall countryside skim past.

"I feel a little guilty leaving dad behind. He said he was OK but I can never be too sure about what he's really thinking. Are you sure your mother was OK with being a tour guide?"

"She was funny at first," replied Francine. "It was as if she wanted to and then she wasn't so sure. I can't recall seeing her quite so, so flustered. But the more she thought about it the more comfortable she seemed to become with the idea. Anyway, she didn't have anything big on her calendar so being with your dad can't be such an imposition. No, I think she was glad they could spend a little more time together."

"Your father is quite a guy. He has, how do you say it, a dry sense of humor?" said Leon.

"Oh, it's dry alright. My poor mother had to put up with it for over forty years. As you might imagine she heard some of his lines more that once. He also has the ability to use humor to deal with tough situations. When my mother was ill he tried his best to make light of things and keep her mind off of her condition. I don't know how it was for her but it helped the rest of us."

"Well, I think he is cute and I love his sense of humor. Of course, I probably don't understand most of his stories but he has such a twinkle in his eye when he tells them," said Francine.

"He's a wonderful guy; stubborn at times but wonderful none-the-less. I can't tell you how much he helped me during my dark days of divorce. When my spirits were at their lowest I'd stumble over to his house and get a boost. I don't know how he did it because he was dealing with mom's illness at the same time, but he did."

"Did your girl friends step up and support you?" asked Francine, while changing lanes in the outskirts of the city.

"My two best friends helped. But others, that I thought were my friends, treated me like a pariah. It was like they figured the breakup must have been my fault because Eric was such a great guy. It couldn't have been his fault. I don't even think they connected the dots when he appeared at a charity event with his little Kimberly just a month after we went public with our separation."

Leon turned to look at Anita in the back seat. "What do you mean, 'connect the dots?'"

"Sorry. It means they ignored the clues. If they paid attention they would have seen I had been traded in on a younger model, that's all."

Francine looked at Leon, "Did your friends abandon you?"

"No. I was lucky. I think some of my friends thought my wife was a bimbo all along so when she ran off it confirmed their old expectations."

"I'm sorry Leon, the woman was a bimbo!" injected Francine.

"I don't think that was a fair assessment of her but, what the hell, she did run off. In any case, I was treated so well by some of our friends that I think some of the husbands were getting jealous," he said with a laugh. "But no matter how you do it, it takes time to become a single again after being a couple for many years."

"I think I will stay married," Francine concluded. "It seems easier than what you two have gone through."

By now they were approaching their hotel, the Parc Central, in downtown Luxembourg City. Familiar with the area Francine soon had her car in the hands of the valet and their luggage on its way to their room. When the traveling trio arrived at the suite they were greeted by Charles Hardenne, Francine's husband.

Francine threw her arms around him and, to his apparent surprise, gave him a passionate welcome kiss. "It's so good to see you darling. I have just spent an hour hearing about the trials of divorce and have concluded that I am happy to be married and fully intend to stay that way."

"Well I don't know what prompted that welcome but," he said turning to Leon and Anita, "you two will need to wait in the hall or the bar. I need some time alone with my wife. It will only take a minute or two."

"Oh, you're awful. It's a wonder I ever kiss you at all. Anita, this is my husband Charles. Charles, this is the woman I was telling you about, Anita Chase, of the U.S.A."

"Ms. Chase; I'm so pleased to meet you and glad you chose to join us on our little trip to the big city. And you Leon? You're looking fit. All ready for your trip to the promised land, America?"

"Absolutely. Absolutely. I could leave tomorrow if needed. But I don't actually make the move for a couple of weeks. Just wrapping up personal and work things in the meantime. Hey, nice room," he said as he walked into the suite and surveyed the surroundings. "I hope you're paying the hotel bill!"

"It is great isn't it? Since I was involved planning this trade show the hotel assumed I was someone important and upgraded me to this suite for the price of a regular room. Look around if you like. I've staked out the big bedroom for Francine and me. You two can fight over the two over there. The only hitch is that you will be sharing a bathroom but I figure you're adult enough to handle that. Though I would advise Anita to lock her door. You can never trust a lawyer."

"I'm familiar with that adage," replied Anita with a laugh. "We feel the same way about them in the states and I should know; I work in an office full of them."

"But you're not a lawyer, I hope."

"No, so you can't offend me when you joke about them."

Charles was not what Anita had expected. He was slightly built, only a few inches taller than Francine, with a neatly trimmed goatee and mustache that gave him an elfin look. His quick wit was matched by his quick movement. He seemed to be in perpetual motion, moving from place to place, directing the bellman with the luggage, answering the phone and sorting through the boxes of brochures that were piled in the corner of the suite near a desk that he had taken over as his trade show headquarters.

"O.K. everyone. Here's the deal for tonight, subject to your collective approval. First, I have appropriated some wine from the displays downstairs and you will find it in the bar over there," Charles said, pointed toward the alcove near the door. "Help yourself. Second, I have to run down and greet some of my clients at a little reception being hosted by a vendor. After I show my face for a respectable period of time I'll slip out and we can go to dinner. I've made reservations at La Rue. It is a nice place with a dance band and good food. Kind of a 1930's motif. I've never eaten there but it comes highly recommended and I had to pull strings to get us in. I'm afraid you'll need a tie Leon. Sorry about that. Anyway, that is the plan. How does it sound?"

"Oh Charles," Francine swooned with a laugh. "You're such a take charge man. Isn't he great?" she said turning to Leon and Anita. "Of course it's fine. Now get out of here to your reception. We will be here drinking until you return so don't be too long."

After confirming the time, Charles slipped off to his reception, leaving the others to unpack, uncork and unwind.

The waiter unobtrusively set down the gleaming coffee press with steam curling from the small pouring spout and then discreetly left them alone at their table, tucked in the back corner of the restaurant. Simone had selected Lombardi's and the meal and ambiance had been exquisite. It was a small family owned restaurant, with just twelve tables, tucked in a narrow space just off the main city square. Frank had passed by the entrance during his daily walks and had not noticed the understated sign. But the locals knew about it and when Frank and Simone arrived they were shown to the only unoccupied table. The owner, a long time friend of Simone's, had greeted her warmly, though Frank could only pick up an occasional word. He wasn't sure how Simone had introduced him but the owner was most enthusiastic when he shook Frank's hand in greeting.

At Simone's suggestion they had both selected the plat du jour, a lamb stew, prepared in a wine sauce that Frank enjoyed but could never have successfully described. The recommended wine was from the Moselle Valley, just a short distance from Bastogne. Dinner conversation had focused on children, grandchildren and other neutral subjects. They both seemed more comfortable not talking about Frank and Simone. But, with the dinner dishes removed, the tables near them vacated and the wine settling in, the atmosphere warmed and they grew more reflective.

Frank was the first to speak, following the waiter's departure. He had been silently studying the woman across the table as the waiter completed his work. "You know, you are an attractive woman."

Simone, startled by the comment and the change of subject, looked up abruptly and then gave Frank an embarrassed smile. "That's just the wine talking, soldier boy. Or maybe it's the poor lighting."

"I've seen you in the light when I was stone cold sober. No, I'm sure of it," he added with a smile. "You are a beautiful woman."

"At my age I don't hear many compliments like that so perhaps I should just accept it. So I thank you Frank Larson. That is a very kind thing to say."

The small room was quiet except for the sounds of classical music wafting from the yellowed speakers high on the wall near their table. He smiled, still studying Simone until she could no longer endure the silence.

"How did you like your meal?" she said, offering him a chocolate from small plate the waiter had brought with the coffee.

"It was really wonderful. It pays to dine with a local. You know the best spots."

She smiled, turning a spoon over and over in her hands.

"It's funny," he continued. "Here we are in 1994 in this wonderful little place but, while I was eating, I found my mind drifting to a different place, fifty years ago. Do you recall that stew we often made in your aunt's kitchen with the meats from my rations, your vegetables and I don't know what all. I can remember working with you, under the watchful eye of your aunt, putting a whole lot of different things in the pot trying to make something palatable. Then we would just sit in the kitchen making the meal last as long as we could."

"That was a long time ago. I too think of it from time to time. We certainly made the best of a bad situation."

"The truth is," said Frank, "that I ate slow hoping your aunt would finish and leave us alone. Those evenings working with you and just talking in the kitchen were the best evenings I'd had since I'd arrived in Europe."

She smiled at Frank over the rim of her coffee cup. "I doubt that but they were nice times. You were just there for a few weeks but after a few days I felt I had known you for years."

"Really? That's how I felt too. For me, your kitchen was a refuge from the war. For months we'd been living in the wet, the cold and the mud. That little kitchen took me away from all of that. You would ask me all sorts of questions about my home, my school, my friends....everything that I had left and hadn't had time to think about for months. Talking to you took my mind back home. At least that's what I thought later. At the time I wasn't prone to be so philosophical."

"We were just kids."

"We were, weren't we? Just kids. And just the year before, when I'd been in high school playing basketball and chasing girls, you were living in an occupied country that I probably couldn't have located on a map. That always seemed so unfair to me. It was as if you had been deprived of your fun years."

"Perhaps we didn't know what we were missing. But you are right. At nineteen I had lived a quarter of my life under the threat of war or actual occupation. But we did what we needed to do to survive.

That is what people do; try to survive. One thing I do remember is talking to you about books and music. We had just met, had to converse in my broken English and came from very different cultures and yet we had both enjoyed some of the same books and music. They were kind of a universal language and made the world seem a bit smaller for me. And, may I say one more thing without you laughing?"

He poured the remains of the coffee into their cups, smiling in anticipation. "No promises, but I'll try not to smile."

"You were such a nice boy. Some of the soldiers, both American and German, were not so nice. They could be rude and pushy. But you were polite and respectful, particularly of my aunt. Maybe I had, how do you say it, a crush on you? Anyway, I think my aunt suspected something which is why she kept an eye on me."

He smiled. "Nice boy! Here I wanted to be viewed as a gallant warrior and you saw me as a 'nice boy.' Now my whole self image is at risk."

"Now don't you make fun of me. You know I thought you were a special boy. You just may not have known when I started feeling that way. I shouldn't have said anything."

"No, I'm sorry. I'm glad you said something. Makes an old man feel good," he said, looking toward the front of the restaurant where the owner stood watching them with a fatherly air. "Looks like they want to close up. Perhaps I should escort you home so we can both get some rest. We have a big day tomorrow."

"Yes of course. And I have to tell you one more thing. I think I even convinced my aunt you were a nice boy. Now what do you think of that? I can't tell you how many times she told the story of the wonderful American soldier that lived with her during the war. She thought you were very special."

"So she concluded I was harmless too!"

"Perhaps, perhaps; but then she didn't know you as well as I did. That might have changed her mind, don't you think?"

Frank studied her intently and then, without words, reached across the table to squeeze her hands.

A small band filled the crowded restaurant with throbbing notes of a dated disco beat, drawing a dozen gyrating couples to the hardwood floor. "Leon seems quite taken by little Miss Anita," said Charles as he studied Leon and Anita moving around the dance floor.

Francine looked at him in surprise. "What are you talking about," she said, her eyes following his to the enthusiastic dancers. "Oh my! They do seem to be enjoying themselves don't they? But really Charles, they are just dancing. I don't think anyone is taken by anyone. They're just dancing."

"Are you blind? He hangs on her every word. He raced to open her car door on the way over here. I thought he was going to trample the valet who gets paid to open doors. And when I offered him the front seat, he said he was sure you wanted to sit with me so he hopped in back. No, I've been watching him. He is taken. I haven't seen much sign from her but I don't know her like I know Leon. The man is in trouble whether he knows it or not."

"I think you are reading too much into his acts of kindness," she said, as she watched the two dancers share a joke that left them both laughing as they headed back to the table glistening with perspiration.

"That was wonderful," gushed Anita as she slid into the booth. "I can't remember having this much fun on a dance floor in I don't know how long. Your brother is a fair dancer and a great storyteller."

"Oh, he can tell stories all right," said Francine, talking loudly to be heard over the music. 'But don't forget he's a lawyer so you can't believe most of them."

"I'll remember that," she said, leaning into Leon as she laughed at a private joke.

"We'll, I don't want to break up the party but, since I have to get up early in the morning and I'm driving, I suggest we head back to the hotel. Anyone care to join me?"

"You are very persuasive Charles," said Leon, sliding from the booth and offering Anita his hand. "The driving part got my attention. I have no interest in walking across the city in the dark. Ladies, shall we go?"

"This was a wonderful place and you all have been wonderful company. Great suggestion Charles. You can make reservations for me anytime," said Anita as she took Leon's arm and left the restaurant.

Frank pulled up to Simone's home and parked in a vacant spot at the curb. Then he bounded around the car to open her door, offering his hand to help her out. She smiled and kept his hand as they walked to the front door, releasing it only when necessary to search for the key.

Frank stood silently behind her until the door swung open. Then she turned, took both of his hands in hers and kissed him gently on each cheek. Still holding hands he leaned back, where he could see her better in the dim light. Their eyes met, their hands slipped free and they embraced, with her head pressed against his chest. Eyes closed he savored the touch of her hair on his cheek and the fragrance of Simone; the fragrance of a woman he once knew. The darkness concealed the tears in his eyes. He couldn't see hers.

"I'd better be going," he said, when they had released one another. "We've had a busy day."

"Would you like to come in?"

"I would love too, more than you know, but your aunt, God rest her soul, wouldn't approve. And if I stay you may change your mind about me being a nice soldier."

"You're probably right," she said laughing and pressing her hands against his coat lapels. "I've had a wonderful evening Frank. It's been fifty years but I still think you are a nice guy. Good night. I'll see you in the morning."

She rose to her toes, kissed him lightly on the lips, turned and retreated into the house.

Short of breath Frank floated back to the car.

Anita sat on her bed with a book closed on her lap. She could hear Leon showering nearby but, otherwise, the suite was quiet.

What a fabulous evening, she thought, staring out of the uncurtained window with the evenings dance tunes tumbling through her head. God, the evening had been magnificent. What was that song, "I Could Have Danced All Night?" Well, she could have. It was wonderful in Leon's arms. He was so solid and in control on the dance floor. Actually he was solid in general. What a great guy; such a gentleman, opening doors, helping with her coat. Was it a European thing or is he being unusually attentive? She decided he was being attentive and let it go at that.

It had been a long time since she'd been in a man's arms on a dance floor. It felt good to have his hand on the small of her back and to bury her face in his chest during the slow numbers. She hoped she didn't feel too flabby when he held her. She remembered wishing the band would stick to slow songs so she could stay in his arms a bit longer. And the smell of his aftershave had been so pleasant; so Leon.

She slipped from the bed and stood at the window, watching the cars on the narrow street below. Well, she thought smiling; whatever he was thinking there is nothing that says I can't let my fantasies loose on their own. What if he came across the hall and slipped into my room like those guys in the romance novels? What would I do? Resist? Swoon? Now that would be quite a picture, with his sister across the suite. But it's the '90s. Maybe I could slip into his room and take charge. Maybe, but I'm a girl from the fifties and that's not going to happen. Oh well. It's a nice thought.

She flopped back into the easy chair with her leg draped over the side. What on earth was she thinking? She wasn't on this trip looking for a man. She was on the trip to be with her father; the father she'd abandoned in Bastogne. Well, that was ok. He would have a good time with Simone. Until tonight she had seen Leon simply as Francine's brother. That was it. But something happened tonight or, maybe it started today, and now she was seeing him as a gorgeous man right under her nose. He was available; she was available and, could you believe it, he was moving across the world to Seattle. How good was that?

But was it good at all? Could it be one of those cruise ship romances where the person looks really good out of their native habitat but when you see them again, after the cruise, you wonder what you ever saw in them. But she was out of her habitat and he is in his and she was thinking he looked pretty good. The risk was that he would not be as enamored with her in her mundane habitat. Well, then she'd be no worse off than she was when they met. And at least she'd have had a wonderful time while she was here.

It had truly been a fantastic night she thought as she dozed off in the chair. And there was no knock at the door.

9

Frank fumbled for the bedside lamp switch in the still darkened room. Squinting at his watch in the new light he saw the numerals 6:30 staring back; no wonder it was still dark outside. He had slept poorly, struggling to get warm thoughts of yesterday out of his head. His teen years were long past but his time with Simone had left him feeling like he'd just returned from a date with a very special girl. Holding her, however briefly, had ignited feelings he'd thought were long burned out with age. He could have stood on the porch until dawn, holding her in his arms and enjoying the fragrance of her body; the touch of her hair.

Was he out of his mind? He was seventy years old, lived half a world a way and was firmly committed to simplifying his life. He prided himself in controlling his emotions. He remembered some politician that warned of avoiding foreign entanglements and yet here he was being drawn into one of a very different kind. He'd successfully resisted all of Sharon Webber's romantic snares and here he was slipping into one all on his own. It was nuts!

He fluffed his pillow, placed his hands behind his head and lay staring at the ceiling as his mind traveled back in time. It was 50 long years ago, as two scared young kids, that they'd first held each other. They'd hid in each others arms during some long and frightening nights while the German tanks rumbled up and down the street above their protective cellar. They thought they were in love. They knew they needed each other. But war and time and distance tore them apart and left them to live separate lives, continents apart.

Am I crazy to do it all over again, he wondered? I mean, am I crazy to have feelings for a woman I will say farewell to in two short days and, in all likelihood, never see again? Maybe last night didn't mean that much to her. Maybe I'm making too much of a simple goodbye hug. These Belgians are a demonstrative people. Maybe a hug at the door means less to them than it does to me. It really doesn't matter. In two days they would be separated, possibly forever. What could it hurt to enjoy her company in the meantime; what could it possibly hurt?

After tossing those thoughts around for a while he dragged himself from bed, showered and enjoyed a quiet breakfast, sitting alone. He was just finishing the newspaper when the desk clerk found him.

"Mr. Larson, I have a call for you. You can take it in the lobby or I can send it to your room."

Frank picked up his half full coffee cup and followed the clerk to the lobby phone. It had to be Simone. He didn't know anyone else in town. He'd felt foolish when he returned to the hotel last evening as he had forgotten to make any plans for today. He assumed he would see her but had not broached the subject. That was unlike him. Hopefully, he reached for the phone.

"Oh Frank, I hope I didn't disturb your breakfast. I tried to leave a message but the clerk insisted he had seen you in the dining room and..."

"Oh, don't worry about my breakfast. I was just sitting there like an old man trying to decide what to do today."

"Well, I have an idea if you don't think me presumptuous. I finally got a hold of Cousin Mark in Wiltz and he is dying to see you. He's invited us to his home for lunch. I told him I'd have to check with you."

"Mark Gelsi; how wonderful. Of course I'd love to see him and lunch certainly works. You're going too of course? When should I pick you up?"

"Yes I'm going; 11:30 would give us time enough. It's a short drive to Wiltz," she replied.

"Could I come early; say 10:30? I'd like to drive around the countryside east of Wiltz and see if I remember anything. You can be my tour guide."

"That would be fine Frank dear. See you then."

Frank dear! The words brought a smile to his face as he hung up the phone. He turned and walked slowly toward the elevator, stopping to generously tip the desk clerk as he passed.

Leon was comfortably seated near the suite's bay window reading a newspaper when Anita walked absentmindedly from her room, still tying her light cotton travel robe. When she saw him she cursed herself silently for not having the good sense to run a brush through her hair before greeting the day. As a consolation she ran her fingers through her twisted curls in a half hearted attempt to fluff them up and make them presentable. It was too late. Leon was about to see the real Anita.

"Well good morning. I hope I didn't wake you banging around out here fetching the paper and making the coffee," he said while rising from his chair in a most gentlemanly fashion.

He was wearing what appeared to be a silk smoking jacket giving him a very continental look, she thought.

"No, no. I didn't hear a thing; I slept like a rock. Did you sleep well?"

"Actually no. Something I ate didn't agree with me. I felt a bit rummy most of the night. I'm feeling better now though. A bit tired but otherwise ok.

"Sorry to hear that. Are you still up for a little touring?" she said while helping herself to the coffee from the small hotel coffee maker.

"Touring yes. Mountain climbing no. Today shouldn't be too grueling so I should be fine. It's probably a good way to tour the wineries. If my appetite is gone I may not drink and eat so much," he said with a laugh.

Just as Anita plopped down on the sofa, with her carefully balanced coffee, Francine and Charles made an appearance with Charles barely pausing on his way down to his conference. "Well, it looks like you two are stuck with me for the day," said Francine, as she stood by the small coffee maker, waiting for it to complete a second brewing. "Charles will be busy until dinner. Is everyone still on for a little wine tasting?"

After a plan for the day was agreed upon Anita excused herself and wandered off with her half a cup of coffee to take a "quick shower."

"Nice lady, isn't she?" Francine asked.

"Hmm, I mean yes, nice lady," said Leon, without laying his newspaper aside.

Francine studied him for a moment, shook her head and returned to her room without comment.

After a lazy breakfast at the hotel the trio retrieved their car and headed out of the city armed with a map and a list of wineries provided by the absent Charles. The weather was misty, putting a damper on the scenery but the picturesque wineries still exuded a certain magic as they drove from one to another up the river valley. As he predicted, Leon was a little subdued but his spirits were sustained by the chatter of the two new friends, Anita and Francine. Leon skipped the last two wineries, choosing instead to stay in the car with the seat laid back, catching a brief nap. All too soon they were winding back down the river valley to their hotel, satisfied with the day's activity.

At 5:00 o'clock Charles returned, sweeping in and giving Francine a warm kiss in passing. "Well, how did the wine tasting work out? You were treated well I hope."

"Actually, a couple of the wineries were closed and at some of the others, the people you suggested we contact were not there. It seems there is a big trade show in Luxembourg City or something," Francine offered, watching for Charles reaction.

"That was stupid of me wasn't it? Of course most of the owners are here for the show. I knew that but with so much on my mind I put their names down anyway. Forgive me for my faux pas.

"You are forgiven," Francine said playfully as she handed him a glass of wine. "Anyway, even if the owners were not on site, dropping their names seemed to get the attention of the staff so all was not lost."

"We tried your name, Charles, and that didn't gain us a thing. Apparently you're not such a big name up in the valley," quipped Leon.

Charles smiled. "I'll have to work on that. Now about tonight? There is a reception followed by the awards dinner. I can get you all in; nothing fancy. Coat and tie for the men and party dress for the ladies. Reception starts at 6:30 and dinner at 7:30.

"Count me out dear brother-in-law. I've been feeling poorly all day and I think I'll just order something light and stay in tonight."

"Your choice. Don't mind him Anita. You're still invited. This isn't a couples thing at all. And most of the attendees are not as lucky as me to have a spouse in town to join them," Charles said, giving Francine an affectionate pinch, which aroused mock indignation and a smile.

"Thank you so much Charles. But I think I'll join Leon, if he can stand company. I'm tired from a busy day and, frankly, I don't have anything to wear that would even resemble a party dress. I'm afraid I packed more for touring than for dining in a fine crowd."

"Are you sure? No pressure but you would be most welcome and there is no dress code. And I've been telling everyone about the beautiful American woman that I have hidden in my room and they are all dying to meet you."

"I hate to disappoint them, but, tonight I think staying in would be the best."

Francine rose from the sofa and headed toward her room. "Well, you all can figure out who is going to what and who is eating where. As for me, the other woman in Charles' room, I need to get dressed. It may take a while to spruce me up so that I don't disappoint his colleagues. You two are on your own."

"I'm right behind you. Don't slam the door," said Charles, slipping in the room behind her.

Anita and Leon were left in the silence that remained.

A misty rain was falling as Frank drove down the narrow Wiltz street where the Gelsi home had been. A shiny asphalt parking lot marked the spot, much to his disappointment. Early for their lunch appointment he continued to follow Simone's directions as he drove on through the town and continued down the winding road to the east; toward the German border. It was a road he had not traveled for fifty years. It was wider and the bridges newer than he recalled but the steep, tree covered hillsides looked just as impassable as he remembered them.

The only car on the road, he drove slowly studying the countryside as if seeking clues to the past. Simone broke the silence. "Are you OK talking about the war or does it bring back too many sad recollections?"

"No, I'm alright. Here, for instance, I just wish I could remember more about what happened after I was blown off of this road. It must have been along here somewhere but nothing looks familiar. It's frustrating having such blank spots in my memory. It's like studying an old photo album that's missing many of the pictures. You know they were there but you can't for the life of you remember what they depicted. On the other hand, perhaps my mind is doing me a favor masking memories of those awful days of uncertainty and suffering. From the time I dug myself out of the snow beside the road until the time I stumbled into Wiltz, my mind is fogged with generalities."

He slowed the car, vainly looking for familiar landmarks.

"That must have been a frightening experience," said Simone, turning in her seat. "And the weather was so awful that year."

"I do remember that I had no interest in surrendering to the passing Germans. At best I would be an inconvenience for them. It would have been too easy just to shoot me and toss me back in a ditch. Who would ever know? No, I didn't want to die an anonymous death beside an anonymous road in a foreign country at the hands of some fascist farm boy. So I decided to head back to Wiltz. I knew it couldn't be more than ten miles away."

"It's strange when I think about it now. You spent nearly a month with us after your accident but I don't ever recall hearing the details of your escape," she said.

"In my one college psychology course they talked about repression; when you bury bad memories deep in your mind. Maybe I was repressing the memories. In any case, when we were together in that cellar, we had our hands full just staying alive."

"I suppose you're right. Well, I'm glad you made it."

"Yes, but those five days sure seemed like an eternity at the time. My problem, as you can see from this road, is that I had few places to hide and the Germans were using it around the clock. Equipment, troops and trucks headed west passing ambulances and empty trucks heading east. I could only travel at night. During the day I had to hide, the best I could, using a blanket and poncho for protection and warmth.

"So you managed to avoid contact with the Germans the whole time?"

"Almost. And how I've regretted it since," he replied, staring down the road.

Simone waited for more but he remained silent. Finally she asked, "But what happened; with the Germans I mean?"

Snapping from his reverie he said, "Oh, it wasn't anything and it was a long time ago. Actually my most vivid recollection is the constant cold and hunger. There was no escape from either.

"I can't tell you how relieved I was when I finally spotted those old industrial buildings in lower Wiltz. I watched them from across the river one afternoon and they appeared uninhabited. I hoped so. I needed cover and warmth. I was wet, cold and out of food. My wound continued to ache and my feet were in constant pain from all the walking and dampness. Of course, you saw me the next day. You know better than I what a mess I was in."

"You were a sorry sight when I first saw you, that is for sure."

"After dark I made my way to the buildings which, as it turned out, had nothing to offer but a dry floor and protection from the wind. But you can't imagine how much I appreciated both. I still needed food so I decided to move up into town to see if, by chance, you all were still in the house. It was a risky move but I was familiar with that part of town and I felt better with the idea of doing something, anything, rather than sitting in a freezing warehouse slowly starving.

"So that's how I ended up on your doorstep and you know the rest of the story."

"Yes I do; I do know the rest of the story," she said, absorbing the story for the first time. "Well, thank you for sharing it with me. Oh goodness; look at the time. We had better turn around. Mark will be upset if we are late. I know he is so looking forward to seeing you."

"You absolutely scared the shit out me, that's what you did. Can you imagine," said Mark, turning to his wife Sabine, "what it was like in the pitch black hearing an English voice calling out my name. And there I was holding several loaves of stolen German bread. I nearly shit my britches."

"Mark, your language, please," said Sabine with an embarrassed look.

Frank and Simone were comfortably seated at the heavy wooden dining table in the Gelsi's Wiltz home finishing a rich and filling lunch prepared by Sabine. The conversation had stumbled at times since, for Frank's benefit, they spoke in English, the weakest of Sabine's three languages.

It had been an enthusiastic and emotional reunion for Mark and Frank; more emotional than either of them would have anticipated. But Simone could see the tears welling in the eyes of the two men who had played such an important part of her early life as they bear hugged each other upon arrival. The greeting was followed by compliments about there respective good looks and a reciprocal chorus of "you haven't changed a bit" followed by denials from the recipient. Despite the five decade separation the reunion had fueled long suppressed memories that threatened to overwhelm his wife, who had not been part of the cellar dwelling party in 1945. But Sabine, hearing some of the stories for the first time, encouraged the story telling with a string of questions indicating a sincere curiosity.

"What did you do with Frank when you got over the initial shock?" asked Sabine.

"I didn't know whether to grab my Lugar and shoot him or take a risk and cross the alley and hug him."

"You were packing a Lugar?" asked Frank.

"Yes. I sort of borrowed it from a German officer. Well, anyway, I see that it is really Frank so I shut him up and drag his sorry ass inside and lock the door behind. It is still so dark I can't really see clearly but there is no doubt it's him. So we made our way into the dim light of the cellar and scared the hell out of the ladies."

"Well what did you expect?" asked Simone. "You should have seen him Sabine. He was a filthy mess. He had this blanket over his head like a shawl; his beard was dark and scruffy; his eyes were sunk into his head in blacken pits and a bloody bandage was protruding from a tear in his Army pants. I had no idea what Mark had dragged in. He was always scrounging strange things but this was a new one."

"I'm sure glad you two recall my arrival. I remember seeing Mark in the alley and that's it. The rest is a blur."

"You were pretty much out of it for a few days buddy boy," said Mark. "You just did what you were told.

Simone continued the story. "We pulled him in by the fire and peeled off his damp clothes. I should have been embarrassed, stripping this young man down to his shorts but it was the natural thing to do and I had stripped lots of wounded boys at the clinic. Anyway he was really skin and bones. I suspect he was always a bit on the skinny side but now he was looking even worse. We gave him some warm broth and put him on Mark's cot, near the fire. We had moved bedding down to the cellar from the upstairs so we were comfortable, if not a bit crowded. Now poor Mark had to go back upstairs and retrieve another mattress for himself for it was clear Frank would not be moving too soon."

"All this time my mother was wailing in the corner," interrupted Mark. "She remembered Frank and liked him well enough but now she was sure his presence would bring the Germans and we would all be shot. She seemed to ignore the fact that I was a deserter living in their midst and the Krauts had less regard for German deserters than for captured Americans. But she had placed her bedding in the enclosed pantry in the back of the cellar so she retreated there and closed the door as if not seeing Frank would make him go away."

"I never knew why she liked that old pantry. It was far from the fire and always colder and damper than the rest of the cellar," said Simone.

"I think she liked having a little privacy. It was fine with me if that made her happy."

Sabine, who was listening to the exchange from the nearby kitchen, soon returned, with a small package of chocolates and rejoined them at the table. "Was Frank wounded or something? You mentioned a bandage on his leg."

"Actually he was," said Simone, deftly unwrapping a chocolate and placing it on Frank's saucer. "And walking ten miles with an open wound had not done him any good. I was afraid his leg wound was infected, as it looked horrible, but medicines were so scarce at the clinic that I couldn't even steal any. But he had some sulfa powder in his own first aid kit and that might have helped. In any case, after a week or so healing he was walking around comfortably, with a limp."

"What on earth did you eat when you were hiding on the road? You must have been half starved," asked Sabine turning to Frank.

"He looked fully starved when we found him," said Mark.

Frank squirmed, a little uncomfortable with the attention he was receiving. "I was lucky I guess. There were a few rations in the Jeep. The krauts had missed them. And I found a couple issue chocolate bars in my jacket. The chocolate ration bars were nothing like the candy bars you might buy at a grocery store. They were hard as stone and not particularly sweet but they were packed with calories. The bars would suffice in an emergency and they made great presents for the local kids. We even joked that we could toss them at the krauts if we ever ran out of ammunition. For me they were like finding a steak dinner! They carried me all those days."

"How long did you live in the cellar?" asked Sabine.

Mark shook his head in disbelief, "For nearly a month. Can you imagine? Frank came just before Christmas and the Germans didn't withdraw until late January. We lived like rats. Simone came and went during the day, walking up to her job at the clinic. I came and went during the night, scrounging food, firewood and whatever else they didn't nail down."

"Simone, you kept going to the clinic? Wasn't it full of Germans?" Sabine asked.

"It was full of all sorts of people. At first it was a mix of civilians and American soldiers. When the Germans returned they captured the Americans and the medical personal that stayed to care for them and moved them east, out of here. Eventually they had us move the remaining civilians onto the second floor of the old wing and then they took over the rest of the clinic for their own wounded. I helped out all over the clinic. The sick and injured look the same once they are in a bed. We cared for them all. Most of the German cases were just passing through or slightly wounded. The serious wounds were treated and sent back to Germany. Others were patched up and sent back to the front. But having access to the clinic gave me access to food and medicine, which was useful when we inherited old Frank here," she added with a smile, giving his forearm a gentle squeeze.

"You should have seen Simone when she left for the clinic. She was the scruffiest thing you had ever seen."

"Mark, that's a dreadful thing to say about your cousin," said Sabine, glaring at him.

Frank smiled, recalling the memory.

"No, it's true," Mark continued. "She didn't trust the German boys and didn't want any of them to develop an affection for a little Belgian lass. Well, with her hair pulled back and hidden under a soiled scarf and a dress and shoes that looked like something my mother would have worn, there was little about her that would have inspired lust."

"He's right Sabine. I did try to dress on the dowdy side. And the baggy dress and coat offered more places to hide purloined goods for my trip home from the clinic. In America I would be called a 'bag lady' isn't that right Frank?"

"Well, you looked like Florence Nightingale to me. I was treated very well by Nurse Simone."

"I remember that special Christmas dinner we had," continued Frank. "Old Mark here goes out on one of his normal evening escapades and comes back with the nicest goose you have ever seen. Claims he just 'borrowed it' from somewhere. Anyway, Aunt Anne attacked it and before you know it she has it plucked and dressed ready for roasting.

But all we have is a heating stove with room for a kettle on top. Now I don't recall how she cooked it but that greasy goose made for the best Christmas dinner I can ever recall eating in the company of these two special people," he concluded, nodding to Simone and Mark.

"Then she added the leftovers to our perpetual soup pot that we just kept adding to each day and we had bits of goose for days after," remembered Simone. "Yes, it was a memorable Christmas."

"Why were you living in the cellar anyway? The house was still standing wasn't it?"

"Yes," replied Mark. "It was standing but the windows on the street side were broken or missing and it would have been terribly difficult to heat. And we feared American air raids might fall on the city if the weather ever improved. In fact, we were bombed in January on several occasions. And besides, it was better to stay out of sight of the Germans. You could never tell what might tempt them. Even Simone tried to be discrete when she arrived and departed so they would think the house wasn't occupied. Of course, there was always a trickle of smoke coming from the chimney but that was in back and not as obvious."

Frank leaned forward, his own memory fired by the discussion. "Do you two recall the night Anne took on the whole German Army? She might have been a bit quirky but that night she was magnificent."

"My mother-in-law took on the German Army? What's the story behind that?" said Sabine, part way to the kitchen with her hands full of dirty dishes.

Mark shook his head and laughed at the recollection. "Well, it was about dinner time, as I recall, because we were gathered near the stove to keep warm and to eat our daily soup when mother heard someone walking upstairs. There was a war on but this was still her house and no one could simply barge in and start walking around her house. So she goes limping up the stairs mumbling to herself about the audacity of the Germans. While she is going up we did our best to conceal our American friend here and hide the evidence of his presence. Then I hid under the stairs where I could overhear the conversation."

"And were they Germans?"

"Absolutely; three of them. They said they needed a place to spend the night and wanted to use the cellar. I think they may have mentioned the smell of the food cooking, but I don't recall. Anyway, she lights into them like you would not believe. There is no room for them in our cellar. It's just her, a crippled old lady, and her poor niece, who has connections with the commandant at the hospital. Her only son is off fighting in the German Army, just like them. What would their mother say if she saw them barging into the house of the mother of a German soldier. What would they say if an American soldier did that to their mother in her home? She would have loved to assist them but she couldn't. Then she told them to get out while it was light enough to find another place."

"They left?"

"They left! Here I am trying to decide what to do with the bodies if I have to shoot them in the cellar and then mother just throws them out of the house, humble and apologetic for having interrupted her evening. I think she could pull it off because she didn't know enough about them to be frightened and she caught them off guard. But Anne Gelsi won the battle of Wiltz that night," he concluded, still shaking his head in disbelief

"Well, that's a side of your mother I never saw," said Sabine.

The amiable conversation went on until nearly 4:00 P.M. when Frank and Simone said their goodbyes and departed in the fading light. It had been a pleasant afternoon that refreshed memories for the three old people who had shared so much in that dark cellar many years ago. Talked out, Frank and Simone silently shared each other's company on the road back to Bastogne.

As they approached Simone's street, Frank broke the silence. "Can I pull that lonesome soldier line again and buy you dinner later?"

She turned toward him, offering a smile. "You don't need to do that. And with the size of that lunch I couldn't face another big meal. But I have an idea. All that talk of endless soup surprisingly makes me hungry for soup. I have all the ingredients for a seafood chowder. Why don't you come back here a little later and join me. Nothing fancy mind you but it should be filling."

"That works for me if it's not too much work for you."

"Soup is easy. I'll be fine. Now, there's no place to park so just stop here and I'll jump out," she said.

As the car rolled to a stop she released her seat belt, leaned toward Frank, kissed him gently on the cheek and then was gone.

And he felt like a teenager once again.

"How much longer are you going to be? I need to get down to the ballroom and check on a couple of things," called Charles, standing in the doorway of their bedroom.

"I'll just be a few minutes," Francine called back, from her dressing area. "Why don't you go on ahead? I will just meet you there in a bit."

"Please don't be too long. I've already lost the American beauty I promised to bring. I don't want to appear without my wife as well. All my colleagues will think that I have lost my touch with women," he said, before turning toward the door.

"Women," he continued as he passed Anita, who was curled up on the sofa in her fleece warm up suit reading a magazine. "Are American women slow in front of a mirror or is that a European genetic trait?"

"Why Charles, it's all relative. Are women slow or are men too fast? I would rather believe that you have simply rushed and failed to fully enjoy the process of preparing for an evening out. And, in answer to your question, American women are not 'slow in front of a mirror,' as you say. But you will find that American men are as impatient as you appear to be."

Leon, who was watching business news on the T.V. smiled as he listened to the exchange.

"Ah, an international women's conspiracy," responded Charles. "Well, I don't have time to engage in a debate I cannot win. Leon, if you don't see your sister in ten minutes perhaps you could go in and blink the lights or something. For now, I must be off." With that he left the suite.

In a few minutes Francine swept into the room looking radiant in a knee length blue dress topped with a tailored white long sleeved jacket. "How do I look?" she asked, walking toward Anita. "I never know what to wear for these business affairs. I want to look business formal and party casual at the same time."

"I think you look great. It's a good thing we don't live closer together. You have a wonderful wardrobe and I would be over constantly wanting to borrow things."

"Well, I had better get on down there. Charles has enough on his mind. I don't need to have him worrying about me. What are you two going to do for dinner?"

"Leon had mentioned doing room service. That works for me. Are you still on for that?" Anita asked, looking at Leon, who seemed engrossed in a news report.

"He didn't hear a word you said. Oh well, have fun and we'll see you later. We shouldn't be too late. Goodbye brother dear," Francine said, as she twisted his ear lobe. "Now take care of our guest."

Anita pushed the room service cart out of the suite entrance and parked it in the hall. She returned to her place on the sofa and curled up, sitting on her feet. "How do you feel after a nice hot bowl of soup?" she asked Leon, who was seated in a comfortable overstuffed chair nearby.

"That was perfect. But I still feel very droopy. I'm afraid I'm not very good company for you tonight."

"Hey, I'm not exactly Ms. Energy either. A quiet evening suits me just fine. And don't think you have to stay up just for me. If you want to go to bed, feel free to do so. I have a good book and some journal writing to catch up on."

"Journal writing! What sort of things do you put in a journal?"

"It's more of a travel diary I suppose, rather than a journal. I like to record where I have been, who I was with, what I bought, that sort of thing. It's amazing how much I forget on a trip. The journal is a memory jogger for me."

He smiled as he listened to her explanation. "Have I made it into your journal?"

"Oh yes," she replied with a laugh. "I have a whole section on handsome princes and you're in there. You see I need to embellish my journal to add a little excitement to the future reading."

"Ah, I see. Now tell me; what do you think of the Belgian people after nearly a week of intense study. Are we what you expected?"

"Based on my exposure to your family and to restaurant, hotel and airport staff I can say you are a delightful and gracious people. I'm not sure that is a very good sample though unless you can tell me that your family is really typical."

"We are the ideal Belgium family. If you like us you will like everyone!"

"But I can't forget you're a lawyer, trained to speak artfully, if not accurately."

"Anita, Anita, Anita! You malign my profession. I always speak the truth, as I understand it. But if you believe as you do, my words will never convince you. So tell me, are you a typical American woman?"

"Oh no," she replied with a laugh, changing position slightly to get more comfortable on the sofa. "I am a one of a kind"

"Like a rare gem?"

"Absolutely! All the other American women you'll meet will pale by comparison."

"Such modesty!" He replied with a laugh. "I like that. I will say that you are much more fun than some of the American women I have met at Microsoft. How would you say it, tight assed or something? They seem to have a chip on their shoulder and are a bit edgy."

Anita clearly enjoyed the description. She had done estate planning with some of the newly rich from Microsoft and knew the type of woman he was describing. "Don't judge all of us or everyone at Microsoft by that standard. I know there are some like that. It is a pressure cooker environment over there. But if you look a bit you will find some American sweethearts tucked around the place."

The conversation continued as it moved from women through music and food to a topic Leon loved; his mountains. Leon experienced a burst of renewed energy as he discussed some of the places he had hiked and climbed in Europe. Hiking, a passion of his youth, had been put on hold during his ten year marriage and then reignited following his divorce. He spoke to her of past climbs and of climbs yet to accomplish. His descriptions were so vivid she could almost experience the view from the summit of his latest conquests.

"I thought you were divorced," she said as he completed a story, "but I actually think you're married to your mountains."

He gave a hardy laugh, pressing back in his chair. "Married to my mountains! Yes, you may be right about that. But a separation is in the offing. With my new job and my creaky knee I will be seeing less of my Alpine lover than I would like. But things do change…."

Just then Francine and Charles returned, interrupting the conversation. "Well, look who's still up," said Francine. "Poor Anita was probably hoping for a nice quiet evening of reading and here you are, brother dear, probably talking her ear off. I thought you weren't feeling well."

"I'm not feeling well but Anita insisted I stay around and entertain her, so what could I do? As a representative of the host country it was my duty," he said while slowly rising from his chair.

Anita moved to the arm of the sofa to better view the brother sister exchange.

"Yes, I'm sure I believe that," said Francine.

"You two can party all you wish," said Charles, passing through the sitting area on his way to their room. "As for me it's off with the tie and into bed with a good book. I've been on my feet all day and could use some rest. Please don't think me antisocial."

"Good night Charles dear. I won't be long," Francine replied, kicking off her shoes and taking over Leon's big chair.

"Well, Anita, I turn you over to my loving sister now. I'm sure you will find her company satisfactory but perhaps less entertaining than mine. Good night all," he said as he closed the door to his room.

There was a raised counter with four stools opposite the gas cook top in Simone's kitchen. Frank sat on one of those stools as Simone, across from him, busied herself with dinner preparations. "When the kids ask what we did while they were gone I'll have to admit that all we seemed to do was eat. I'm not complaining but it won't strike them as too exciting I suppose.

She leaned over the cook top and placed a basket of sliced bread and plate of cheese on the counter near him. "Well, I've had a very nice time the past two days. It's been plenty exciting for me. I'm not looking for too much excitement at my age anyway.

Frank studied her as she leaned back against the sink, arms crossed with a glass of wine in her hand. Since she returned home from lunch she had changed into a white blouse and dark slacks and both were covered by a burgundy colored apron. He was very aware and appreciative of her clothing choices. She was always a head turner, looking very classy. Her hair was still carefully in place, as it had been at lunch, with just a wisp or two flying loose near her temples.

"Remember yesterday, when I said I thought you were beautiful."

"Yes I do Frank. And I blamed it on the lighting and the wine. Have you reconsidered in the light of day?"

"No, in fact, you're more beautiful today. And you can't blame the lighting or the wine. I've barely had a sip. Anyway, I make it a policy of mine to notice beautiful women and I can definitely say you qualify."

"Why thank you Frank. You're way too kind but I don't have to agree with you to appreciate your remarks."

"You know with all of the talk about living in the cellar I couldn't help but think of the wonderful times we shared in that little space. But it didn't seem quite right to bring them up today. You do know what I'm talking about don't you?"

"Yes Frank, I remember. Those were special times for me as well. And don't think I haven't ever thought of them myself.

"Simone, you may not realize how hard it is for an old man to talk like this but the older I get the more I realize that, if I don't say what's on my mind now, I may never have another chance."

"What is on your mind?" she said, taking a stool one over from his and setting her wine on the counter near the cheese platter.

"In case you never figured it out, I was crazy about you back in that cellar. I knew you were a beautiful young woman no matter how you looked when you left for the clinic. And you were beautiful the way you cared for me; held my hand by the fire, talked to me, dreamed with me and kissed me when we were alone. I wouldn't have recognized it for what it was back then but, Simone, I think I was in love with you in a deep and indescribable way."

"Frank, any woman would love to hear you say that. I'm deeply touched. I really am. You were very special to me as well. I have to confess that I was glad Mark left at night and that Anne slept in the pantry behind a closed door. Not that we did anything we would be ashamed of but it was still nice to have some privacy."

"I always figured you thought me a cad for running off to the states and never writing but I did write. I tried to get a hold of you after I got home but I never heard from you. I don't know how many letters I wrote. I was like a love sick puppy for months. Now it seems so easy to keep track of people; just hop on a plane or pick up the phone but…. "

"The mail was very unreliable right after the war. And I moved around some."

"I tried Wiltz. I tried Bastogne. I figured in a small town someone would know who you were but nothing. Then of course I began to wonder if you just didn't want to write. You had a life of your own after all."

"Frank, trust me. I never forgot you. I never forgot the times we shared together. They were and always will be special to me."

"Does your family still have that little hunting lodge we visited that time?"

"Yes we do, though it has grown a bit since that time we visited there. It's more civilized and a gravel drive goes right to it; no more long hike."

"Would we be able to visit it? I have often thought of that cozy little place with the knockout view. I never thought I would see it again but, if we could..."

She reached across and took his hand in hers. "Of course we can. We could go tomorrow if you wish. I could pack a lunch and we can have, how do you say it, a picnic?"

"A picnic would be more than I could ever hope for. Yes, let's do it tomorrow."

They sat in silence, still holding hands, until Frank continued. "Have you ever wondered how our lives would have been changed if we had tried to get together somehow?"

She smiled, lowering her eyes.

"I have. It would have been crazy. I was broke and going to school. And you were living half a world away in a world that was still trying to recover from the war's disruption."

"Those were very different times. And, yes, there were many obstacles for two young people like us.

"We both seemed to have good lives so there should be no regrets I guess."

"No Frank, we should have no regrets. Instead we should enjoy each other's company now. We are very lucky to have this time. Let's enjoy it. Now, are you ready for some dinner?"

Francine curled comfortably in the big overstuffed chair and laid her head back, as if exhausted from the long day. "Well, tell me, did you and my brother have a nice evening?"

"Yes, actually we did. Or at least I did. I can't speak for him. He is really a delightful person; so easy to talk to. I don't know how to explain it."

"He's a dear man, even though we give each other a hard time. And, except for that wife of his, he has always done well. I know mother is very proud of him.

"Was his a messy divorce?"

"Not any messier than the marriage. Now even he would admit the marriage was a mistake. I think his loins overruled his brains for once and he had to pay the price. You see, she was about six years younger, gorgeous, and dumb and had a body that stopped traffic. I think that's what stopped Leon and I told him so before he married her. I don't think they were unhappy all the time but she spent the whole marriage trying to change him to fit what she thought he should be. Mountain climbing was out. Fast cars were in. Quiet weekends in the country were out and big parties in the city were in. That sort of thing. Oh he went along with it but those that knew him knew Leon was working too hard to conform to her idea of an ideal life. The only surprise for some of us was that the marriage lasted ten years."

"How did he handle the divorce? Was it hard on him?"

"I'm sure it was but he was always Mr. Upbeat. Separating from the kids was the worst part for him. He loved the children dearly and soon found himself estranged from them. His ex promoted that. When she remarried, someone more her style, it grew even harder for him to maintain contact with the kids. They seemed to be traveling every chance they had. So he lived for the law and the mountains."

"Is he seeing anyone special?"

"Except for you, no one that I know of. He has lots of friends that are ladies but not many lady friends, if you know what I mean."

Anita blushed and shifted uncomfortably on the sofa. "Except for me? What do you mean 'except for me?' I'm sure I'm not 'special' to Leon. I've known him less than a week!"

"Oh, I'm sorry," said Francine, leaning forward and speaking in a conspiratorial tone. "I didn't mean to embarrass you and that was unfair of me but I think he would consider you 'special,' as you put it."

Anita blushed more, squirmed more and shook her head in disbelief.

"Charles, bless his heart, was the first to see it," Francine continued. "He mentioned it when he was watching you dance last night. And I was watching Leon today. Yes, Anita dear, there are signs. There are definite signs."

"Now I don't think I can face him again. And I was so enjoying our little talks."

"Anita, don't worry about him. I don't think he knows. Just act natural. It may take him days or weeks to figure it out. In the meantime, enjoy each other. We sure enjoy having you with us. You're like one of the family."

"You've all been wonderful to dad and me. I mean all of you. I'm so glad I met you. So much has happened in a few short days. I can't believe that good fortune."

"Nor can I," said Francine, finishing her wine. "Now I best retire to my husband's chambers. And don't worry about Leon. He knows not his own heart. I'm not sure who said that but it sounds nice doesn't it?

"Yes it does. And thank you for everything."

They headed to their rooms and were just about to enter when Anita turned and said, "Francine. Just for the record, I think your brother is pretty special too."

Francine paused, sent her a warm and loving smile and slipped into her own room.

Frank ambled down the now familiar sidewalk from Simone's to his hotel. The intermittent rain had stopped but the pavement still glistened, reflecting the lights of passing cars. He was grateful he'd walked to her home as the walk back would give him a chance to gather his wits and, he feared, he may have consumed too much wine to safely drive the route.

He'd arrived at her home that morning resolved to enjoy her company while controlling his emotions. His resolve had been shattered when she greeted him at the door and remained in shambles the rest of the day. It had been a wonderful day which seemed to end too soon. And her casual good night kiss had curled his toes.

Why was he feeling like such a fool around her? Was it their history together? Was it something about her; God she was an attractive woman. But some of Sharon Webber's friends had been attractive in a way and, yet, he had dodged all their emotional bullets. But holding Simone in his arms, however briefly, was absolutely electrifying. And it was so natural; so right.

A gust of cold wind sent a chill up his spine as he quickened his pace. It must be down in the low 40's he thought; damn chilly. He smiled thinking that maybe it was God's way of giving him a needed cold shower without the water. Anyway, he was glad he'd worn his heavy coat.

For the past 50 years chilling cold and snow had reminded him of the cold of 1944. But tonight the cold reminded him of the welcome warmth in the cellar where Simone and Mark had saved his life and of the exquisite times he'd spent with Simone alone.

He jammed his hands deeper into the warm pockets and paused at the hotel entrance, gazing blankly down the darkened street.

Their time together had been so natural; not at all unseemly. In the evenings, after Mark departed and Anne retired to her little pantry room, they'd huddle together on a cot near the fire; talking, dreaming, touching and sharing. His heart had screamed for more but good boys and girls didn't do that. So they'd traveled new ground together but never went into forbidden territory. It might seem prudish by current standards but it wasn't then. They shared dreams of going to school, getting married and having big families. They both longed to run free through the green hills without the fear of guns or mines or death. They had been simple dreams but they sustained two young people in those difficult times. They'd given Frank the hope of a better tomorrow.

Frank smiled. If "Tomorrow," that song from the play "Annie," had been written we would have sung it, he thought. We truly believed the sun would come out tomorrow and we would see a new day; start a new life.

S. J. Dennis

It's ironic in a way. Here I am, years later, drawn to another impossible relationship with the same woman I futilely pursued back then. I guess I'll never learn.

10

After her late night conversation with Francine, Anita was nervous about seeing Leon. It was one thing for her and Leon to be friends. It raised her anxiety level to think that she might be considered special. But the relaxed banter that characterized Anita and Leon's previous encounters continued when they met the next morning. Perhaps Francine was wrong about Leon's feeling toward Anita. Or perhaps she was right; Leon did have feelings but he hadn't noticed them yet! Anita could detect no signs either way.

After sharing a cup of hotel room coffee in the comfortable sitting area the new friends went different directions, relieving Anita of any discomfort she may have felt in Leon's presence. Charles left for his morning meetings in the conference center while Leon retired to his room to place a series of business calls.

"Looks like we're on our own this morning," Anita said to Francine. "Any ideas?"

"How about wandering in the shopping area? I think you call it 'window shopping.' And I know a charming little coffee shop we could visit."

"Window shopping; perfect. My suitcase is too full to do any real shopping."

The two friends were soon heading out of the hotel into the bright sunshine of a crisp fall morning. Anita had always found it difficult to "shop" with another person. Some people raced through stores, rarely stopping to look at anything. Others would get caught up in the first shop visited and never move on. It was a question of pacing, she'd concluded long ago. You needed to find someone who had a similar shopping pace if you wanted to shop together. Like much of their relationship she and Eric were not compatible at the mall. But what man ever could match a woman's pace? She and Francine seemed to be made for each other; their shopping styles meshed perfectly. When they finally sat down in the pastry shop with their small coffees and delicate pastries Anita explained her shopping theory to Francine.

"So I think it's interesting that we seem to have the same shopping pace," Anita concluded with a smile.

"I can't say I ever gave it much thought. But you're right about men. Charles goes to a store to buy, not to shop. When we're together, he prefers shops with a comfortable chair so he can read while he waits. Or, better yet, I shop alone."

Anita responded with a laugh. They'd enjoyed a wonderful, relaxing morning and the pause for coffee promised to be a perfect finish. As she stirred the sugar into her coffee the door chime announced the entry of a mother with her young daughter. Both were dressed as if they'd soon be posing for a family portrait. As Anita watched them take a seat near the front window she turned to Francine and said, "You're sure lucky to have your mother living. I miss mine. We used to talk nearly every day."

"Mother is a dear isn't she? I probably take her too much for granted. She has just always been there for me."

"She's such an attractive woman. Was she always as beautiful?"

"It's funny. You don't see your mother as beautiful but, now that you mention it, I guess you're right. I know she was very pretty when she was young. In pictures her face was thinner but she was still pretty with thick dark hair."

They sat quietly for a few moments, smiling as they listened to the animated conversation of the mother and daughter across the nearly empty shop. Anita could clearly recall the special times that she and her mother had made the trip to downtown Seattle to go shopping. They would even dress up for the occasion in anticipation of the special lunch at the restaurant on the eighth floor of the big department store.

Breaking from her reverie Anita said, "I hope Simone doesn't mind looking after Dad."

"I don't think your father needs much looking after. He seems pretty independent and very sharp. I'm sure Mother's fine."

"Just think, if you and I hadn't met, Dad might have never run into Simone. That would have been such a shame considering all they went through together. Up until he saw her he'd been feeling kind of down. He didn't expect to see anyone he knew and I think that was bothering him. It's tough on guys his age knowing that so many of their buddies are dying off every day just from old age. I imagine it's very sobering."

Francine listened closely to Anita and shook her head in agreement.

"Had you ever heard about Dad living with them and all of that other stuff about hiding him from the Germans?" Anita continued.

"I don't remember any details. Her cousin Mark used to tell stories about that time but he's quite a storyteller and I never knew how much to believe. Mother never said much at all."

Anita set her pastry down then licked her sticky fingers. "I'll never forget the look on Dad's face when your mother walked in the other night. I thought he was having a coronary or something. And then I thought he was going to kiss her. That would have been just so unlike Dad!"

Francine laughed and shook her head in agreement. "Well, I better get back to the hotel and get changed. Charles wanted me to join him for lunch with a client and his wife. But this has been fun. As you say, we have a compatible shopping pace."

They made their way back to the hotel, entering the suite just as Charles was leaving.

"Oh good, I had just about given up on you. Can you meet me in the lobby in about five minutes?" he asked as he slipped out.

Agreeing, Francine performed a quick change and raced from the room leaving Anita and Leon to fend for themselves.

With quick movements Frank dressed, eager to be off on the day's planned adventure to the hunting lodge. He'd been there one other time, in July of 1945. He never thought he'd see it again. It had been summer then and warm….

Lt. Frank Larson slowed his Jeep as the battered town of Wiltz came into view. It had been seven months since the town was liberated for the second time. Nothing was familiar. Hills that had been snow covered and barren last December were now a lush green as if Mother Nature was working to paint over the scars of war. Rusting evidence of the violence lay beside the road with grasses, encouraged by the warm summer sun, pushing upward in a vain effort to soften their sharp edges.

Since he'd left his basement refuge with the Gelsi family he'd been consumed by the chaos of war and had little time to reflect on his time there. But, with the end of hostilities and the switch over to occupation duty, the memory that time and of Simone had teased his soul. He desperately wanted to see her again though fearful that she might want to put him and the memory of war behind.

He struggled to find his way. Buildings he'd used as landmarks were gone, turned to rubble. Bricks and stones, gathered from the tumbled heaps were stacked in places, waiting to serve as foundations for new homes that would rise above the desolation. He made two wrong turns before he found the Gelsi's street, easing to a stop at their front door, relieved to see the block that contained their home still standing. The homes across the narrow street were gone with remnants of foundations standing as stark evidence that they were once there. But the Gelsi home, with several windows covered with wood scraps, appeared lived in.

It all felt so different. He'd known the winter Wiltz, a cold, snowy place huddled under gray winter skies. He'd known war time Wiltz. Now the war memory was fading and the people of the scarred town were moving forward under a peacetime summer sun. Would they remember him? Would they care? Without the war as a common bond would these people who had saved him now seem like strangers?

With those thoughts rolling through his mind he knocked on the heavy wooden door.

"Frank. Well I'll be damned. It's really you, Frank," exclaimed Mark Gelsi, stepping onto the porch to bear hug the startled soldier.

Switching from English to French he pushed Frank though the house to the kitchen where his mother, Aunt Anne, was struggling to rise from the table with a welcoming smile on her face. With tears in her eyes she kissed Frank on both cheeks, pushed him away as if examining him and then repeated the cheek kissing again between utterances in French which Frank did not understand.

"Sit down, sit here," a still excited Mark said, pushing a chair toward Frank. "No, wait. You don't want to see us. You'll want to see Simone and she will be so surprised to see you, her soldier. Come on. It's almost 4:00 and her shift at the clinic will be over."

"We can take the Jeep, Mark. First, I've brought some things for your mother. Give me a hand if you will." Returning to the kitchen each young man set a wooden crate on the table near a curious Aunt Anne.

"Tell her this is for her," said Frank as he began to remove items from the box. Many were Army issue rations in familiar olive drab containers.

"Oh my God," Mark exclaimed. "Flour, sugar, coffee and, what's this, processed meat?"

"That's the GI's favorite, SPAM. It's not too bad. And here is some stew. I can't recall what all I tossed in. I thought you might be able to use it. I'd heard that some things are still in short supply."

"As in non-existent. Mother will be your slave when she figures out what you've brought." Mark turned to her describing what was in the boxes as she rubbed her hands on a cotton apron as if afraid to touch the booty. Then she kissed Frank again.

Mark, freeing Frank from his mother's embrace, steered him back to the Jeep. "Drive on or we'll miss her," he intoned.

The Jeep ground up the hill to the clinic where Frank came to a stop across from the entrance. This part of town seemed less damaged than lower Wiltz and nearby shops were catering to the city's needs. He had just set the brake when he saw her. Still tall and trim, without a coat, clad in her white uniform she looked like a stiff breeze could lift her from the stairs. Eyes on the ground she was nearly past the Jeep when she glanced over, catching sight of the driver.

"Frank, Oh Frank," she cried, lunging toward the Jeep and Franks arm's. She kissed his cheeks in quick succession before Frank cradled her face in his hands and kissed her lips in return.

With her head buried in his chest they stood beside the Jeep, oblivious to the passerby's. Mark interrupted their embrace. "Excuse please. Aren't you happy to see your cousin as well?"

With tears on her cheeks but still clutching Franks hand she stepped back. "Did you know he was coming? Are you in on this surprise Mark, you devil."

"No way. I'm as surprised as you. Now let's get this little tableau on the road before the entire town is talking about Simone Challon and her shameful behavior with that American GI. Hop in front cousin. I'll sit in back."

"So, I figured Luxembourg City wasn't really that far from Wiltz so a little detour would be in order and here I am," concluded Frank, explaining how he'd connived a trip to their town.

Frank and Simone were seated on the front step of the Gelsi home with Mark perched on a wooden crate on the nearby sidewalk.

"How long can you stay? A long time I hope," Simone said, clinging to his arm and resting her head on his shoulder.

"A couple of days, if you'll have me that long. I should head back to post on Monday at the latest. It's about an eight hour drive."

"So," Mark said, "you drive to Luxembourg City, take a three day course in civil administration, stop here for two days and then head back to your post and no one will think you've gone AWOL? Won't you be missed?"

"What can I say? Discipline is a little lax since the Nazis went kaput. Occupation duty is just one long boring day after another. So don't worry about me. No one is taking attendance. The big question is, can I have my old place in the basement back for a few days?

"Don't be silly. You can have the best room in the house. Top floor, shady side. And, since the window is missing, it stays nice and cool," she concluded, giving his arm a squeeze. "Now tell us where you have been since January. Until the surrender I, err, we have been so worried about you."

"Well, after I went from "missing in action" to alive and well; when was that? About January 10th or so?"

"About that," replied Mark.

"Anyway, the Army re-liberates Wiltz and I rejoin the Army. They confine me in an aid station a few days to see if I'm healthy enough to be shot at and then I'm lucky enough to be reassigned to my old unit. Of course, by that time so many I'd known had become casualties that I felt like a stranger in my own Company."

"Did you have another chance to kill Krauts," asked Mark, leaning forward to hear the reply.

"And they got another chance to kill me. No, I'm convinced the best place to spend a war is right in the basement of this house. At least it was for me.

The trio sat silent for a few moments before Simone changed the topic. "So, we have our GI back. What shall we do with him for a few days?"

"Why don't you two go up to the Lodge and see if it's still standing? This Jeep should be able to negotiate the road."

"That's a wonderful idea Mark. Frank, you remember me talking about the little cabin, we call The Lodge? It's not far from here in the forest. None of us has been there since the war. I don't even know if its standing but it would be a wonderful excursion." Turning to Mark she continued. "And you dear cousin must come along."

"Don't 'dear cousin' me. Frank didn't come here to see me, did you Frank?"

Frank squirmed and visibly blushed.

"Besides, I promised Renee I would help him set the new center beam on his house tomorrow. But I do have an idea. Mother would be worried if you and Frank were without a chaperon so I'll leave with you and you can drop me off at Renee's on the way out of town. Pick me up when you return, the beam will be installed and Mother will not worry.

With the front hubs locked and all four wheels struggling for traction, the little Jeep ground its way up the narrow road. Twice they'd been stopped by fallen trees. Frank pulled one aside with the cable he found coiled in the rear and the second was dispatched with the ax mounted on the Jeep's side.

"Looks like the end of the road," said Frank as they pulled into a small clearing.

"Stop over near that opening. I think that's the start of the trail."

Retrieving the picnic basket from the rear seat they struggled down the narrow, overgrown path, to the cabin. While out of the trees the cabin was surrounded by out of control brush. With Frank in the lead they finally burst through the underbrush and climbed the leaf covered stairs to the creaking porch.

"Oh wonderful," she exclaimed, running down the porch like a school girl. "It's safe. The Lodge is safe. I was so worried someone or something would have been here but...." She pushed the door open and went into the darkened room. "As you can see it's more a cabin than a lodge and more for relaxing than for hunting but it's been in our family for nearly one hundred years. Oh, how I loved coming here as a little girl."

The cabin's rough wood siding was exposed on the inside; covered in places with old pictures, book shelves and other odd bits, the likes of which seem to migrate to old cabins. None of the wood showed evidence of paint. The lodge contained little more than two bunk beds at one end and a counter, which served as the eating area, on the other. The most memorable feature was the generous covered porch that ran along the view side and gave the cramped cabin a spacious feel. The view was incredible that summer day in 1945. From that porch you could see for miles across rolling, tree covered countryside that showed no signs of the death and turmoil that had taken place beneath its green canopy just a few months before.

While he sat the picnic basket and blanket on the counter she twisted the rusty hasps on the window shutters, flinging them open so light flooded the cabin. Then, with Franks help, she managed to open the two windows that looked out to the distant mountains. The soft breeze melted the mustiness of the closed up cabin.

While she stood gazing at the view and drinking in the mountain air Frank stepped close behind and wrapped her in his arms. Resting her head on his chest the two swayed, each lost in their own thoughts.

Without words, she turned and, with her fingers brushing his cheek, they kissed with a rising fervor so different from their furtive tries in the wartime cellar. They didn't stop.

As if fearful of parting again they clung to each other. His lips found her lips, her eyes, her neck. Like a starving man he craved for more and she matched his passion.

She wrestled free of his embrace and, in a fluid motion, pulled the light cotton blouse over her head. She placed his hand on her breast and rose again to kiss him.

He had never touched anything so beautiful, so soft and responsive. Her body pushed against his hand. His body was responding to hers; he was certain she could feel it as she pressed so tightly against him.

He struggled with the buttons of his uniform shirt before shedding it, letting it slip to the floor. She helped remove his tee shirt and then began kissing his chest while her nails dug into his bare back.

His mind was in turmoil. But his body knew exactly what it wanted to do even if he wasn't sure how. But they moved as one and the answers came.

She twisted from his embrace, took the picnic blanket and spread it over the musty looking mattress on the lower bunk. Sitting on the blanket she turned, beckoning him to join her. Their inexperienced hands worked with a clumsy efficiency to remove her skirt and his trousers. His lips explored her breasts while his hand slipped into her panties where it found her moist and ready. Her warm body pressed against him as he explored and pleasured her.

His body was charged and ready. Alarmed that he might come too quickly he removed the remaining clothing before moving over her.

Would this hurt her? He didn't know much more than he'd read or heard about from barracks chatter. He didn't want to hurt her but he didn't want to stop.

She reached down and guided him into her most private place. He plunged and she winced before pulling him closer. The rhythm of their movement quickened and then exploded as their bodies pulsed as one.

God, how he loved this girl....

The hotel restaurant was still very quiet; the breakfast rush had not begun. Frank sat his coffee down and glanced at his watch again. God the time was moving slowly, he thought. He was anxious to leave for Simone's but didn't want to make a fool of himself and arrive too early. But they were going to the Lodge today. He'd awaken early with thoughts of his previous Lodge visit vivid in his old rusty mind. They filled him with warmth and made him feel foolish at the same time. The last visit was fifty years ago. Today would be very different. But still, what a memory....

He found Simone busy in the kitchen loading a wicker picnic basket. Several small blocks of cheese and a sausage, each wrapped in a bright colored napkin, were tucked in to support a bottle of wine. Two bottles of water, apples and an orange followed. A long baguette was balanced on top.

"I think that is all we need. There are dishes and silverware in the lodge. So that should do it. Can you think of anything else?"

"You appear to have enough food for several days. Perhaps we will need more wine," he offered with a sly smile.

"One bottle will be quite enough thank you very much. And besides, I suspect there is a bottle or two hidden up there but I can never be sure. Francine, Leon and cousin Mark all use the place from time to time so I never know what food or drink has survived the last visitors."

Soon Frank was behind the wheel of his Passat following Simone's directions to the little retreat. "I would never have found this on my own," he offered as she directed him to turn off the highway onto a narrow gravel road that ascended along a winding course into the thick forest.

"Turn down this next driveway and take it easy; it is steep. Do you remember the footpath we had to go down to reach the cabin?" Frank nodded while negotiating the turn and shifting to a lower gear. "This is it. Father widened it into a driveway back in the fifties."

The sun was brilliant against the clear blue sky but the air was decidedly chilly, propelled by a strong and steady breeze as they emerged from the forest into a small clearing.

"Well, here we are. Do you recognize it?" she asked as he came to a stop.

"Not at all," Frank answered, in disbelief. "I don't recognize anything but that view."

"Father added on to the place when he retired. He and Mother would come up here for weeks at a time in the summer. He so enjoyed it. He added running water, inside plumbing and gas cooking and heat. It's really quite civilized. Let's go on in."

Carrying the basket Frank followed her up the moss encrusted paving stones that outlined the path to the deck and front door. Yes, he thought, the view and this porch look familiar but nothing else is the same. It was all much more civilized than he remembered it.

With practiced hands Simone opened valves and twisted knobs on a primitive gas wall heater bringing it to sputtering life. Its radiant blue flame pressed against the cabins damp and chill as Simone, still in coat and gloves, laid out their luncheon fare on a nearby table.

"Now, what can I do to help," asked Frank, wrapping his arms around her slender shoulders from behind.

Bread in hand she twisted, gave him a light kiss on the cheek and wiggled from his embrace. "My, this place seems to bring out your romantic side," she chided. "Why don't you heat some water for tea? That should keep your hands busy for a few minutes."

"Hey, what can I say? I guess your aunt was right. You can't trust a soldier with a beautiful woman."

She smiled, shook her head in mock disbelief and dove back into the lunch basket.

Later, finishing the last of the cheese, Frank turned to view the distant hills through the nearby window. "God what a view. Now that I do remember. Same view and same woman but everything else is so, so different."

She smiled and reached across the table for his hands. "We're different too Frank. We're fifty years older and our whole lives different."

"But the memory of what we shared fifty years ago hasn't changed," he said, returning her gaze. "It is still very clear to me. Simone, I may sound like a sappy old man but, I loved you deeply then and what we had here. That can never be changed."

She gazed into his eyes and held his hands a little tighter.

"I wish I had my old letters to you," he continued. "I think I expressed myself better in those days. Maybe I was hopelessly in love and made no sense but I do know I labored over those letters to get the words and feelings right. You see, writing has never been my strong suit," he added with a humble smile.

"I know. Your letters were wonderful. I can't tell you how wonderful."

"What?" he said, sitting upright as if stunned by an electric shock. "How do you know? You said you never received them."

"I'm sorry Frank. I misled you a little when we talked about your letters yesterday. It's true, I never received them. But I did find them in my mother's things after she died in '58. There were twelve of them, a perfect dozen, all unopened and neatly tied with a yellow ribbon. All addressed in your hand."

"Your mother intercepted my letters? Why? Why would she do that?"

"I can't answer that. We can't unring a bell. What was done was done. You wrote them and I never received them; at least not when you sent them. But I've read them Frank. I've read them many times. They are quite beautiful."

"What did you do when you read them? I mean, did you consider writing me?"

"Not for a minute. I assumed you were married. I knew I was. No, after thirteen years there was no purpose in writing. I did feel better about you. I had always been saddened to think what we shared meant nothing to you. I couldn't believe you could go from the feelings you had expressed when we were together to nothing at all. But I didn't know. The letters answered that. They touched me deeply."

They sat quietly, each lost in their thoughts. Frank was tossing "what might have been" ideas around in his head with full knowledge that nothing that happened in their lives could be changed. The book of his life was nearly written. All he could influence was the "rest of the story" as one old radio commentator used to say.

What if she'd received the letters? What if she'd come to America? What if....?

They spent the rest of the afternoon at the lodge, leaving only when the light began to fade. Few words were exchanged. They communicated with looks, gestures and touch. He stood with his arms around her as she repacked the picnic basket following their lunch. They walked to the top of the nearby ridge, holding hands like children. They wrapped in old wool blankets and sat on the wooden bench on the porch and watched the sun turn the sky a rainbow of colors as it passed behind the scattered clouds on its way to the distant horizon. The bench was as comfortable as a church pew but they didn't seem to notice. Together they shared the anguish of knowing the day would have to end.

Finally, after a fleeting afternoon of incredible warmth and happiness, just being together, they made their way back to the car, loaded the basket in the back seat and began the homeward journey.

Silently Frank gripped the wheel as he steered back to Bastogne under a darkening sky.

We made love in that old lodge on a glorious day, fifty years ago, he thought. It was the first time for both of us. We didn't plan to. But the day, the love we had for each other, the view, the sun; all the complex forces of nature came together in a glorious burst of passion that remains fresh in my mind to this day. Life doesn't grant you a second chance for a first time. We didn't need a second chance. We fulfilled our expectations that first time.

She was beautiful, white, soft and lovely, lying beside me in the sun. We were happy. We spoke of possibilities without considering consequences. We ignored the barriers. We lived in different worlds. I was living from payday to payday. I needed to go to school. I had no post war job prospects. None of that mattered. What mattered was that we were in love and in each other's arms and had given everything that meant anything to each other that day.

And after that, except for the long lost letters, nothing but silence passed between us.

"Could we get together for dinner tonight?" she asked. "We could get back into Lombardi's if you like. They always do a nice job.

Her voice brought Frank back to reality. He was not living in the distant past. He was living in the present and Simone Challon Chauveau was sitting beside him. He needed to focus on that for now. Time was too precious to lose at their age.

"Of course. Yes, Lombardi's would be fine."

It was mid-afternoon when Anita and Leon returned to the hotel room, following a late lunch. Both were still laughing about an eccentric woman with a dog they'd encountered on the elevator.

"It was all I could do to contain myself when I saw her coming," laughed Anita as she flopped into the big chair, kicking her shoes off in the process. "At first I thought she must be going to a costume party or something but..."

"Now, now Anita; she could be royalty from some old duchy or something. You can never tell in Luxembourg. Just because she was dressed like a rainbow doesn't mean anything," he continued with mock seriousness.

"Yes, right. I'm sure she was someone famous. And did you see that dog. Where would you find a dog that ugly? I mean, really."

Leon picked up her coat from the back of the sofa and hung it, with his, in the nearby closet. He then removed his shoes, eased onto the sofa and put his feet on the sturdy wooden coffee table.

"I hope your feet hurt," said Anita. "Mine sure do. I'll have to be more wary when you suggest a 'short walk' in the future. I guess short is a relative term, especially for a mountain climber."

"Yes, well, I am sorry about that. It was a bit further than I remembered it. But wasn't the food excellent, particularly for such a modest looking place?"

"I have to agree with you on that."

"Now, are you ready to teach me that card game we talked about?" asked Leon.

"OK, you're on. Why don't you clear a spot for us on the table and I'll see about a deck of cards."

She pushed out of the chair and walked barefoot to her room, carrying her shoes and purse. She thought about changing into her comfortable nylon warm up outfit but paused first, studying it on the hanger. What would Leon think if she changed? Perhaps she looked better in the sweater and khaki pants. But what did it matter what he thought? They were just friends. Or did he really think she was special and, if so, what exactly did that mean?

Trying to stall for time she stuck her head out of her bedroom door, calling out, "Leon, give me just a minute. I'm going to change into something more comfortable."

"Good idea," was the response. "Maybe I will too."

Good, she thought. That bought some time but didn't answer the question. With her mind in a swirl she went back to the closet to review the choices. Do I think he's special? Perhaps that should be the question. Oh, of course he's special. Who am I trying to fool here? He's smart, handsome and available. I feel like a teenager when I'm with him. Oh God, now I'm not sure I can even face him. Breathe Anita.

Breathe. Standing with sweaty palms, she finally took a deep breath and removed the nylon warm up suit from its hanger.

When she returned she found Leon looking very comfortable in a pair of well worn jeans and a blue polo shirt.

"You look nice and relaxed," he said, looking up from a business magazine.

"I hope you don't mind the casual look. But if I'm going to beat you at a game of cards I need freedom of movement," she said, swinging her arms in wide circles like she was warming up for a fight.

"Oh, so the lady takes her cards very seriously. OK teacher. I'm ready for my first card lesson."

The afternoon flew by and the conversation wandered widely. He was a quick study, very competitive and soon had mastered Anita's version of the classic game of gin.

"You scoundrel! You must have played this before, the way you're beating me," she moaned, pushing the deck toward him for the shuffle. "I bet you have a card partner waiting for you in Brussels."

"How do you say it; beginner's luck? No, truly. I have never played games. We just didn't find the time."

"I'm not so sure," she said, watching him deal.

Picking up her cards she teased, "So tell me, how many women are going to be broken hearted when you leave Brussels for the states? You must have a string of lovelies waiting for you back there."

"Oh yes, dozens," he replied, studying his hand. "Actually I'm quite sure the women of Brussels will not notice my absence, except for the one that cuts my hair of course. She will be very disappointed as I have been generous with my tips over the years."

She smiled at his reply. "That would surprise me. I just assumed the women would declare a national day of mourning when you boarded the plane to leave the country."

"How about you? Will there be a string of men at the airport when you return, fighting for the privilege of driving you home?"

"Now that is a picture I'd like to see!"

"Well, don't forget, you have promised me a grand tour of your city when I arrive. I plan to take you up on the offer."

"The offer remains open. But we'd better do it as soon as you arrive. Once you hit the Microsoft campus one of those millionaire woman managers will snatch you up and I'll become a distant memory," she said with a mischievous twinkle in her eye.

"Thanks for the warning. I will try to resist them at least until we have our tour"

And so it went as the afternoon wound down. The conversation remained on a lighter vein but both used the banter to learn a bit more about the other. But the minefield of serious conversation was never crossed and, if Anita was special to Leon, he didn't reveal it or didn't realize it himself.

Simone succeeded in getting them back into Lombardi's for their farewell dinner. The maitre d' courteously seated them at "their" table, near the back. An old friend of hers, dining near the front, even bought them a bottle of wine. But the black cloud of his imminent departure hung over the otherwise exquisite meal. Frank nervously pushed a small vase back and forth across the crisp white tablecloth as they talked of children, food and wine but avoided talking about Frank and Simone.

The restaurant was nearly empty when he paid the bill, retrieved their coats and they stepped into the cool night air. They drove the short distance to Simone's in silence. Frank knew the sand in their hourglass of time together was running out but was unable to stem the flow. It troubled him in a way he couldn't describe.

When they reached Simone's Frank opened her door and offered his hand as she ascended from the car. She fumbled for her keys and could only unlock her door when he put his hand on hers to calm the shaking. Together they stepped inside and stood, holding hands like young lovers. Then, in a motion that surprised even Frank, they fell into each other's arms in an embrace that released fifty years of pent up passion. Their lips met, as they had so many years before. He kissed her lips, her forehead, her neck, her hair; not wanting to stop. But, in moments, as if the storm had passed, he found himself standing quietly in her embrace with her head pressed against his chest. Frank wasn't entirely sure of what they had or where it was going but knew he didn't want to release her for fear of losing it.

"I want to see you again," he whispered. "We'll find a way."

"The heart of this old woman says we're crazy. We really are."

"If I write, will my letters get to you this time," he asked, with a smile, lifting her chin up so he could see her eyes.

"I'm sure they will. I'm quite sure they will."

"Good night Ms. Challon," he said, squeezing her hands.

What should he do? Stay? Leave? Profess the love he thought he felt? While his mind spun his body slipped out the door and walked back toward his car, with the darkness concealing the moisture in his eyes.

The four roommates returned to the hotel from a leisurely dinner at a nearby Chinese restaurant. After settling on plans for the next day Francine and Charles said their "good nights" and retired to their room leaving Anita and Leon behind.

"I've had such a wonderful few days. I can't believe we're leaving tomorrow," said Anita, as she wandered slowly toward her room with Leon at her side.

At her bedroom door Leon surprised her by taking her hand. When she turned, he raised the hand to his lips and kissed it gently. "Ms. Chase, I have enjoyed making your acquaintance. I'm looking forward to my Seattle tour."

She smiled an embarrassed smile. "Just give me a call big guy; you just give me a call. Good night," she said retrieving her hand and slipping into her room, easing the door closed.

Alone in his room, Leon changed into a heavy terrycloth hotel bathrobe, hung up his clothes, sat on the bed and tried to read. Unable to concentrate, he set the book aside, grabbed the remote and previewed the choices on the TV. An old movie captured his attention for a few minutes but, when a commercial appeared, he clicked through the rest of the channels and then turned the TV off. He eased from the chair and paced between the window and the bed, as if lost in deep thought. Finally he headed down the narrow hall to take a shower.

Leon stood in the shower, much longer than normal, with the hot water pelting his body and steam filling the small hotel bathroom. When the mirror and walls were thoroughly obscured by a thin smear of condensation he shut off the water, toweled dry and stepped from the shower into the lingering cloud of steam. Finishing at the sink he stood for a moment with both hands on the edge of the counter, staring at the condensation on the mirror as if he could actually see himself. After staring for nearly a minute he shook his head with a confused look and opened the door to the hall.

Alone in her room, Anita found herself standing barefoot in the window humming "I Could Have Danced All Night." When she thought about what she was doing she smiled to herself. They hadn't actually danced at all. But they had a wonderful evening and she felt a wild exhilaration as if Leon had been guiding her across a grand dance floor to the sounds of a full orchestra.

She finally retied her bathrobe and flopped into the only chair in the room with the TV remote in her hand. She paused on world weather, clicked by the news and then gave up on the TV.

In the quiet room the sound of the water running in the nearby shower resonated through the common wall. It was pleasant to think of Leon luxuriating in the shower just on the other side. Get a hold of yourself girl, she thought. You shouldn't be sitting around thinking about Leon in the shower. Perhaps she would opt for a cold one when it was her turn. Then the sound of the water ceased, snapping her from her reverie.

She turned on the bedside light, fluffed her pillow and crawled onto the bed with the novel she had been working on since the plane ride from Seattle. Why can't I get into this thing, she thought? The book was a best seller and yet she was having trouble reading it for more than five minutes at a time. Tonight she didn't make it five minutes.

She glanced at the alarm clock. It was late and tomorrow was going to be a tiring travel day. It was her turn to use the now silent bathroom. She removed her clothes, placing them in plastic laundry bag, retied the heavy hotel robe, grabbed her nightgown and opened her door

---

In the rush down the hall she nearly collided with Leon as he emerged from the bathroom with its light filling the hall from behind. "Oh, you surprised me," she gasped as she stepped back.

He reached out taking her by the shoulders as she regained her balance. But he didn't let go. He held her for a moment before pulling her toward him, his lips touching hers. The first light kiss was followed by others, each firmer and more passionate than the last. Not a word passed as they pressed tight, separated only by their lumpy robes.

Then they paused, still clinging to each other, with Anita resting her head on his partially exposed chest.

"I was on my way to the shower," she said softly.

"You didn't make it did you?"

"Someone got in my way."

"Are you sorry?"

Without responding she released him, took his hand and led him into her dimly lit room, latching the door behind them. Leon's hand tilted her head up to meet his lips as his body pressed hers against the door.

Her mind raced. Oh God…what had she done? What was she doing? As she felt him come alive beneath his robe the answers came.

She buried her head on his exposed chest and began carving small circles around his nipple with her nails.

With a fluid motion his hands pressed her back and then her hips to him and then, with ease, he swept her from her feet and carried her to the bed. When he lay her down she stiffened as pain shot up her back.

"What? Are you ok…?" he said pulling away.

"Ah, I think so," she whispered, rolling to the side, pulling the novel from beneath her back and pushing it to the floor. "I don't care for that book anyway."

His look of concern was replaced by a smile. "Anita Chase, why am I so lucky? I find you…."

She silenced him, pulling his lips to hers.

His hand slipped into her robe caressing a breast as if savoring its silky surface. His gentle touch drew ever tighter circles on her full breast until his fingers enclosed her hardened nipple sending waves of delight through her body.

Her mind tried to grasp what was happening but her emotions were moving too fast. She wanted him to move into her. She wanted him to slow down. She wanted to feel the thunder that was so long absent from her life. She wondered if she was still able to feel the thunder.

While her mind tumbled he moved over her, leaning forward to kiss and caress first one breast and then the other before kissing her throat and ear lobes.

Her hands wandered down his body searching vainly for the hardened soldier she'd felt against her before. But the tangle of robes, ties and knots frustrated her reach.

"Oh Leon. Leon, can we get theses damn robes off. I want to feel you against me."

He gave each breast one more kiss and then rose to his knees. His fingers opened her tie and spread the robe to either side like angel wings. Still on his knees his hands traced her breasts before slipping down her body with the reverent gaze of an art aficionado.

"Do you want to kill the light?" she asked.

He leaned forward, circling her navel with his tongue. "I don't want to lose this view," he replied leaning back with a smile.

"Well then, I'd like a view too," she said pulling on his robes tie. But, instead of falling open the tie locked in a neat knot. "Oops."

As he leaned back to work on his robe her hand slipped beneath its folds finding her prize erect and full. He groaned as she stroked him with a firm hand. "Take your time with that knot," she teased.

"Oh God Anita! If you keep that up I won't have much time," he replied, opening the tie and flinging his robe from the bed.

Oh God yourself, thought Anita, as she gazed up at the heavenly body that hovered over her. The vision lingered for a moment and then disappeared as he slid down her, pausing at her navel again before sliding lower. Her hands, now free, curled through his hair as his kisses explored her body sending fire through her soul.

"Oh Leon, I want you. I want to now!"

With a fluid motion his tongue traced a line from her loins, across her tummy and breast as his body rose. He thrust into her in a way so new yet so familiar. Bodies choreographed in a dance of love they moved as one to a glorious explosion of long restrained passion.

She felt the thunder.

Frank was sitting up in bed with an unopened book on his lap. His emotions were in a heap. His torment was interrupted by the ring of the bedside phone.

"Frank here."

"Frank, it's me, Simone. I hope I didn't wake you."

"I was just sitting here thinking of you."

There was a pause at Simone's end and then, "Oh you sly old soldier. I have a favor to ask. Francine has invited me to spend a few days with her in Luxembourg City. Would you mind awfully if I rode down with you in the morning?"

11

Anita wandered into the sitting room with a lightweight travel robe neatly tied over her nightgown. She had taken time to run a brush through her hair but the rest of the barefoot package was all Anita, without her confidence building makeup. Leon had seen her without more than her makeup so there would be no surprises there, she thought to herself, smiling.

"Good morning Mr. Chauveau," she said, padding silently towards him.

Seated at the table with his newspaper and coffee he looked up, surprised. "Anita! I didn't hear you. How are you doing this morning," he said, rising to greet her.

They kissed and embraced, swaying gently in each others arms. "Here, sit down," he said finally, leading her to the sofa. "May I pour you a cup of fine imported coffee?"

"No," she laughed, "but you can pour me a cup of that hotel stuff I see over in the pot."

"Ah, you caught me. Well, never mind; this is the best I have to offer," he said, joining her on the sofa.

She sat for a moment, her gaze focused on the steaming cup in her hand. "About last night..."

"Yes," he replied, "it was very nice."

"Do you really think so? I mean I don't want you to get the wrong idea about me or..."

"It was wonderful. We are wonderful together. Sorry I slipped out while you slept but I thought it best, with my dear sister nearby, if you know what I mean."

She nodded.

"Though, I admit I felt overpowered by you. I mean I just lost the strength to resist. You American girls are everything I had been led to believe," he said with a mischievous smile.

Her look went from alarm to mock indignation. "You're terrible; and taking advantage of a woman like that. I may just tell my father when he gets here. He's sort of old fashioned, and he may insist that you marry me and make an honest person out of this fallen woman."

Leon smiled but contained his laughter, not wanting to disturb the others in the quiet suite. "Marry you? That might not be too bad a punishment but there is just one problem."

"Really; now what would that be?"

"Are you a millionaire?"

"Are you kidding?"

"You're the one that told me to look for a Microsoft millionaire. So your relative poverty could be a problem."

"You are a horrible man!" she said, thumping him on the arm with her fist. "My mother warned me about men like you."

"Good morning," said Charles, stepping from his room. "I hope I'm not interrupting anything but, I quite agree with you Anita. Leon can be a horrible man."

Overcoming their surprise they greeted Charles with nervous laughter. What else had he heard, wondered Anita.

Bathed in fall colors the rolling countryside slid by as Frank and Simone made their way along the winding road to Luxembourg City. They'd shared a light breakfast at Simone's before embarking on their short journey. Now the miles, or kilometers, were slipping by as they moved closer to their destination. At Frank's request the trip was to include a short detour to visit the Luxembourg American Cemetery and Memorial near the city's airport. Emory had encouraged the visit saying, "If you see nothing else, you must see that. It's both magnificent and gut wrenching."

The cemetery lay on a treeless ridge, facing the mid-morning sun which reflected off the light colored stones of the plaza and memorial.

Leaving Simone behind Frank descended from the plaza and walked among the rows of white marble headstones that were precisely arrayed across the sloping grassy field. The even pattern of Christian crosses was occasionally interrupted by the crisp outline of a marble Star of David. According to the brass plaque at the entrance there were over five thousand of the marble headstones spread across the ridge. From the dates carved in the stones Frank could see that many of the young men had fallen during the Battle of the Bulge but, despite the fact that he found several from the 28th Division, there were no familiar names. His eyes moistened as he thought of all the young men around him, buried so far from home; so far from loved ones.

With his chilled hands tucked firmly in his jacket pockets. Frank turned and looked back up the slope toward the silent memorial tower. There, at its base, he could see Simone, looking so small in the fall sunshine. He was glad he came. It was time to go.

When he rejoined her she stood beside him, her arm in his, and together they looked out over the somber field. "Thanks for coming with me. It's both beautiful and sobering but I needed to come here. Do you understand?"

She squeezed his arm and leaned her head on his shoulder. After several minutes of silent reflection they moved toward the gate. There they stopped, turning to take a last look. "You know, we were all so young. We all had full lives ahead. Some of us were able to live out our dreams and others just.... It just doesn't make sense does it?"

"No Frank. It didn't then and it doesn't now."

"I'm glad we stopped. Thank you," he said, squeezing her gloved hand.

They walked slowly back to the car sitting by itself in the large empty lot. While the sun was out, the air was cool and the car was a welcome warm refuge when they climbed inside. As he was reaching for his seat belt Simone removed the key from the ignition and laid it upon the dash board.

"Frank, what are we going to do?"

"Do?"

"Do with us? What are we going to do with us? I mean you have been here less than a week and now I feel all confused. You would think I would learn but, no, here I am falling for the same man a second time. It's all so impossible; so futile."

"We can figure something out."

"Frank, this is serious. My good sense says we need to be honest with each other. I can't pretend we will be able to see each other again and again when my mind says that is not going to happen."

"Would you like to be together 'again and again'?"

"Yes, no, I don't know. Oh, there you go again; confusing me. I just think that, perhaps, today should be goodbye. Then I won't struggle with the false hope that something more will come to us and then be set up for disappointment when it doesn't. I just think it would be better not to fool ourselves; for me to fool me."

"Do you really want this to be goodbye?

"No, of course not but…"

"Then give us a chance. Give us six months. Give us a year. But don't try to decide now."

"Oh Frank, I thought I had all my arguments worked out. Why can't you be logical? You're impossible," she said as they leaned together and kissed.

Damn bucket seats, he thought. He'd always hated bucket seats.

It was approaching noon when Frank and Simone arrived at their children's hotel room door. Francine responded to their bell. "Mother; Frank, you made it. Come in, come in."

Anita appeared from down the hall and gave both of the new arrivals a warm hug. "I hope he wasn't too much trouble, Simone. I have had a wonderful time with your family and I feel guilty for saddling you with the crotchety old guy," she said as she gave him a second hug around the waist.

Simone smiled, looked at Frank and then back to Anita. "Well, as you might imagine, I live a very active life and he did slow me down some but, it was the least that I could do for the U. S. Army after all they did for us. But he's all yours now. Do I need a receipt or anything now that I have delivered him?"

Leon soon joined them and, after sharing a few more laughs, they crowded into the elevator and moved upstairs to meet Charles in the hotel restaurant. The familiar noise and aroma of a busy restaurant, crowded with business people, greeted them as they stepped from the elevator. Located on the top floor of the hotel its windows overlooked the city, with its gray stone buildings which nearly looked attractive in the bright fall sun. Their reserved window table, near the back of the dining room, isolated them from the worst of the business chatter.

The lunch was a boisterous affair as everyone shared tales of their recent activities. Some were tall and some were true but all evoked laughter and the mealtime passed quickly.

Finally the reality of the imminent departure of Anita and Frank set in and plans were made for the trip to the airport. Leon, since he was familiar with the route, suggested that he and Anita take the rental car and return it at the airport. Francine could then take Frank and Simone and they could all meet at the check-in area. Charles, with meeting obligations, would simply bid everyone farewell at the hotel.

"We'll be down in a minute," said Charles, as the others rose to leave the table. "Francine, why don't you stay with me while I finish this last cup of coffee?"

Sensing he had something on his mind, Francine remained at the table with Charles as the others departed.

"Well, what do you think of my love meter now, dear," said Charles when the others were gone.

Francine laughed. She too had detected the new level of attentiveness displayed by Leon toward Anita. "Charles, you truly amaze me but, yes, you were right about my little brother. I think there is something going on there."

"Your little brother! How about your mother?"

"Mother?"

"Yes, your mother. Didn't you notice her and Frank. Good Lord woman, you must be blind. It was a bit more subtle but they're as bad off as Leon and Anita. I'm not sure it was good idea to leave them home together without a chaperone!"

"There was something familiar about the way they were acting but do you think it's more than just being nice to each other?"

"I would put money on it. In fact I wonder if I have a special gift for spotting love struck couples. Maybe I could find a way to sell my services," he said with a laugh.

"Mother and Frank; Leon and Anita? Do you really think so? Well, if you're right, Frank and Anita have sure stirred up our little family in just a week."

"I'll bet you my body that I'm right. Winner takes all!" he said with a seductive glint in his eye.

"What a prize," she replied, beginning to rise from the table. "Come on Romeo, I need to get some people to the airport."

Francine and Anita were seated near the ticket counter while Simone and Frank tended the luggage in the check-in line. Leon was nearby visiting with an old college friend he hadn't seen for many years. Crowds swirled back and forth and conversations were interrupted from time to time by scratchy announcements on the airport public address system.

"Well, Charles is now firmly convinced that you've captured Leon's heart. Are you seeing any signs?" asked Francine.

Anita fidgeted and blushed. "Oh Francine, I don't know. I just don't know where this is going."

"Where what is going?"

"Us, I mean, Leon and me. We did…ah, we did talk some last night after you and Charles went to bed."

"And?"

"We'll just have to see. Francine, he's a wonderful guy. We'll just have to see what happens when he comes to Seattle. At least we enjoy each other and I can have fun showing him around and then, well, we'll just have to see."

"Oh Anita, I'm so glad for the both of you. You will write me won't you, and let me know how things are going?"

"Francine, if 'things are going' I'll let you know. But don't get your hopes up. We've only known each other a week."

"And look at your Father there in line. Charles thinks there is something going on between them too."

"That Charles of yours is a real romantic isn't he," Anita said, studying her father in the nearby line. Simone was holding his arm and their heads were close together as they engaged in a very private conversation. "They seem to enjoy each other. I think it's cute, at their age."

"Don't let mother's age fool you. She is still a good looking woman, don't you think?"

"Good looking? She is drop dead gorgeous. I only hope I look half as good as your mother at her age."

"Here comes Leon. Now you remember what I said about writing. I don't want to lose touch with you or him."

Reinforcing Francine's best hopes, Leon walked up to Anita and kissed her gently on the cheek as if Francine wasn't even there.

It was dark when Frank and Anita arrived in Copenhagen on their flight from Luxembourg. They'd exchanged small talk during the flight and subsequent layover but the banter never moved beyond the superficial. Now they were again side by side, belted into their big leather seats as the heavily loaded flight to Seattle lumbered down the runway and reluctantly lifted off into the nighttime sky. They would chase, but never catch, the sun for the next nine hours as they curved over the frozen northland on their way home.

After fiddling with his headphones, flipping through his book and exploring the information in the seatback in front of him it was Frank that broke the self imposed silence.

"So, did you enjoy the trip? Was it what you expected?"

Anita, who had been studying the electronic map on the screen in the front of the cabin, thought for a moment before responding. "Oh, I don't know. How about you?"

Just like her mother, he thought. Doris had a habit of answering a question with a question. It must be genetic, handed from mother to daughter. He could have bounced the question back to Anita but, instead, he used the same approach that he had used with Doris for all those years. He just gave in. "Yes, I surely did enjoy it. I'm glad Emory pushed it. And you too of course."

"Was it what you expected?"

"Hmmm. I guess so. The museums, the veterans and the war stuff were much like I expected. Of course Simone and her family were a huge surprise. I never thought I would see her again. Now that was not expected. But how about you?"

"How about me what?" she asked, turning her head toward Frank.

"Did you enjoy yourself?"

"I had a wonderful time Dad, though things didn't go quite as I expected. I'm still sort of trying to digest the experience. I do know it was nice learning more about my favorite father," she said, giving his hand a squeeze as it lay on their shared armrest.

"You and Leon seemed to hit it off. From the looks of your farewell embrace you seemed to hit it off very well," he said, watching her for a reaction.

She blushed and looked up the aisle, flustered. "Well, yes, he's very nice. And we had a wonderful time, we really did. But, dad, he was just being hospitable saying goodbye. Or maybe he was following his mother's lead," she said looking back at him. "You and Simone seemed to be very—how should I say it—friendly, at the departure gate. In fact I thought I saw a tissue in her hand."

"Yes, well, you know what they say about Army guys. I guess we just have that impact on women."

"I wish they didn't live so far away. There was—oh I don't know how to describe it—a chemistry between Francine and me. Maybe she's the sister I never had. We seemed to get along like long time friends. I wish I had a friend like her at home."

The discussion was interrupted by the dimming of the cabin lights and the announcement that the first movie was about to begin. They both seemed relieved.

"I think I'll watch it. I want to stay awake as long as I can or I'll never sleep when we get home," said Anita.

Frank settled back but didn't respond.

Anita's nose was pressed to the cabin window as the plane touched down in the Seattle darkness and splashed its way across the taxiway to the glimmering terminal building. The groggy couple, father and daughter, wandered through the customs gauntlet and were soon settled in the back of a cab, weaving their way through the airport traffic. Each would find their homes just as they had left them. But both would walk into their homes buoyed by an optimism that had not existed one week before. The meeting with the Chauveau family had changed everything.

12

Frank shuffled from the elevator in his fur lined moccasins and terrycloth bathrobe. He normally wouldn't visit the upscale lobby of his condominium building in his pajamas and robe but he knew there were few residents up and about at six in the morning. He'd been home from Belgium for a week and he still found he was waking up at odd hours. He took the blue air mail envelope from his robe pocket, reexamined the address and inserted it into the shiny brass mail slot. Out of habit he checked his own mailbox even though he knew he'd emptied it the previous afternoon as soon as Ethel, the mail lady, had finished her box stuffing exercise.

This was his third early morning run to the mail this week. Once his body clock adjusted so he didn't wake up at zero dark thirty, as he liked to say, he would be making his runs to the lobby later in the day, properly dressed.

He re-entered the elevator and pushed the button that would carry him back to his top floor unit where he knew the coffee he had brewed before his departure would be gurgling its last drops into the Pyrex pot.

The smell of fresh coffee greeted him when he opened his front door. He poured himself a cup, grabbed his book and the TV control, turned on the gas fireplace and settled into his favorite chair to begin the day.

It was eight-thirty when Frank awoke with a start. His book was open on his lap and a talk show had replaced the morning news on the TV, which was barely audible in the corner. Frank squinted at his watch and shook his head in disgust pushing himself from the chair. He didn't like to sleep during the day. In his opinion old people and small children slept during the day; he didn't believe he qualified on either count.

After showering and dressing Frank retired to his office, located in the smallest of the three bedrooms. It was a crowded little room, jammed with the books from his old den that were too good or memory filled to dispose of when he moved. He fumbled with his dog eared little phone directory, found a number and then reached for the phone.

"Emory here," came across the line, followed by a spasm of coughing.

"Frank, Frank Larson."

"Frank, you old bastard, you're home. Hey how was it? Did you see any guys you knew?"

Frank was alarmed by the sound of Emory. His voice seemed weak and raspy and his frequent coughing spells made it difficult for him to converse. But he wanted the details and Frank provided them; at least most of them.

"And you will never guess who I did run into," said Frank, who then went on to tell about Simone, Mark and the time spent in the cellar in Wiltz.

"Geeze that's great Frank. That's great. Did you take any pictures? God I would love to see some pictures."

"Anita did. I'll have her make duplicates and then I can send you copies. You can enjoy the reunion without the jet lag," he said with an attempt at humor.

"Geeze that would be really great," he replied again, between coughs. "Hey, gotta go. Lenore says I'm tiring; like talking on the phone is tiring. Hey buddy, stay in touch."

Frank would never speak to Emory again. He just hoped the pictures got to him in time.

Anita and Leon, warmed by fleece jackets beneath their rain shells, walked down the deserted Whidbey Island beach hand in hand. The empty mussel shells crunched beneath their feet as they wound their way between the incoming tide and the tangle of driftwood that lay twisted where it had been placed by the last great storm. The gray clouds seemed trapped between rain and sun in that middle nothingness that characterizes Washington weather in November.

Leon had been in the states just two weeks and, during that time, he had spent as many nights with Anita as he had spent at his hotel room near the Microsoft campus. Their second weekend together they were spending at Anita's island home. "I can see why you like it up here. It is so quiet. Is it always like this?" asked Leon as two gulls glared at them with suspicion before lifting off the beach to clear their path.

"It's busier during the summer; more boats, more people, just more going on," replied Anita.

"How long have you had the place?"

"Dad built it about ten years ago. He said it was for him and mom but I knew he was hoping we would use it and bring our boys up here in the summer. And we did for a few years. But you know, as boys get into high school they get into activities, girls and jobs and it just got too hard to break them away."

"Did you and your husband use it much?"

"Not really. The only sand Eric liked was the kind you find in sand traps. There are a few good courses on the island but it wasn't the same as playing his own course with his cronies."

"I've never golfed," offered Leon. "But then I've never spent much time at the seashore either."

Reaching the end of the beach, where the high bluff crowded down to the water's edge, they climbed over the accumulated driftwood and took the wooded path back to the cabin. The cabin sat back on a small rise, overlooking the water. Large windows surveyed the quiet cove and a wood stove drove the fall chill from the great room. They left their sandy shoes on the protected back porch and hung their coats on hooks near the entry.

"This is so great," Leon exclaimed, flopping onto the sofa near the fire. "It is so different from anything I have experienced before. Growing up our parents would take us for short stays at a little cabin in the hills near Clervaux; my grandfather built it originally. We had to haul everything nearly a thousand meters down this narrow path. It seemed much further and the path seemed to enhance the remote feel of the place. But this is so different from that. The smell of the sea is very...I don't know how to describe it."

Anita joined him carrying a bottle of merlot and two glasses. "Well I'm glad you're here," she said with a kiss on the cheek. "This can be a very nice place if you just want to be alone but it's much nicer for two."

She poured the wine and then curled up on the far end of the sofa where she could have a good look at him. "Here's to our international relations," she said, raising her glass. After taking a sip she continued, "I feel a little guilty leaving dad. We usually have dinner a couple of nights a week. You've disrupted my schedule Mr. Chauveau."

"We just saw him last weekend so don't try to make me feel guilty." He paused before continuing. "I spoke to Francine yesterday. She says mother hasn't been her old self since you two returned home."

"Do you actually think there is something going on with her and Dad? He hasn't said anything to suggest it but then he's never too gabby."

"Francine sure thinks so and she is better about that sort of thing than I am. I didn't even know I was falling for you," he concluded with a smile.

"Oh you," she said nudging him with her foot. "Do you think they've spoken since we came home?"

"I don't know. Francine didn't say."

Anita stared absentmindedly out the window at the grayness of the water. "You know, I think your mother is a dear person. But I have trouble thinking of my father with another woman. Isn't that crazy? My God, he's a seventy year old widower and mom's been gone for five years but...."

Simone was looking forward to Francine and Charles's arrival for dinner. It had been nearly a month since Simone had returned from her short stay in Luxembourg City and the days had been hanging heavy for her. She'd returned to her normal schedule of activities but the memory of the time spent with Frank was a frequent distraction. She could picture his surprised look in the entry on that first night. She could still see him sitting on the kitchen stool while she prepared the fish stew. She'd hoped the feelings and visions would fade with time. They had not.

The past Sunday Mark and Sabine had come for dinner, churning more recently stirred memories. The three of them enjoyed a delightful evening together but, the entire time she had a feeling that someone was missing from the room and conversation.

She hoped that writing to Frank would normalize their relationship and stabilize her feelings. It hadn't. She tried not writing for a few days. That hadn't helped either.

She was standing in the kitchen, knife in one hand and lettuce in the other, staring at the stool, his stool, when Charles and Francine burst into the kitchen, exchanging warm greetings with Simone. As they were heading back to hang up their coats the phone interrupted.

"Would you get that dear and take a message. I don't want to speak with anyone right now."

Francine stepped to Simone's tidy desk, near the dining room, picking up the phone. As she took the message her eyes were drawn to the neat pile of blue air mail envelopes sitting on the corner of the desk. She didn't have to pick them up to read Frank's name on the return address sticker. She smiled to herself and wondered if Frank had a similar pile at his end of the mail route.

Anita surveyed her dining room table; three places set with her best china for the Thanksgiving dinner that was taking shape in the kitchen. Not too bad. Mother would have approved, she thought as she adjusted the napkin at her father's place.

Anita had become hostess for family holidays following the death of her mother. Often the only guest would be her father. Today was special. Leon would be joining them. Her sons would be spending the day at their father's. They'd promised to spend Christmas with her. She always missed them during holiday dinners but, six years after the divorce, she was resigned to the arrangement. She knew that future girlfriends or wives would further complicate the holiday commitments; she would deal with that situation when it arose.

Her father was first to arrive, cheeks red, wearing a ski parka and carrying his ever present umbrella. "Good Lord Dad, did you walk?"

"You bet. It's only a mile or so and, if I'm to eat your great dinner I figured I needed to assuage my conscience with some healthy exercise."

"Well, at least it's not raining," she said, hanging up his coat.

"Who all is coming today?"

"Just you and Leon. The boys are with Eric. I invited Liz but she left for the weekend; so it's just the three of us."

"Suits me," said Frank, settling into a chair.

The door bell soon announced Leon's arrival. Frank watched as Anita greeted him with a kiss in the entry.

"Happy Thanksgiving Leon," Frank offered when Leon entered the room. "You are about to experience a delightful American tradition prepared by one of Seattle's best cooks. Her mother trained her well."

"Yes, I am looking forward to it. I have eaten a variety of fowl but don't believe I have ever eaten turkey," he said as he greeted Frank with a firm handshake. "And I have had occasion to sample your daughter's cooking and I know it is good. At first I assumed that all Americans were superb cooks but I now understand that may not be the case. I am lucky to be in the company of a kitchen artist."

"Well, this artist doesn't want anyone messing in her studio so I suggest you both get comfortable here and I will let you know when I need a big strong arm to mash some potatoes."

"You play backgammon Leon?"

"I do indeed."

When Anita returned with hot cider she found her two men engaged in a heated game that would continue until she asked for help in the kitchen.

"Anita tells me you are quite the skier. Any ski holidays planned for the winter?" Leon asked, between moves.

"Oh, nothing firm. I can usually wrangle an invitation to my friends' places in Sun Valley and at Whistler. But nothing's on the calendar yet."

"You ought to plan a trip to Europe. Mother would love to see you."

"Mmmm, I suspect your mother is quite done with being my tour guide. I'm sure she has a full plate of activities."

"Don't be too sure. No, don't be too sure. I'm sure she could find time for an old veteran like you."

Frank gave Leon a smile and then refocused on the game board.

Dinner was a great success. The turkey, stuffing and pumpkin pie were all new treats for Leon and he seemed to savor every course.

As was his nature, shortly after dinner Frank became restless and insisted on heading for home. Since a lazy mist was falling he consented to Leon driving him the short distance down the hill. Leon was soon back, joining Anita in the kitchen where she was packaging up the left-over food. He gave her a big hug from behind since her hands were greasy and fully engaged in her task.

"This has been a most pleasant day Ms. Chase."

"Yes, it has," she replied, turning her head to kiss him on the cheek. "We will make an American out of you yet. Anything on dad's mind during your time alone?"

"Nothing memorable," he replied, pausing before he spoke again. "Do you think your father would consider going skiing in Europe this winter? Francine was wondering. She is putting a tour together to St. Moritz and was going to encourage mother to go along."

She snapped the lid on the last plastic container and wiped her hands on a paper towel as she turned to face Leon. "I don't know. He and mom skied Europe several times. But it's a long way to go by himself."

"He wouldn't be by himself when he arrived. There would be about twenty-five people on the trip. Francine always puts together good trips. And it would be a chance for, you know, a chance for him to see Mother."

A chance for him to see Mother. Why does that bother me, she thought as she gave the countertop a final swipe with a damp cloth. It's good he has a friend. But is it more than that? And if it is, why do I feel this way; uncomfortable with the idea.

"I guess it doesn't hurt to ask him. I just feel funny playing cupid for my dad."

"Playing cupid?"

"Trying to fix my dad up with a woman. We call that playing cupid. Let me think about it."

"Fair enough; I can get more details from Francine when I am there next week. But enough about them. How about us," he said, taking her into his arms.

Anita no longer looked forward to December. Where holiday depression was concerned, November was just the preliminaries. The finals came in December. You couldn't avoid December. Advertisements, decorations, music, TV specials, parties.... Christmas just kept staring Anita in the face screaming "you're alone, you're alone."

And her father wasn't helping her mood. He'd slumped into a morose crankiness that even his friends commented on. When it was just Frank and Anita, no Leon, his cantankerousness blossomed. The waiter was too slow, taxes too high, politicians too crooked, traffic too slow and most people were, as a rule, no damn good. He hadn't mentioned Simone to any of his friends so none even suspected heartache as the source of his malaise.

In the past the holidays had been a time of family, friends and holiday parties. The divorce and loss of her mother had changed all of that. Now her boys had to split their time between her, Eric and their own lives and friends. There was an occasional party where she felt comfortable alone but, for the most part, she skipped the party scene. And she felt an obligation to insure that her father was not alone.

She had hoped having Leon in her life would brighten the holiday season but his schedule and family obligations precluded that. He spent the first week of December in Belgium, on business. He returned for a few weeks and then left again on the twenty-second to spend the holiday with his mother and extended family. Anita was disappointed but could hardly object to the call of his family and long time traditions.

So she smiled, wore Christmas colors, decorated the condo and made the best of things. The middle of the month she had Frank and Liz in for a casual dinner. She enjoyed preparing it and the evening was a success. But now even Liz was out of town with relatives.

The office party, her only party for the year, went as anticipated; too much booze and too little restraint. She'd slipped in, avoided the most aggressive divorced senior partner, and then slipped away without incident. The next morning the office was abuzz with stories about what happened, or allegedly happened, at and following the party. She was not the subject of any of the discussions.

She was a survivor. Leon had given her something she hadn't been looking for; hope, love and companionship. He would be back soon. She could survive until the holidays were past. Who knew what the New Year might bring.

A heavy New Year mist obscured the view of the bay when Frank opened his living room curtains on January first. It didn't matter too much what was going on outside. It was bowl day on TV. His only outing would be to the 8th floor for the Rose Bowl and dinner with the Webbers.

The ringing of the phone broke the morning silence.

"Happy new year; this is Frank."

"Happy new year to you too."

The accent could only be one person. "Simone, good morning, or I should say good evening to you. It's good to hear your voice."

It was good to hear her voice. They had exchanged a few phone calls since he returned from Belgium. But they'd both been raised in a letter writing generation and still felt the use of the phone for transcontinental communication an extravagance. So they had exchanged many letters since the reunion, but the letters were filled with information, not emotion. A phone call always trumped a letter in his mind.

They talked about their holiday activities, all the food they had consumed and of their children. She reported that Leon had left for the states that morning; information which Frank was sure would please Anita.

"Francine is trying to convince me to come to Seattle in June when she is leading a tour group that will go on to Alaska. Do you think that would be a good time of year to visit?"

"Absolutely," he replied, both buoyed by the prospect of her visit and dismayed by the six months that must pass before it occurred. "It will be wonderful to see you. And, if Leon will let me, I'd love to reciprocate as your tour guide."

"Frank, that would be wonderful. I'm sure Leon wouldn't mind and it would free him up to be with your daughter. I fear she was on his mind during his entire holiday visit. He seems quite taken by her."

"And she by him. Yes they make quite a couple. Even if nothing comes of the relationship I may adopt him. I enjoy having him around though I know it's more to see her than it is to see me."

"I hope they know what they are doing?"

"You mean Anita and Leon?"

"It is just that, oh I don't know; I don't want to see either of them hurt. After all, his home is here and hers is there. Do I make any sense?"

"I think I understand," he said, confused. "Anyway I don't have much influence over my daughter when it comes to her social life."

"I suppose that is true. Perhaps I shouldn't have said anything. Now tell me how will you spend the first day of this New Year."

The sound of her voice on the line fueled an emotional fire that he had difficulty subduing.

When the call was completed he just sat in his favorite chair with the TV controller on his lap. His mind was in such a state that he missed the first quarter of the Peach Bowl. Why did he feel this way, he questioned himself. Nothing can come of it. He was here and she was there. But, he did love hearing her voice.

The Saturday morning call caught Anita by surprise. "Anita, Francine."

"Francine, it's good to hear your voice."

"I just spoke with Leon and he thought I might be able to catch you. How's my little brother treating you?"

"He's doing just fine. We were going to run up to my cabin today but he probably told you we're getting our mid January snow storm."

The comfortable conversation rolled forward. Each updated the other on their recent activities, the conditions of their families and an assortment of other girl to girl topics.

Switching topics Francine continued, "Say, I wanted to run an idea by you. I think Leon told you I was putting a ski trip together for the first week in March. I have convinced mother to be my roommate and was going to invite your father along. I thought they might enjoy seeing each other again. But when I mentioned it to Leon, over Christmas, he said you might not be comfortable with that kind of arrangement."

"Oh, now I'm embarrassed. I did express some concern to Leon but, well I just don't know…"

"Please don't think I'm trying to play matchmaker here but, as you may be aware, there is something going on between them. The volume of mail going back and forth is astounding."

"Really? I didn't know that. I…"

"Trust me. You should see the stack of letters that mother keeps on her desk. That father of yours is a prolific writer."

"Maybe they're exchanging recipes," Anita offered.

"That would surprise me."

"Me too. I was just kidding. Look, dad would love to go skiing in Europe. You should definitely call him. He's never been too spontaneous before so he might not agree but it doesn't hurt to ask."

"You are a dear friend Anita. I know this will please my mother very much, even though she doesn't know about it; yet."

"I'm going to turn Leon into a football fan yet," said Frank as he took his seat at Anita's well laid table.

"What'd you think of your first Super Bowl? Did it live up to all the hype," asked Anita setting the fragrant pork loin beside her father's place and joining the men at the table.

Leon smiled while helping himself to the green salad. "Well, there is still much I don't understand. Like, if San Francisco is playing

San Diego why do they play in Miami instead of California? It seems so inconvenient for their fans."

Frank explained the intricacies of Super Bowl siting to Leon while Anita filled their wine glasses.

"OK, OK, OK," said Anita. "Football has already occupied too much of the day. Let's change the subject. When are you going to Sun Valley this year?"

Frank leaned back in his chair. "First week in February. Say, that reminds me; I got a nice call from Francine this morning. She said to say hi to the two of you."

Anita smiled and kept her eyes focused on her plate.

Leon looked up in surprise. "What's on her mind?"

"Oh, she's planning a ski tour in Switzerland and wondered if I had any interest in going."

"And…," said Anita, fork suspended in midair.

"And what…."

"And are you going?"

"Haven't decided; probably not. It's a long way to go when we have such good skiing here."

Anita's perplexed expression was missed by Frank as Leon asked, "Where is she going this year?"

"St. Moritz."

"Oh Frank, that is a fabulous resort and my sister puts together excellent tours. I'd go if I didn't have a little thing like work to deal with."

"Leon's right. You should go. It would do you good and I'm sure you would have a great time. Simone's going isn't she?"

"I suppose so," he replied.

"You suppose so," she replied, her exasperation level rising. "You suppose so! You would have a great time and be able to see Simone and all you can say is you suppose so? Francine was kind to think of inviting a crotchety old man like you. You'd better accept before I tell her what you're really like."

Leon's concerned look went from father to daughter and back again, unsure of the seriousness of the discussion.

"It's a lot of work, traipsing all over the world just to go skiing when I can ski right here in the U S of A. Anyway, I didn't say I wouldn't go. I just said I'd think about it. And I will."

"You'd better, you stubborn old man. You'd better…."

13

Lulled by the drone of plane's engines Frank watched the cabin crew prepare the business class section for the first meal of the nine hour flight to Copenhagen. He still wasn't certain that going on this ski trip was a good idea but Francine had been so convincing and the thought of seeing Simone, well…, how could he describe that? For the last six weeks he'd been rationalizing his decision to take this European ski vacation. He told his friends the trip was all about skiing but he knew better. It was the thought of spending time with Simone that melted his initial resistance to Francine's sales pitch. And now, as the big jet drew him closer to another encounter with this woman from his past, his mind was again tangling with his heart for control of his old body.

During his pre-trip internal debate his mind kept saying stay home, relax and enjoy the memories of the past. But his heart kept clouding his mind with thoughts of Simone; her voice, her touch, her caring.

Emory's death lowered his last wall of resistance. During the five weeks since the funeral a black cloud had hung over his soul. The grim reaper was harvesting closer and closer to home.

Maybe the trip would be good for him, he thought. Maybe he could get Emory out of his thoughts and her out of his system at the same time. Yes, that was it. They lived oceans apart. She was European. He was American. She had a life and so did he. So while their orbits might intersect once in a while, they were light years apart. But it sure will be nice to see her again.

Frank tipped the bellman, closed the door to his compact room, stepped around his bulging bag and slumped exhausted into the overstuffed chair by the window. Copenhagen, Luxembourg, Zurich…the cities he had passed through the past two days, were little more than a smudge in his memory.

The recent vision of Simone was much clearer. He could see her waiting to greet him at the Luxembourg airport. He could recall the touch of her hair and the smell of her perfume when she gave him that first gentle hug in the terminal. And the memory of her warm hand in his during the long and winding bus ride to St. Moritz was fresh indeed. Now it gave him a warm feeling to picture Simone and Francine in their room, just down the hall, busy unpacking; mother and daughter.

He knew the worst part of the trip, the getting there part, was over. With a little rest he would subdue the effects of the jet lag and be feeling his old self again, ready to tackle the ski slopes of Switzerland. From his small window he could see fragments of the snow covered hills above town and the tops of several tram towers, linked by thin strands of cable. But his view was nothing compared to Francine and Simone's. On the other side of the building their spacious room offered a view of the Alps that seemed to extend all the way to Italy. He would have gladly traded places with Francine and not just for the view, he thought to himself, smiling.

His own room, in the old wing of the hotel, was more "old European" in size; which meant it was small. With the two beds, a table and the chair he was now sitting in, there was little spare space to navigate around the place. He was certain his room was about the size of Simone and Francine's generous bathroom! But he could live with it. He hadn't come on this trip to sit in his room.

He was confused. He had arrived in Luxembourg convinced his mind was in control. Seeing her had changed all that; his heart took over. It was as if they had been apart for a few days; not a few months. He was so comfortable with her. Despite his exhaustion they had talked and laughed and seemed to pick up right where they left off in October. Be careful, his mind intervened, as his eyes slipped closed. Don't lead her on. You have too much respect for her to do that.

Having fallen asleep in the chair Frank was startled by the knock on his door. Opening his eyes and orienting himself he was surprised to see that daylight had escaped and the darkened outside scene was a sea of twinkling lights from the nearby buildings.

"Coming, I'm coming," he grunted as he pushed himself from the comfortable chair in the overheated room.

Opening the door he found Simone and Francine, looking like sisters, standing side by side in the hall. Both were dressed casually in dark skirts and bulky light colored sweaters of some sort. Frank was never sure about women's clothing. "We were just heading down," said Francine. "It's almost time for the manager's reception."

"Frank, have you been asleep?" asked Simone.

"Just resting my eyes a bit," he replied, with a sheepish grin. "But I'll just be a minute. Why don't I catch up?"

"Don't let her fool you Frank. Mother took a little nap too, while I was down taking care of an unhappy customer. It always happens. The Bouchers were put in a room just like yours and they didn't take it very well. So I raised a little stink with the manager and everyone, except perhaps the manager, is happy now. Anyway, we will see you down stairs in a bit."

"Why don't you go ahead dear? I'll wait and walk down with Frank."

Francine glanced at her mother, "O.K. you two. But don't be long now, do you hear? I don't want to start any rumors so early in the trip."

The next morning, following breakfast, the group gathered in the hotel's ski room, ready for the first day on the slopes. There was considerable confusion as everyone seemed to arrive at once. It was always like that on a first day, Frank thought, as he struggled to find a place to sit to put on his boots. No one knew where they were going. No one knew where to buy the lift tickets. No one knew why this person or that person had yet to arrive; or if they had already departed. Someone forgot their ski poles. And so it went. But he took solace in the knowledge that every other day would be an improvement as people developed their own routines and learned their way around the mountain.

Accompanied by Simone's old friends, Bernie and Alice Laclaire, they were soon tucked into a swaying gondola with the bustling town disappearing below. It was an ideal day for skiing with sea blue skies, little wind and snow groomed to a corduroy perfection. "Simone is an amazing skier," offered Bernie, in broken English. "She will give us a real workout."

"Actually, I'm a bit rusty, but on a day like today, with such forgiving skis I can perhaps even fool myself," she responded with a laugh. After hearing a translation of the exchange Frank smiled and nodded his concurrence.

Bernie and Alice lived in Brussels. They spoke some English but tended to speak in French when conversing with Simone. That was more difficult for Frank but, if they were all compatible skiers, that would make up for any communication lapse.

Francine had stayed behind to finalize meal arrangements with the hotel and tend to other business details. Being a tour leader interfered with her skiing but it was a business for her and she understood her responsibility to the guests.

After a couple of runs Frank had worked out his first run kinks and was feeling good. And Simone had turned out to be as beautiful on skis as he'd imagined.

"Maybe I should find a slower group," said Frank as the gondola swayed gently, suspended from its thin cable on their third ride to the top. "You three ski like teenagers!" He didn't actually feel that way but he tended to understate his own ski prowess.

"Nonsense," replied Bernie, as the others laughed and Simone gave Frank a nudge with her shoulder. "I've been the last one down the hill on each run. I will be recovering in the spa by two o'clock."

"Tell me about this 'Frank' gentleman," said Alice as she and Simone pulled down the footrest on their chair that swung from its cable as they glided up the hill for their first run after a lazy lunch at a mid-mountain restaurant.

Simone sat quiet with her face barely visible beneath a quilted nylon hat and above the turned up collar of her black Bogner one-piece suit.

"There is not much to tell I'm afraid. I met him, or re-met him to be precise, at a reunion last October. I had first met him during the war. In any case, when he heard about this trip he signed up and here he is."

"Oh, I see; that's all there is to it then. He is just another guest on your daughter's tour. Did Francine ask you to hold hands with him at dinner last night so he would feel welcome?"

Simone stopped midway through applying fresh sun protection to her lips.

"I'm sorry," Alice continued. "That was gossipy of me wasn't it?"

Simone turned smiling. "Don't be sorry Alice. I know that you're no gossip. It appears you can still see through me. You're right. There is more. I'm not sure how much more but we do enjoy each other very much. My feelings are very confused and I'm not sure about his. I wish there weren't so many miles between us, that's all."

"So you've kept in touch since October?"

"We've exchanged letters some. They're mostly about the weather, where he's been for dinner, how his daughter is; that sort of thing. And I don't suppose mine are much better. But he's here and that's nice. Perhaps he just came for the skiing so...." Simone finished, with her voice trailing off.

"Well, I'm glad you're out enjoying yourself. You are too vibrant a lady to languish at home alone. I was so pleased when I saw your name on the trip list. You haven't come since Jules's passed away have you?"

"No, but I have done some trips with Francine and her husband so I haven't forgotten how to ski but, no, I haven't done her tour. At first I couldn't bear the thought of going on one of her tours alone."

"Well, I'm glad you came this year. And it doesn't appear you will be alone much."

Simone gave her friend a guilty smile, slipped on her gloves and prepared to lift the footrest as they approached the upper lift station.

"Tell me how you came to know Simone," said Bernie as he and Frank pulled down the footrest on their chair, gliding up the hill for their first run after a leisurely lunch at a mid-mountain restaurant.

While Bernie was self conscious about his English, Frank found him to be quite competent and understandable.

Frank sat staring at the tips of his skis with only his face visible between his baseball hat, with 'Sun Valley' embroidered above the bill, and the turned up collar of his brilliant yellow North Face parka.

"What's to tell? I met her, or re-met her to be precise, at a reunion in Bastogne last October. I had first met her during the war. In any case, when I heard about this trip I signed up and here I am."

"Mmmm, I see. So you have been staying in touch with her since the reunion?"

"Yes, well you see, her son, Leon is living in Seattle now. Small world isn't it?"

Bernie nodded, watching Frank as he spoke.

"Well," he continued, "my daughter Anita has been seeing Leon a great deal since he arrived last November. They really enjoy each other and she is introducing him to life in the U. S. of A. So it's easy to stay connected to the Chauveaus through Leon."

In response to Bernie's polite questioning Frank outlined his wartime experiences in Belgium and the occasion for his first meeting with Simone. But, uncomfortable doing all the talking, he took the first opportunity to become the questioner and learn about Bernie.

It turned out that the Laclaires were about sixty-five and married for only fifteen years. Alice, an old friend of Simone's, had been widowed and Bernie divorced when they met on a ski trip in Austria. They hit it off, enjoyed the same foods, the same music and many of the same activities. So they were married after a three month courtship. "We figured that, at fifty, we didn't have much time left and, if we were meant for each other, we needed to get started as soon as we could," he concluded with a laugh. "My adult children thought I was a bit impetuous but here we are, fifteen years later, happier than ever and she is still a hot skier.

Happier than ever. Now that is a lucky man thought Frank as they approached the upper lift station.

The second day on the slopes was much like the first, except for the weather. The clouds, promised by the forecast, covered the upper reaches of the resort and by the end of the day the first traces of new snow were blowing around the streets of town propelled by an increasingly persistent wind.

"I don't mind coming in a little early," said Frank, as they removed their boots in the hotel's basement ski room.

"I hope not," said Simone. "You didn't have to come in with me. I wouldn't have minded if you and Francine took a few more runs."

"Are you kidding Mother? I just hope I can ski as well as you two when I'm in my sixties. You and the Laclaires are amazing. My thighs felt like Jell-O on that last run. If Frank wanted to ski more he would have to find another partner."

Frank smiled but didn't respond. In fact his legs were a bit tired as well; but he would keep that information to himself. Anita would have called it a 'guy' thing.

As they stepped out of the suitcase sized elevator Simone said, "Frank, why don't you pick up a couple bottles of wine. Then we can have a little pre-dinner drink in our room and not have to sit in that smoky bar another night. Would six-thirtyish work for you?"

"Say no more. I'd invite you to my room but I don't have space for the bottles, let alone any guests," he said with a laugh while continuing down the hall.

At 6:30, dressed in his khaki pants and blue turtleneck, Frank tapped on Simone's door carrying a plastic bag from the local market. "Well you're right on time," said Simone, her lips brushing his cheek. That simple act still thrilled him more than it should, he thought.

"We're all set for a small party. I have wine, cheese, some crackers and my Swiss Army knife with a cork screw," he announced laying out his treasures on the coffee table in their sitting area. "Boy, this weather is sure going downhill," he continued as he walked to the window. "The weather man said we could expect snow showers the next twelve hours. If this is their idea of snow showers I'd hate to see a real storm. You can't even see lights across the lake anymore."

After a glass of wine, Francine rose and excused herself. "As much as I dislike that smoky bar I need to mingle with the guests; customer service and all that, you know. You're coming to dinner, aren't you?" she said as she left the room, casting a suspicious eye toward them.

"Shame on you, naughty girl," said Frank, tossing a cork in her direction.

In the now quiet room Frank rose and took another walk to the window while Simone topped off their glasses.

"What do you want to do tomorrow, if this keeps up?"

"I don't know Frank. But if it's like this I would prefer to take the day off. I don't like to ski when the visibility is poor. How about you?"

"I agree. No see, no ski is my motto." He returned to his seat and helped himself to a small piece of cheese. "The concierge had some ideas for a little outing if you have an interest. We could take the train to Davos and wander around there a bit. Or we could take another one to Italy. The scenery on that run is supposed to be spectacular, though we might not be able to see much of it unless the snow lets up."

"Frank, both are wonderful ideas. I was hoping we would be able to spend a little time with just the two of us but, except for now, that hasn't happened. I would love to take a day trip with you. Which place sounds the best?"

"Italy. There is a little town of Tirano a few hours from here. We could go there, grab lunch and then catch a return train mid-afternoon. The concierge said there is not much to do in Tirano but the mountains are breathtaking and the route is a real engineering marvel with lots of twists, turns and tunnels."

"I guess that appeals to the builder in you. Well, let's do that then. And Frank..."

"Yes," he replied, taking a sip of wine.

"Let's keep our plan to ourselves. If others hear about it they may want to join us. I would rather not share the trip with anyone else."

He smiled, gazing at her over the rim of his glass. Yes, it would be nice to be away from the group, he thought. Very nice indeed.

It was like riding rails through a cloud as the train wandered south in a swirling blizzard toward the Italian mountain town of Tirano. The vaunted scenery remained a promise for Frank and Simone as they sat comfortably in the overheated coach, swaying ever so slightly as the undulating tracks passed beneath the carriage.

Traveling alone had been no issue. To meet the demands of the railroad timetable they had been the first from their group to arrive for breakfast and departed the dining room before most of the others arrived. Francine had made no effort to impose herself on their plans, seeming to understand their desire to be alone. The Laclaires, arriving midway through their breakfast, had expressed some interest in joining them but concluded they couldn't be ready in time for the train departure. So Frank and Simone were gliding alone through the snow clouds of the Swiss Alps, sharing the carriage with strangers.

"It's lovely isn't it Frank," she said, sitting forward, staring into the swirling abyss.

"Uh uh," he replied, sitting back, staring at her profile and holding her ungloved hand.

She turned to him, smiled and gave his hand a squeeze. Sliding back on the seat, she laid her head back and studied the man beside her. "Do you want to hear something silly? We have spent so little time alone; alone together I mean, that I've sometimes worried about what we would have to talk about if we finally got to be alone. And yet, here we are and it doesn't seem to be a problem at all."

"I think I'd enjoy being here with you even if we said nothing at all."

She linked her arms in his, slid closer and rested her head on his shoulder. "I love how you think. You're really an old romantic, did you know that?"

"I can't recall being called that before," he replied, as he felt his resolve inexorably slipping away.

The dark shape of the station platform and the slowing of the train were the only visible signs of their arrival. They gathered their hats and gloves and stepped from the car, greeted by an icy blast of winter air and swirling snow. They walked across the covered platform with the few other passengers who shared their destination as the train eased from the station and disappeared into the persistent blizzard. In an effort to orient themselves they stopped and studied a city map mounted on the station wall near the entrance. Then, hoods up to slow the blinding snow, they headed into town.

From a tourist brochure Frank knew Tirano was an ancient place, tucked in a small Alpine valley. They could see little of that as they wandered the narrow empty streets, barely able to see the gray toned buildings that surrounded them. The few shops they passed seemed closed. Seeking a warm refuge from the storm they ducked into a small hotel near the station. Since it was approaching noon, they decided to have an early lunch in the hotel restaurant.

"If we eat slowly we can hang out here until our departure time," Frank said, after shaking the snow from their parkas and hanging them near a gurgling radiator. "I can't see wandering around in this storm anymore. I thought it would be over by now."

Frank studied Simone over the top of his menu. Despite looking a bit bedraggled from the effects of a fleece hat, parka hood and melting snow she still cut a striking profile. His mind and heart jabbed at each other as he thought how natural this all was. What had Bernie said; he was happier than ever? Well, thought Frank, I'm happier than ever right now.

Enjoying the warmth of the hotel they lingered over lunch. After nearly two hours, and growing stiff from the inactivity, they gave up their table in the uncrowded restaurant and settled onto a well worn sofa in the lobby. Finally, as departure time approached, they bundled up and headed out into the unrelenting storm.

The station was quiet, with small groups of passengers scattered about on the hard wooden benches. "That's funny," said Simone, "It seems quiet so near a departure time. Perhaps we should check to see if there are delays."

Simone took the lead when they arrived at the ticket window. Her Italian was limited but adequate. Frank's was non existent. He watched her expression change and frustration level rise and fall as she engaged in an animated conversation with the attendant. Finally she thanked him, Frank understood that, and taking Frank's hand, walked to the middle of the waiting room.

"Dear Frank. We have a little problem. There is a slide in the pass and the line into Switzerland, the route we used this morning, is closed. They haven't even begun to remove the slide and can't until it stops snowing. The route to Switzerland is closed and he has no idea when it will be cleared."

"You mean were trapped in Tirano?"

She nodded, staring into his sparkling eyes.

"I guess we should try to call Francine so she doesn't worry about us," he suggested.

"Yes we should, but first we should try to find a place to spend the night. We may not be the only people trapped in town and I didn't see many hotel choices on our walk. Then we can worry about my daughter."

They trudged back to the hotel, fearful there would be a rush on rooms but the lobby was still quiet with a few business types chatting in a cloud of cigarette smoke in the far corner.

Hearing them at the desk, the clerk came from a back room and greeted them in English, to Frank's surprise.

"Do I look that American?" Frank said, with a disarming smile.

"A little sir, but I saw your Sun Valley hat," he replied, pointing to Frank's forehead. "I actually worked there one season when I was younger."

"Your English and your observation skills are very good," Frank responded, leaning forward on the registration desk. "We need a couple of rooms for the night. What do you have available?"

"We have deluxe and economy rooms sir. The deluxe are larger with a small sitting area but all the rooms are quite nice."

"Deluxe then."

"Fine sir. And you said two?"

"One. He meant one," said Simone, as if interpreting for Frank.

"Very well," the clerk said turning to retrieve a room key while Frank studied Simone with a surprised look frozen on his face.

Simone took the little pen, connected by chain to the desk, and began filling out a registration card while Frank paid for the room. The clerk returned to the counter with the credit slip, passing it to Frank while retrieving the completed card from Simone. He glanced at it, made a notation of the room number and then looked up at his new guests. "Good, everything seems to be in order. Will you need any assistance with your luggage Mr. and Mrs. Larson?"

Frank was speechless, staring at Simone, while she explained the situation with the cancelled train and their lack of luggage to the sympathetic clerk who suggested that they might find a few toiletries and other necessities in the shop next door.

Key in hand, the new couple made their way across the lobby to the small elevator and was soon ascending to their fourth floor room, the best in the house according to Alessandro, their new friend at the front desk.

Simone dropped her purse on the bed nearest the door and examined the dimly lit room. Two beds pressed against each other and covered with down comforters, dominated the center of the room. It had once been an elegant chamber but was showing signs of age; the carpet was worn in spots and there were permanent stains on the upholstered chairs. But for a small town in an emergency, it was more than adequate.

She strode to the sitting area, across the deluxe room, where she flung open the heavy curtains letting in the muted winter light. Turning she saw Frank standing motionless, back pressed against the door.

"Are you OK?"

"OK? Yes, I'm fine," he said, trying to look relaxed. Taking a few steps into the room he continued. "It's just that, are you alright with this; with this room arrangement I mean?"

She smiled, kissed him on the cheek and led him to an overstuffed chair near the window. Sitting on the ottoman near his feet she took his hands in hers. "Dear Frank. Please don't think of me as too bold but we only have a week together. The thought of spending it alone in a strange town in different rooms on different floors did not appeal to me. If you're concerned about what people might say…."

"No, that isn't it," he interjected, appearing embarrassed.

"Well, if it is, people don't need to know. And," she continued, gesturing toward the center of the room, "there are two beds so we can be quite proper."

Frank slumped back in the chair as if overcome by her argument.

"Are you feeling ill?" she asked, reaching for his forehead.

"Simone, Simone, Simone. If you detect any fever it won't be caused by illness; it'll be caused by you."

"What's troubling you then? Should we get a second room?"

"Second room?" he replied, kissing her hand. "No, No, No. You're going to think me a confused old man but, well you see, part of me is saying run you old fool. You're slipping down a dangerous path that can only result in two broken hearts. And the other part of me thinks this is as close to heaven as I'll likely ever get. In fact, that snow slide must have had divine intervention. So here I am, alone in a hotel room in a small Alpine town, with the woman I…with the woman I think I love and I'm acting like an old fool. There, I've said it."

"Your words warm this woman's heart. It sounds like you're as confused about us as I am. And Frank…"

"Hmm?"

"I do love you."

"I guess that makes us lovers then, doesn't it?"

"Yes it does Frank. Yes it does."

Fearful the few stores in town might close they soon headed out again to purchase some "necessities," as Frank called them. Returning from a successful shopping excursion they were both happy to abandon their boots and parkas and settle into the room to relax.

The bed nearest the door was now covered with their purchases; an assortment of toiletries, two extra large tee shirts silk screened with an Alpine scene, two bottles of wine and a corkscrew.

Simone was seated in the larger of the two chairs, trying to place a call to Francine. After some frustrating moments the connection was completed. Frank sat on the foot of the nearest bed, watching CNN International.

'Francine, it's Mother," she said in French.

"Where on earth are you? Are you OK?"

"Yes, yes dear. Frank and I are quite safe here in Tirano. But it seems we will be here for a while from the looks of things. The storm has shut down rail service."

"We heard. When you were late I had the front desk check with the station and we learned of the closure. So you are stuck in a small mountain town in Italy? Mmmm, sounds romantic. Are you sure you didn't plan it this way?" Francine teased.

"Quite sure."

"Are you sharing a room?"

"The accommodations are quite adequate dear. Quite adequate."

"You didn't answer my question."

"And I don't intend to. Now don't worry about us. We can take care of ourselves. It's quit snowing here so perhaps they can get things cleaned up before tomorrow's train."

"Mother, I love you. And, if you have to be trapped with someone, I can't think of a nicer person."

"Neither can I dear. Neither can I. Good night."

Upon arrival Frank and Simone were the only guests in the hotel restaurant. Frank ordered a local wine assuring their waiter they were in no particular hurry. At his recommendation they selected the daily special which, in multiple courses, arrived at a relaxed pace. They lingered over coffee and dessert, listening to the pianist play for a small but appreciative audience. Frank's emotions were still in a tangle. He had never felt closer to Simone. Yet now, with her arm in his as they walked across the quiet lobby, his nerve ends were fraying in anticipation of what might take place up in his deluxe room in a few short minutes. The elevator was waiting and soon they were standing in front of their room while Frank struggled to engage the lock in the dimly lit hallway. A sharp click signaled success.

Entering the room Simone surprised Frank by turning and kissing him so fervently that he nearly lost his balance and ended up leaning against the now closed door. "Thank you for dinner. It was wonderful," she whispered.

As he caught his breath she turned, set her small bag on the dresser and sat down to remove her boots. "I don't normally wear after-ski boots to dinner but I'm sure glad I was wearing them the rest of the day."

This woman is full of surprises, thought Frank, as he walked nervously to the window, parting the sheer curtains to look at the snow covered town. The reflected glow of the street lights filtered into the room. "It's stopped snowing. I think I can even hear the sound of snow plows working."

She joined him at the window, her arm entwined with his. "Do you normally shower at night," she asked.

"Usually, but I don't have to if…"

"No, I was just wondering. We haven't shared a room like this before you know. Whenever you are ready why don't you hop in? I'll go after you because I plan to take a long hot bath in that big old tub. I don't want you worrying about me using all the hot water," she said with a laugh, releasing his arm and plopping down in the nearby chair. "Now, will you pour this old lady a glass of that vintage wine we picked up this afternoon?"

Soon he was sitting across from her as they shared what turned out to be a fair glass of wine. The room was silent except for an occasional gurgle in the cast iron radiator beneath the window and the growl of the far away snow plow. Frank was the first to break the silence, studying her over the rim of his glass.

"Is this really love?"

She thought for a moment before reacting. "Is what love? The way I feel; the way you feel or the way we feel when we're together?"

"Yes, any of them; all of them."

"I can only speak for myself. I think it's love; the feelings I have for you. You are a wonderful man," she replied, raising her glass as if beginning a toast.

He smiled, acknowledged her toast, and then took a sip.

"Why don't you take your shower Lt. Larson? Between the hour and the wine I might fall asleep and drown in that tub and you would have a lot of explaining to do to the Italian authorities."

"That would be messy. No, I wouldn't want to deal with that," he said as he rose and leaned over to kiss her on the forehead before gathering his meager belongings and retiring to the bathroom.

In their room, illuminated by the dim light cast up from the street below, Frank lay alone, studying the peeling paint on the ceiling. Wearing his new tee shirt and old boxers he was covered to the waist by the fluffy white down comforter, as much for modesty as for warmth. Muffled plowing noises could not mask the subtle sounds of Simone bathing in the next room. The sounds of a squeaky valve, water filling the tub and the bather moving into the steaming water triggered visions of the young girl he had made love to in that lodge, so many years ago.

The thoughts inspired subtle movement in his boxers and brought a smile to his face. He hoped the little soldier would come to attention if called on later that evening.

After a few minutes of silent reflection the ever active Frank Larson sat up, placed both pillows behind his back, switched on the bedside lamp and reached for his Newsweek. That was the scene that greeted Simone when she emerged from the bathroom wearing her new tee shirt, which hung loosely, reaching nearly to her knees. Gracefully she moved to the bed where she took her comforter and placed it over her shoulders like a heavy shawl. She climbed onto the foot of her bed, which was still pressed against his, and adjusted the comforter until nothing but her head was visible, protruding from the white cocoon.

"Hello soldier."

Frank let his magazine slip to the floor while he placed his reading glasses on the bedside table and switched off the light; all the time looking into Simone's shadowed eyes. He smiled, taking in the puffy elegance of her pose.

"How would you like to show a girl a good time?" she continued.

"I, um, I…," he uttered, stumbling for words.

She smiled at his apparent discomfort.

"I mean, what do you take me for? Don't you realize I'm known as a nice boy?" he responded, tossing back an innocent smile.

"Yes Frank. I know that. And I'm sure you'll be nice to me tonight."

She relaxed her grip on the comforter, rolled to her hands and knees and moved to Frank. He could drink in the fragrance of her hair and feel the warmth of her breath as she kissed his neck and throat. Laying back he cupped her face in his hands as his lips found hers. They kissed softly at first then with a passion built up over a half century of living apart.

Her slender body pressed against his from ankle to lips as his hands found their way to her bare and chilly bottom. Concerned for her warmth he paused, stretching to reach for the castoff comforter.

Her hand found his, placing it back on her thigh. "Really darling, I'm fine. Just help me with this ridiculous tee shirt," she whispered.

When the shirt slipped over her head he found his lips pressed against her small white breasts. She quivered as his tongue curled around a nipple. His hands explored each rib on her back moving ever lower.

As she pressed against him, firm but willowy light, his mind flashed back to the first time, at the cabin. So much in their lives had changed and yet this, the passion, the scent, the love of this woman poured forth as if only a day had passed since their last loving.

She rolled to his side and her practiced hand slipped from his cheek, making ticklish swirls down his chest before slipping naturally into his bulging boxers. Her touch sent a surge through his body. He wanted her to touch him more. He wanted her to stop. He wanted to make love to her. He didn't want to lose the moment.

As she worked the shorts down his legs he managed to extricate himself from his own ridiculous tee shirt.

"Well, I guess there are no secrets now. You're in bed with a pale, wrinkled old man."

'Please shush and make love to me soldier," she breathed as she took his hand and guided it to her most private place.

Her body rose to meet his touch as his lips returned to her ready breasts. Time suspended he moved over her and, with her hands as a guide, felt her warmth close around him.

It wasn't the hot and clumsy love of two young lost souls alone in a mountain retreat. It was the measured mature love of two people who had lived and loved and learned about passion and pain; joy and sorrow; gaining and losing.

It nearly brought Frank to tears.

Afterward, as he lay beneath the down of the comforter with Simone beside him, head resting on his shoulder, he gazed toward the ceiling without seeing it at all. His mind was trying to lock in the reality of the evening; the beauty of it; the smell, touch and taste of it. He could still recall her last words. "I'm nearly seventy and I'm feeling feelings I thought were reserved for twenty-year-olds. Frank, we feel so right."

He had wanted this night to happen; he had wanted her lying beside him; he wanted to feel he was her protector; her knight in shining armor. She had made it happen. She had broken down any fears he might have harbored. She loved him.

And he hoped the snow slide blocking the tracks was a big one.

14

Hand-in-hand Frank and Simone trudged from the St. Moritz station toward their hotel. Piles of dirty snow littered their path and covered stretches of sidewalk. The storm had passed leaving gray skies and knee deep snow in its wake. Front end loaders grunted and growled in the narrow streets as they placed their loads of gray snow into the waiting trucks.

Frank had been both disappointed and relieved when he learned the Tirano train would be heading for St. Moritz on schedule. His heart feared the separation from Simone which he knew was just days away. Yet his nervous mind viewed their time together like a live grenade which could blow up at any moment. To resolve the conflict he applied a well tuned Frank Larson technique; he ignored it. For now he was with Simone. For the future, well he thought, he'd deal with that as it came.

As they approached the hotel they were hailed by the Laclaires, a half block away. When they caught up Alice gave Simone a sincere embrace. "I'm so glad to see you two. We were a little worried when you didn't return yesterday."

"Oh, we were quite safe; Italy is very civilized," Simone said with a slight laugh.

"I know that. But what an adventure; stranded without your luggage in a foreign country. And no chaperone…it has an exciting ring to it."

"Actually, he was a very good chaperone. He protected me from those legendary Italian rakes, didn't you Frank?" she said, giving his hand an extra squeeze as they entered the lobby.

"And it was no easy task! I can hardly wait to turn her over to Francine. I need some rest," he replied.

"Whoa," said Simone, noticing Bernie's sling as he removed his coat, "what happened to you?"

"I'm a bit embarrassed by the whole thing but, we decided to try the fresh powder this morning and made a couple of discoveries. First, I don't ski powder very well and, second, you should never use your shoulder as a brake. It's not built for that. I just fell over and planted my shoulder in the snow; it was as simple as that."

"Anything broken?"

"No, but something is stretched and it hurts like hell when I do certain movements. But I'll survive."

"He keeps saying he needs to do all these things before he is too old to do them," offered Alice. "Well, this might be a message for him to stay on the groomed trails. He just waited too long to become a powder skier, that's all."

Stay on the groomed trails; good advice, thought Frank. Very good advice.

"O.K. Mother. I want to hear it all. What did you two do in Tirano?"

"Please Francine. You make it sound like it was some sort of a tryst. The train was cancelled, we stayed overnight and we took the next train back. That's it. Yes Frank is a wonderful man and yes I thoroughly enjoyed our time together. Now I just want to clean up and change clothes."

"Why don't you marry him?"

"Because he lives in another country and..."

"Ah, so you talked about marriage?"

"We did no such thing. You're as bad as that lawyer brother of yours; tricking me into saying things I don't intend."

"Whatever you say, Mother. Whatever you say."

The next morning Frank walked down the narrow stairs to the breakfast room and was delighted to see Simone waiting at a small table with the Laclaires. When he sat down he felt a nearly irresistible urge to give her a "good morning" kiss but contented himself by giving her knee a gentle squeeze under the table.

"Well you look like you are ready to hit the slopes this morning," Bernie offered.

"I feel great. I'm glad prudence sent me to bed early last night. I'm ready to go. Are you up for a bit of skiing today?" he asked, turning to Simone and nearly ending his sentence with the word "dear."

"Absolutely! After taking two days off I'm more than ready. Francine would like to ski with us as well if you don't mind."

"Mind? Of course I don't mind. I hope to pick up some tips from her. How about you Alice, you're not going to miss out on the new snow?"

"I wouldn't miss it. Bernie can take care of himself."

"You don't need to worry about me," said Bernie, returning from the buffet. "I'll be fine. I can't ski but I can still walk. I may even look into the spa downstairs and see if they have any of those cute Swedish massage girls working today."

Thirty minutes later the four skiers were bundled in a swaying gondola gliding up the hill. After a second gondola ride and two on a high speed quad chair they moved to a run served by an older, slow moving double chair. Frank and Francine, arriving first, boarded together.

Frank turned around, satisfied himself that Simone and Alice had arrived safely and then turned to Francine. "Thank heaven they still have a few of these old chairs around. The new ones are so fast I don't get a chance to rest," he said with a chuckle.

"Don't think you're the only one that appreciates the slow chairs. I just don't like to admit it."

They sat quietly for a moment soaking in the scenery before Frank spoke. "This may sound funny but, do you think Simone has a problem with the Leon-Anita relationship?"

"How do you mean 'a problem'?"

"It's just little things she says and the way she says them. It's hard to describe and maybe I'm misreading her. But I thought she would want to encourage the kids...."

"Actually you are very perceptive. I have noticed a few remarks myself and let them pass but if you have sensed it too; I just don't know. I do know she thinks Anita is a dear."

"Hmm. Here I am at 70 and I still don't understand women," Frank said laughing while he fumbled for a worn trail map in his coat pocket.

Francine continued. "I can tell you I am delighted that you came on the trip. I know it's a long way to travel just to ski. Of course I enjoy seeing you but you can't believe what a tonic you are for mother. When I told her I had invited you she seemed a little flustered but when you agreed to come I thought she would never come down out of the clouds. She'd be unhappy if she thought I was telling you this, but it's true. You are very special to her. I hope you realize that," she said with a serious look.

"Your mother is a beautiful lady."

"I hope it's an inherited gene," she replied with a laugh.

"Is she, or I mean, does she see anyone?"

"You mean, does she have a special male friend?" she responded, turning to him.

Yes, he nodded.

"No worry there. She has lived like a female monk since Father passed away. Oh she goes to charity things and sees friends for dinner and theater but there is no one special, if that is what you mean. No one except you that is."

Frank nodded again and then turned to focus on his map. The words "no one except you" echoed through his head. What had he and Simone started? Before the trip he labored to convince himself he'd only come for the skiing. He knew that was a charade. He wanted to see Simone. But why? Was it for one last look at this world so he could then put her out of his mind and move on with his insulated life? If so, that plan was in a shambles. Things had changed; and he was confused.

As they passed a lift tower a glomp of snow fell on Frank, shaking him from his reverie. They shared a laugh while he brushed the snow from his lap and tried to refold his now damp map.

As they approached the unloading area Francine grew more serious. "I hope I haven't said anything to make you uncomfortable. I don't want to sound like I'm playing match maker here."

"I am very comfortable, thank you. And, if you don't mind me saying so, Simone is very lucky to have such a delightful daughter. If your mother would give you up I'd adopt you in a minute. I don't think a man can have too many daughters," he said with a laugh. "Now let's go skiing."

"Isn't this wonderful snow?" Simone exclaimed as she settled into the chair with Alice. "Too bad Bernie can't be here to enjoy it."

"Oh he is probably down in the spa lusting for one of those cute Swedes. And I suspect they will know how to handle a foxy old gentleman like him," Alice replied with a laugh.

"Bernie is quite a fellow. How long have you two been together now?"

"Can you believe it? It's been fifteen years; my God the time flies."

Yes it does, thought Simone. Yes it does. She met Frank fifty years ago; a lifetime ago. She saw him again five months ago. They made love two days ago. But it was all in the past. For them it was all about the past; they never seemed to have a future, only a past. Yes, Alice is lucky to have Bernie; to have Bernie here in Belgium with her now and in the future. The gods seemed to be teasing her.

They rode without words for a few moments, Simone studying the shadow of their chair as it glided across the fresh snow below. The only sound disturbing the silence was the subtle hum of the guide wheels on each lift tower they passed.

Alice finally broke the spell. "Frank seems like a nice fellow. If I didn't know better I'd think you two had been together for ages."

"He is a special person," Simone said, as she put new sun screen on her cheeks. "And in a way I have known him forever. When you think about it I actually met him before I met Jules. Isn't life funny? I meet him, then I don't see him for fifty years and then he comes back into my life and it's as if he just left yesterday."

"What are you going to do now? You surely can't let him get away for another fifty years."

"First of all I don't think I have fifty more years to worry about. Secondly, I just try not to think about it. After all, we are just friends and he has a life in America and..."

"Simone! Who are you trying to fool? Not your old friend Alice I hope. I've known you too long for that. It looks like more than a 'friendship' to me. You two are so happy together. You can't let something that looks so good slip away."

"But don't you see how impossible a relationship with him would be? At my age I just can't see complicating my life. I have no regrets. I had a wonderful marriage, have three great children and lots of grandchildren. If he lived in Belgium maybe something would make sense but..."

"Listen," Alice said, turning and gripping Simone's arm, "when Renee died a part of me died with him. We had a good marriage, great kids and a lovely collection of grandchildren. I could have spent the rest of my life as the merry widow, skiing with friends, gardening and being the good grandmother. But then I met Bernie and, when you are a fifty year old widow, there aren't that many Bernies around. We were so fortunate to find each other. Individually we were both doing fine. But together we just, I don't know how to say it, we just seem to magnify each other somehow. Am I making any sense?"

"Alice, you are a dear friend. But don't you see how different this is? I am nearly seventy, not fifty. My family, my entire life is in Belgium; his is in America. And I suspect he is quite content with his life just as it is so thank you for your thoughts but I just need to value him as a wonderful friend and not set myself up for a big disappointment."

As they raised the footrest at the end of the ride Alice turned again to Simone and said, "Forgive me if I have been a bit presumptuous but I'm only bugging you because I love you so. Do think about what I have said. If you really love the man there must be a way."

They raised their tips, made contact with the snow and glided from the lift station to where Francine and Frank were waiting.

The rest of the week was a whirl for Frank and Simone. They skied, shopped and dined together but were rarely completely alone, just the two of them. They joked about running off alone, but knew they couldn't abandon Francine, the Laclaires or others from the tour group.

Sunday, their travel day, arrived far too soon from Frank's perspective. He arose early, packed his bags, set them out for the porters and then made his way down to the last breakfast in St. Moritz. He took a place at Francine's table, ordered coffee and awaited the arrival of Simone who soon made her way gracefully into the room.

She kissed Frank with just a glance and smile and took an empty seat across from him at the table.

"Well, shall we tell him our little surprise?" said Francine, returning from the buffet with a full plate.

Simone nodded her approval while Frank gave each of them a surprised look.

"We hope you don't think we are being pushy but we couldn't bear the thought of leaving you alone in Luxembourg until your flight tomorrow afternoon so we're going to spend the night and give you a ride to the airport."

Frank smiled and shook his head in surprise. "That's very nice of you but you really don't have to stay on account of me. I was just planning to eat early, sleep late and then grab a cab to the airport. And what about Charles? I'm sure he is dying to see his lovely wife."

"Oh, right," responded Francine. "I'm sure he is and he's in luck. He's meeting the bus and spending the night with us in Luxembourg. It will be a mini trip to the big city for us as well. I've booked us all in the hotel where you're staying so we can have a nice dinner somewhere and enjoy the last night together. Anyway, I always need to unwind after a week of worrying about my tour clients."

"You don't mind do you?" said Simone, with a hint of alarm in her voice.

"No, no. Of course not; of course not. I'm delighted; I'm speechless; I don't really know what to say. I was resigned to the fact that this was our last day together. And now I get another one. I'm reprieved! You're too kind to me, all of you," he said reaching across the table and taking Simone's hand.

Francine smiled like an approving mother.

It was late afternoon when the bus full of weary skiers stopped in front of the old Majestic Hotel in Luxembourg's city center. A slight breeze moved the large flags representing a dozen European nations displayed on the front of the gray stone building. As he stepped from the bus Frank's glance paused on the German ensign, third from the left. Times do change, he thought. Fifty years ago his army had kicked the German conqueror out of this very city and now German tourists were being welcomed back. He shook his head incredulously in a gesture unnoticed by others.

"I'll wait here and supervise the unloading," said Francine. "Why don't you two see if you can find my husband somewhere?"

Frank and Simone entered the grand lobby through the polished brass revolving door and spotted Charles, sitting in a comfortable chair in a well lit corner of the ornate lobby, engrossed in a book. Frank liked Charles. He seemed like a solid business person, good husband and he had a subtle sense of humor that played well against Francine's. Frank liked a good sense of humor.

"Good afternoon favorite son-in-law. Have you been waiting long?"

"Mother, Frank," he said, standing to greet them each with a hug. "I haven't been here long at all. What have you done with my wife?"

"She's performing her last official acts as a tour director. She should join us shortly," replied Simone.

"Well, how was the trip?" asked Charles.

While awaiting Francine, Frank and Simone brought Charles up on some, but not all, of what went on in St. Moritz. Their report was interrupted by Francine's arrival and soon, after agreeing to meet in the lobby bar for drinks at 6:30, the tired travelers headed to their rooms on three different floors of the classic hotel.

Frank took a quick shower and then lay on the bed in his comfortable room, just three floors below Simone's. The seven hour bus ride had gone smoothly but, none-the-less he was tired. Travel did that to him.

The next sound he heard was the ringing of the phone on the nearby nightstand. "Frank here," he answered, rolling over and focusing on the bright red numerals, 6-4-0 on the bedside clock.

"Hey, are you going to join us?" rang Francine's voice on the line.

"Mmm; I see the time. Must have dozed off. Be down in a minute."

"If not we'll send a porter up for you," she said with a laugh.

That was the start of a delightful evening. They moved from the bar to the hotel restaurant which, according to Charles, was considered one of the best in town. Their meals did nothing to tarnish that reputation. Francine, relieved of her tour responsibilities was full of energy and humorous anecdotes from the trip. Simone, rested from her own nap, appeared to be enjoying the company of her happily married daughter and husband. The conversation was so brisk, the meal so good and the wine so pleasant there was little time for Frank to focus on his impending departure.

On the way to the elevator Francine, always the planner thought Frank, brought them back to reality. "What time should we meet for breakfast?"

"There is one thing I need to do in the morning," said Frank, to the surprise of the others. "I need to visit the American cemetery. I can just grab a cab and pop out there. I won't be gone long."

"That's no problem and you don't need a cab," said Charles, as the elevator arrived, opening its doors to greet them. "If you don't mind company we could just leave for the airport early and make a stop."

Frank paused for a moment then replied, "That would be fine if you don't mind. Yes, the company would be fine."

Everything else happened too fast. As the elevator began to rise they agreed to meet for breakfast at eight o'clock and stop at the cemetery on the way. As the door opened for Frank's floor Simone squeezed his hand, kissed him on the cheek and bid him a good night, in French. Then he was alone in the quiet hallway. And he felt very alone.

"Your mother and Frank seemed to be getting along well," offered Charles with a smirk and raised eyebrow. "That Larson family seems to have quite an attraction for your family. First Leon and now your mother!"

Francine kicked off her shoes and plopped onto the bed, leaning against the pillows and the headboard. "I feel so bad for mother. Yes, you're right. They do get along well. And he is such an old dear. Mother seems to enjoy every minute they're together and yet they live an ocean apart. Tomorrow is going to be a hard day for both of them. It seems so unfair somehow."

"Unfair?"

"Yes, unfair. Their story should have a happy ending and how can it when he is climbing on a plane and mother is coming home with us?"

"Why doesn't she marry him?"

"I kidded her about marriage the other day but I just don't see that happening."

Charles, rummaging around in the mini-bar produced a small bottle of cognac and two glasses, removed his shoes and joined her, sitting on the foot of the bed. "Why not? We live in the nineties. He could move here or she could move there. If they're happy together why not? The two places are just hours apart and I suspect they could both afford an airline ticket now and then."

"Oh Charles; they're a little late in life to be traipsing around the globe, don't you think? Belgium is her home. She could never leave. And I doubt he would want to leave America. No, I just think I am going to have to come up with some ways to keep mother busy when we get home."

"From the looks I saw them exchanging tonight you are going to have to keep her real busy. Yes, very busy indeed."

Frank sat in the windowsill of his room, watching cars pass on the street below.

What a fool I am, he thought. I should have stayed on that elevator. I should have gone to her room; or maybe invited her here. Of course, it was a little awkward with her daughter on the elevator. Why do I feel like a teenager sneaking around behind the parent's backs? Francine is her daughter, not her mother. Maybe I should call her. God, the way I'm acting she'll think I'm just a horny old man.

Lost in his thoughts he nearly slipped off his perch when the phone rang. He glanced at his watch. Mid-day in Seattle, he thought. Anita must be checking up on me.

"Good evening," he said as he picked up the receiver.

"Hey soldier, there's a little party in room 907 if you want to come up," said Simone.

"What? Oh, wonderful. Of course, a party. No GI would ever turn down a party. Do you need anything; glasses or anything?"

"Why don't you bring the Merlot from your mini-bar?"

Frank was soon standing in front of room 907, gripping two mini-bar Merlots. Simone greeted him with a kiss on the cheek wearing a lavender dressing gown that reached to the floor and billowed behind when she moved.

"I'm so glad you called," he said as he set the wine on the narrow bar and turned, gathering her in his arms. "I've wanted to hold you all evening. I'd better get it out of my system before the other guests arrive."

"There are no other guests," she said, resting her head comfortably on his chest. "This is a party for two."

"Charles? Francine?"

"Should I invite them?"

"No, I mean yes; I mean…Oh I don't know what I mean." He held her close and savored the familiar scent of her hair. "No; definitely no. This room looks just right for a party of two."

She gave his cheek a light brush with her hand then slipped from his embrace, reaching for two wine glasses on the bar. "Good. I can see them most any time. Now, bring the wine."

Settling on the brocade covered love seat Frank twisted the cap from the small bottle and filled their glasses. Handing Simone a glass he took her free hand in his and raised his wine. "To us, to whatever brought us together and to you, you beautiful lady."

Like bashful children they sat in silence between sips of wine. Franks eyes met hers as the tears began to trickle down her cheeks. He touched her cheek and wiped a tear away with his thumb.

"What is it?"

"Oh Frank, forgive me my muddled emotions. I'll be all right."

He set his wine on the table and brushed another tear away.

"It's just that, when you propose a toast to 'us' I can't help but wonder what 'us' means. When you board that plane tomorrow will there still be an 'us'?" It seems like it will be you and me; you in Seattle and me here. The oneness we've shared will end as we go back to our separate lives an ocean apart. I just, I just can't bear that thought."

He set her glass on the table, against his, and pressed her head against his chest. "We'll figure something out. We'll figure some way to shrink that damn ocean."

The words were meant to sooth the woman in his arms but, he feared, they might just be words. He'd always been honest with her but could he really say that this might be their last night together, ever. Could he say that? Could he say they were crazy to think of anything long term? Would either of them be happy if months would always separate their rendezvous?

Turned slightly to face one another each sampled their wine while they seemed to speak without words.

After a moment that seemed like an hour Frank broke the spell. "You are a woman of never ending surprises. A few minutes ago I was moping alone in my room and now this; now here," he said, making a sweeping gesture with his wine glass hand.

"Maybe I was moping, as you say, like you," she offered, giving his hand a gentle squeeze. "In any case I think I'm pretty predictable. Just ask my kids."

"Should I call them?" he said, reaching for the phone with a smile.

"Don't you dare!" She caught his hand in mid-air and placed it on her breast. "Now make me feel twenty again."

He could feel the gentle curve of her body beneath the silky fabric as he slid closer, placing a kiss on her exposed neck beneath her ear.

"Take me to bed Frank," she whispered. "Take me to bed now."

Awkwardly they rose together, bumping the small table and sloshing their wine into a common puddle.

"Oh my, let me get that spill while you get, ah, while you get ready."

He kissed her hand as she slipped away and then, after fumbling with his belt, removed his pants, formed a nice crease for the legs and then laid them over the back of the love seat. As he pulled his golf shirt over his head he gave silent thanks that he hadn't worn a shirt with time consuming buttons to contend with.

As Simone dabbed up the sloshed Merlot his eye caught sight of his boney vision in a mirror. Feigning disgust he killed the room lights leaving only the filtered light from the bath to guide him to the bed.

She welcomed him seated upright, arms outstretched, with her back against the fluffed pillows. Childlike he snuggled against her, head against her breast. Her fingers slipped through his thinning hair as she pressed him to her.

His practiced hands began to explore and draw warmth from her body. The small of her back, the curve of her leg from hip to ankle and, after slipping the tie of her robe, her shoulders and breast. His lips followed his hands to the firm nipple as she lifted to meet them.

For Frank, at that moment, life stood still. Simone and only Simone mattered; nothing else. He wanted her to know, by his touch, by his caring, by his love that she had his love; all that he could give.

To his surprise she rolled him to his back, rolling over him, pressing her body against his. Her fingers, then her lips, traced lazy patterns on his chest as she hovered above him, casting a lavender shadow from her open gown. His hands again found her breasts which swayed as she moved above him. His little soldier, now at full attention, sent waves of pleasure as it sensed the warmth of her loins as they flowed over him, her hips astride his.

He wanted to speed up while not wanting this moment to end. She lowered her breasts to his lips as her body pulsed and then, guided by her hand he was in her and they burst to life together. She rose, slipped from her robe, then, hands pressing his chest, let her body's rhythm carry her to a private peak of passion.

Frank, his body and soul in her hands, followed her.

They were sure the earth moved.

Frank awoke to the shrill ringing of the phone on the nearby nightstand. He rolled toward the sound and reached toward the receiver.

"Don't touch that phone!" whispered Simone as she reached out, restraining his in-flight arm. Half crawling over him she picked up the receiver, silencing the phone.

"Good morning."

"Oh, good morning mother," came Francine's voice. "I'm glad I caught you before you went downstairs. Say, Charles and I just got up so we are going to be late to breakfast. I didn't want you waiting for us down there. We are probably about thirty minutes behind you. I'll give Frank a call as well."

"Actually, dear, I'm still in bed too. Like mother like daughter I guess. Let's not rush. Why don't we say 9:30 and that will give us all lots of time? And don't worry about Frank. I'll track him down. He can find something to do to kill the time," she said while twisting the gray curly hair on his chest.

"9:30 it is then. Love you mom."

Simone placed the receiver back in its cradle, and rolled onto an elbow.

"That would have been hard to explain," smiled Frank as he pondered his near miss with the phone.

"Yes it would. Yes I'm afraid it would. Did you forget where you were?"

"It seemed so natural and comfortable. I guess I sort of did," he said while rising slightly to kiss her neck.

She wriggled free and turned to him, "It was wonderful and now you need to gather your things and be gone or we might have some explaining to do. The last thing I want to do is to send you away and that is exactly what I'm going to do. Besides, I must look positively frightful. Now be gone."

"I think you look wonderful," he said as he slipped back into his rumpled clothes.

"Thanks. I don't believe you but it's nice of you to say," she replied, kissing him gently as she pushed him toward the door.

Frank was seated by a window in the ornate dining room, sipping his first cup of coffee, watching passing pedestrians struggle against the chilled wind that roamed the city streets. In his travel clothes, khaki pants and sport shirt, surrounded by well dressed business people, he felt underdressed. He smiled to himself as he watched heads turn when Simone entered the restaurant. Elegant was the word that came to Frank's mind as he observed her walk toward him as if she owned the room. Her dark blue silk blouse was topped with a large bow at the neck that seemed to float as she walked. Her narrow ankle length skirt made her look taller and even more regal.

Frank rose to greet her with outstretched hands and a kiss on the cheek. He was sure he was the envy of the entire room. "Why don't you sit across from me so I can get a good look at you," he said as he pulled out her chair.

He poured her a cup of coffee and ordered another pot from the attentive waiter. "I had an incredible dream last night. I dreamed you invited me to your room and that I spent the most glorious night in your arms. It must have been a dream because it was too good to be true."

She studied him over the rim of her cup as he spoke, smiling as he concluded. "Yes, I know that dream too."

"I'm going to miss you tonight."

"Let's not think about tonight," she replied.

"Between last night and Tirano we have a great deal to think about, don't we?"

"Yes darling. And, just so you have no doubts, I thought Tirano was wonderful too. I just get a little lost when I try to think 'what's next' for us. Do you ever think about that?"

Frank set his cup down and reached across the table, taking both of her hands in his. "I think about it all the time. It's driving me crazy because there's no simple solution. I like to have things orderly in my mind and, right now, we are in a state of wonderful disorder. I just want to smash my watch against a stone so that our time together will stand still but the practical side of me sees the futility of such a move. Besides, it's a good watch," he concluded with a smile.

"So it sounds like we are in a romantic conundrum."

"Come with me, Simone."

"Still under the spell of last night's Merlot?"

"Perhaps I'm under your spell but I'm OK with that. Come with me and then all of our nights can be together and it won't matter who answers the phone."

"It's a lovely idea. Really it is. But my rational side says, think of the complications. Different countries; different families, different obligations….."

He leaned forward earnestly, taking her hands in his. "I just don't want to leave you for another 50 years. You know, Bernie said something to me that has been tumbling around in my mind ever since. He said that when he and Alice decided they were right for each other they also decided they needed to begin their life together as soon as they could. They didn't want to waste a minute. That's how I feel. I don't want to waste a minute."

"I know but...oh, here come Francine and Charles."

"Will you think about it, please?"

"Yes, darling. I will think about it," she said, releasing his hands and adjusting her hair with a nervous gesture as Francine joined them.

With skis strapped to the roof and luggage squeezed into the back, Francine's Volvo station wagon was riding low as they pulled away from the hotel. Frank sat in back by Simone with a small plastic shopping bag on the floor between his feet. Francine did her best to keep a conversation going but the ominous cloud of the pending departure overcame her best efforts.

After a short drive they arrived at the American Cemetery. Frank was relieved to see the parking lot empty when they came to a stop near the gated entrance. Curiously clutching his bag Frank joined the others as they walked through the gate to the plaza overlooking the green hillside, spotted with brilliant white marble monuments. The persistent wind tugged at their coats as they paused in front of a large stone wall covered by a stylized map of Europe. After a few moments a distracted Frank excused himself from the group and walked down the steps to the headstone covered slope. Simone's eyes followed him seeming to sense that he wanted to be alone.

She watched as he walked past rows of marble testaments to the cost of war before pausing in the middle of the white marble sea, nearly 100 meters away. After a moment he swung his arm in a sweeping motion, releasing a white cloud of dust that was picked up by the wind and just as quickly disappeared, settling among the monuments.

By now, Francine and Charles had joined her, each clinging to the arm of the other, sensing something significant was unfolding before them. As the white cloud disappeared Frank turned his back to the wind and gave a crisp salute. Then, head down, he began a slow walk back toward the others. He nearly made it.

As he neared the base of the wide stone steps he grabbed the heavy carved balustrade with both hands, staggered and then, half stumbling and half turning, slumped to a seated position on the bottom step.

When the others reached him he was sobbing unabashedly, head in hands, with tears streaming down his cheeks. "Frank, darling, are you OK?" asked Simone as she joined him on the cold step with her armed draped over his sagging shoulder.

"Yes, yes, I'll be fine. I'm sorry about this," he said between the sobs, while trying to stem the tears.

Charles took Francine's hand and began to walk away turning only to say, "Take as much time as you like. We are in no hurry."

Frank and Simone sat silently while he struggled to regain his composure. Finally, in a soft and trembling voice he said, "That was Emory out there. You know, Emory Rushing that I've told you about. Those were his ashes. God, that was the hardest thing I've ever done."

"You just spread Emory's ashes?"

He nodded. "He told his wife he wanted to be with his buddies. He wanted to be here. She just didn't think she would be up for such a long trip so she asked if I would do this for him; for her."

"Oh Frank. Why didn't you tell us what you were doing?"

"I wanted to. But I was afraid you might try to talk me out of it. I don't even know if what I did was legal. No, it was just something between me and Emory," he said, sitting more upright and regaining a measure of self-control. "We used to talk about it." He paused, wiping his eyes with a tissue from Simone. "Why were we spared? Why weren't we buried here so some other guy could live a full life? Whose side was God on? Who decided who lived and who died? Pretty morbid stuff, don't you think?"

"Oh Frank, I wish you had shared it with me. What do they call it, survivor's guilt?"

He nodded. "I've even thought about us. Some of these guys never had one chance at happiness. And now, with you, I'm having two. Isn't that something?"

Simone retrieved another tissue from her purse; this time for herself.

Finally they rose and, rocked by the wind, embraced warmly, as if holding each other up. They stood there, trancelike, until a fresh gust brought the first announcement of rain.

And then it was time to leave.

Frank mindlessly studied the milky grayness of clouds that slipped beneath the big plane as it chased the sun toward icy Greenland, far below. His seatmate, a businessman, still looking crisp in his white shirt and blue patterned necktie, was silently poring over a thick document of some kind. That was fine with Frank. He wanted to think, not talk.

His breakdown at the cemetery still bothered him. It reminded him of how painful it is to give up some one you care for. Just another reason to avoid doing exactly what his heart wanted him to do with Simone.

There was a song from the musical "My Fair Lady." How did it go?

"What a fool I was. What an elevated fool. What a mutton-headed dolt was I…?"

Or something like that. Was he being a fool feeling like he did for Simone? Was he just setting himself up for future suffering?

Come with me Simone! He had actually said it. Did she take him seriously? They were never really alone after that. At the gate he had whispered it into her ear once again, as they embraced for the last time.

"Let's talk," she had whispered back. "Let's talk soon."

Now what did that mean? Did it mean she wanted to remind him of the obstacles? Did it mean she wanted to figure some way to be together? Could she be right? Were there just too many obstacles? Would he feel the same way when he returned home and started living normally again?

He didn't have the answers. But he did know one thing. The prospect of not seeing her when he got off the plane was not a pleasant one. What was that other song from the same musical? "I've grown accustomed to her face; she almost makes the day begin….."

There had to be a way.

15

Frank stood, leaning against his kitchen counter with the phone cradled on his shoulder. "So that's about it Lenore," he said, with a firm voice but moist eyes. "On one hand that cemetery visit was the hardest thing I think I've ever done and on the other, it was sort of exhilarating. I'm sure Emory would have been pleased."

"You are such a dear friend. Thank you for calling and giving me the details. I'm sure you're right; Emory would have been most pleased," said Lenore Rushing from her Portland home.

"I wish I could have arranged a headstone for him. Somehow it seemed incomplete without a headstone but…."

"Nonsense. You did exactly what Emory wanted and I'll be eternally grateful to you for doing it."

"How's everything else going for you?" he asked as he shuffled to the stove, placing the tea kettle on the back burner. "Do you need help with anything?"

"Well, I feel bad for asking after all you did but there's one thing you could do. But if you were uncomfortable doing it I'd understand but…"

"You just tell me what it is and I'll decide."

"Well, my oldest girl, Kathryn, is quite upset with me for sending Emory's ashes with you. After his memorial service here she had just assumed his remains would be interred at a local cemetery. She had no idea what Emory wanted. Now she speaks about a lack of closure or some such thing and remains very angry with me for not speaking to her beforehand. Anyway, I was wondering if you might speak with her. I'd understand why you might not want to do it; it could be very awkward. But you knew Emory in Europe and you might be able to give her a better idea why it was so important to him to be buried in Belgium. I've tried to explain but I'm afraid I haven't been very successful."

"Kathryn; I think I spoke to her at the funeral."

"Yes, of course, you would have. She was standing with me most of the time. Well, she asked me about the ashes about the time you returned from your trip. Of course there was nothing I could do about it then, even if I wanted to. And she's been very frustrated with me ever since."

"Hey, I would be happy to speak with her. Would it help if I met with her? I'm coming to Portland next weekend. Perhaps we could get together then?" Carefully, still cradling the phone, he made himself a cup of tea and, while trying to avoid a spill, moved to the table.

"Would you? You are such a dear. Yes, a face to face meeting would be so much better. Say, why don't you plan on coming here for dinner. I'll invite Kathryn and Rex and you can talk to her here. But wait; would that interfere with other plans you have?"

"Not at all. I'm just coming down to pick up some new electronics for the boat. I'll save enough in sales tax to cover the cost of the drive," he said with a chuckle. "I'll just stay the same place I stayed for the funeral and plan on dinner at Chez' Lenore."

"You're a dear man. I'll make your special dessert. Thank you, thank you, thank you."

Anita, morning coffee in hand, stood by her small kitchen window watching the lazy April rain slowly turn the streets dark. Behind her the partially read Sunday paper was scattered in uneven piles on the table. She always enjoyed this time of year, with the first signs of new growth appearing on the trees in the park across the street. That meant ski season was over and summer couldn't be far away. Her quiet reverie was interrupted by an early morning call. Leon had been out of town for a few days so she leaped at the phone, hoping it was him.

"Anita, it's Francine."

"Oh, it's so nice to hear your voice. I've been meaning to give you a call. How are you doing?"

For several minutes the two friends caught up on each other's activities before Francine moved to the main reason for the call. "How's Frank doing?" she asked.

"Funny; I wanted to ask you the same question about your mother but, whenever I think about it, it's the wrong time to call," Anita said with a laugh. "As for dad, he's OK I guess. Leon and I took him to Whistler a few weekends ago and had a good time but I had a feeling he was keeping a veneer on his real feelings. Why do you ask?"

"Has he told you much about the trip over here?"

"A little and he showed us some of his pictures. It was quite an adventure they had in Italy! And I heard about the visit to the cemetery. That must have been an emotional experience. He even had trouble telling me."

"It was an incredibly emotional experience. Your father is a wonderful man; full of surprises. And as for him and mother, well, I don't know what all happened between them but Mother is acting like a love sick puppy since he left. I've been trying to find excuses to visit and to keep her busy but nothing seems to be working. I can only attribute it to Frank, that foxy old father of yours."

"Dad foxy?" she said, as she boosted herself up on the tile counter near the phone, leaning back against the upper cabinet. "It's hard to think of my father as foxy but he is a cute old fellow, isn't he? Well, he has seemed a little down since he returned. The skiing with us helped. And he has been puttering around on his boat but that's mostly busy work. There really isn't much to do at the boat this time of year. He doesn't talk about Simone unless I ask but I know he has a stack of letters from her piling up on the back of his desk. I'd love to take a peek at them sometime but I've behaved myself so far."

"Anita, I don't want you to think I'm trying to play cupid here but I have an idea for a trip and Leon suggested I discuss with you before I mention it to them."

"I don't think you are playing cupid. And besides, I think it is nice Dad has a pen pal. Of course, with the distance between them I can't imagine anything coming of it but the letters give him something to look forward to. I think he has even joined the 'lobby lizards' in his building."

"The lobby lizards!"

"Oh, that's what he used to call the old folks who would sit in the building lobby every afternoon and wait for the mail to be delivered. That's what he used to call them and now he's one of them!"

"Anita, I suspect Mother is more than a pen pal to your father. And I'm not the only one that thinks so. So anyway, here is my idea. I am bringing a group over for an Alaska cruise in late June. We will be flying into Vancouver and sailing from there. At Christmas Leon suggested she consider a trip to the States so she could spend some time with him. So I'm thinking I bring her to Vancouver with us, put her on a plane to Seattle and let her spend a week with Leon. It would be good for her and I know she would enjoy seeing you all again."

Anita paused before replying. More than a pen pal. I wonder what that means, she thought, as she twisted the phone cord around her finger. At Dad's age, what could it really mean? "It would be wonderful to see her and dad could save a little of the postage he's now spending. If you're asking if I think it's a good idea, the answer is yes." she finally said with a nervous laugh as her eyes came to rest on hand painted ceramic canister set on the far counter that once graced her mother's kitchen.

"Wonderful. I thought you would be OK with it but, well you know, Leon didn't want me to do anything you were not comfortable with. I will make the arrangements and she can decide when and how to tell your father."

They spent a few more minutes discussing dates, Leon, work and an assortment of topics before Francine signed off, leaving Anita in her quiet kitchen with a mélange of thoughts tumbling through her head. She walked across the room and evened out the spacing between her mother's four canisters.

What was making her feel odd about that call? She loved Francine like a sister. She wished she lived closer. She was happy her father was enjoying his correspondence with Simone. Simone was a wonderful lady. It would be fun to see her again. What was wrong with the picture?

Her mind continued through it's thought maze as she unloaded the dishwasher and straightened up the already tidy kitchen. Satisfied with her work she refilled her coffee cup and sat at the table, flipping through the front section of the paper. As her eyes settled on an advertisement for the Bon Marche, the department store where her mother took her to lunch each holiday shopping season, an idea slipped from behind the curtain in her mind as if theater lights were shining on it. Could her mother's memory be the issue fogging her thoughts? Seattle was her mother's hometown. Bastogne was Simone's. It was one thing to see Simone in Belgium. But Simone would be coming to her mother's place and spending time with Frank in Mother's home, violating Mother's space. No, wait, she thought. That wasn't quite true. Very little in Frank's condo had come from his home with Doris. That was good. And the home itself was new since her mother's death.

Despite her best effort, tears began to well and spill on the Bon Marche ad. What was going on? If a visit from Simone was good for Frank shouldn't that be good enough for Anita? It should be, but still there was something about the whole idea that was discomforting; somehow unfair to her mother's memory. But, for Dad's sake, if Simone was coming, she would have to deal with it.

She rose, retrieving a tissue. Yes, she would learn to deal with it, whatever "it" was.

"Do you have to rush off or can I fix you something to drink?" said Lenore, as the lights of her daughter's car disappeared down the driveway of her condominium complex. She closed the front door and followed Frank back to the living room, a room papered with memories of her long life with Emory. Family photos covered the inside wall; decorative plates from a variety of vacation destinations were lined up on the mantel; Emory's easy chair, reading light and magazine rack stood as if ready for his return.

"I'm sure the Holiday Inn can wait a bit longer for my return. How about just a drop of Scotch, if you have it. Then I can help you with the dishes."

"Nonsense; I didn't invite you here to do the dishes. Sit yourself down and I'll be right with you," she said, as she selected two glasses from the small buffet.

Frank glanced at Emory's chair and then selected a seat on the sofa, near the fireplace. Lenore returned, handed him more than a drop of Scotch, and switched on the gas fireplace which was soon radiating warmth. Lenore sat in her chair near the sofa and pulled a multihued afghan over her lap. "Frank, I can't thank you enough for coming down and talking with Kathryn. I really think it made a difference."

"Well, I did the best I could. Since I don't always understand why Emory and I felt the way we did about the war I'm not sure how well I can explain it to others. It was good of Rex to leave us alone to talk. That helped."

"Her husband is a good man; my Mr. Fix-it. Whenever I need something repaired he's more than willing to help. I've been wanting those pictures hung in the den for the longest time."

"Do you really think our little talk helped Kathryn?" said Frank, leaning forward to adjust the ottoman so they both could reach it.

"Oh yes. We spoke in the kitchen while I was preparing dessert. She gave me the warmest hug that I've had in months and apologized for her behavior the last few weeks. I don't know what you said but it worked. I can't thank you enough."

"Having a Lenore-cooked-meal is thanks enough for me," he said with a smile while raising his glass in a toast.

They sat quietly with Frank studying the blue flame of the fire and Lenore studying Frank. After a few silent moments Lenore spoke. "How about you; how are you doing?"

"Huh? Me? Oh, I'm doing all right. I stay out of trouble and Anita nags me like a good wife; see the doctor, take your vitamins, put on your jacket; that sort of thing," he offered with a gleam in his eye.

"How about that woman from Belgium? Do you keep in touch with her?"

"Ah yes, that woman from Belgium." He removed his feet from the Ottoman and leaned forward with his elbows on his knees, clasping his glass with both hands. "Yes, I keep in touch with her."

"Is there a problem?"

"It depends on how you define the word problem. But it's nothing I should burden you with. You have enough to deal with now."

"I'm getting along just fine. You don't need to worry about me. I'm no Anne Landers but I can be a good listener if you want to talk. And, candidly, it looks like old Frank Larson has something on his mind," she said, studying him over the rim of her glass.

"You're just like Doris; she could see through me pretty easily. I guess living with Emory gave you good training."

She smiled without comment.

"I do miss having someone to talk to. I just can't bring myself to discuss this with Anita. Seems like there are some things you just don't discuss with your daughter."

"Well, I'm not your daughter and I can keep a confidence so I'm here for you if you want to talk. What's the problem with your Belgium friend; it's Simone isn't it?"

Frank sat silent, squeezing his temples with his fingers as if fighting a headache. Then, leaning back on the sofa he turned to Lenore, "OK, you asked for it." He squirmed uncomfortably before continuing. "To understand, I need to go back in time a bit. You see, Emory and I were alike in some ways. We lost a lot of friends in the war; that was hard. We buried the memories pretty well and went on living. But the past few years it's been starting all over; the loss of friends I mean. I'm sure you see it too. You look at your Christmas card list each year and cross off another few names; names of people who have meant something to your life. And then loss strikes close to home, or worse, in your home and you lose your spouse. So here I am again, the survivor; the grieving survivor."

He paused, thinking, searching for the words he needed to tell the rest of the story.

"Losing Doris was the last straw. I was running out of grief. I simply didn't want to deal with more losses. So what's my solution? I decide to close up shop; keep to myself, enjoy the friends I have and not reach out for more. It worked during the war. Then we quit getting close to new guys so, if they were killed, we could handle it. Then along came Emory to upset my plan."

"Emory! What did he do?"

"He talked me into attending the reunion. If I hadn't gone I wouldn't have seen Simone and I wouldn't be sitting here today with my feelings in knots. Oh, don't get me wrong. Of course I'm glad I attended but seeing Simone again has completely foiled my plan to lay low emotionally."

"Wow. This woman must be quite a lady to turn the head of stalwart Frank Larson."

On an emotional roll, Frank told Lenore of first meeting Simone, the time in her cellar, his return trip, the missing letters and the picnic at the hunting lodge, omitting key details. She listened intently, urging him on with well timed questions, smiles or nods.

"Isn't there a song," he continued, "that goes something like 'You made me love you, I didn't want to do it; I didn't want to do it...' or something like that? Well, against my better instincts I think I love this woman and wish, oh how I wish, that she didn't live so darn far away."

He rose and walked to the window, stopping to stare at the inky darkness, with her eyes following his every move.

"So, what are you going to do about it?"

"What can I do? She lives half a world away. I can't change that. Sometimes I think I should just take a cold shower, get on the boat and sail to the edge of the earth. It must be out there somewhere."

"Oh, that's nonsense. This is the nineties. There is plenty you could do. You have your health. You have the means. Go to this woman, sweep her off her feet and run off to a castle somewhere. You could do it. You just need to decide to do it!"

"You don't understand. Things are more complicated than that. I have responsibilities in Seattle."

"Frank, speaking as a friend, are things really that complicated for you or are you just afraid to try?"

He turned and stared at Lenore.

She continued, "When Emory was so ill he would talk about the things he wished we'd done; the places he wished we'd gone. We talked of 'should haves' and 'could haves' over many days. All that talk was bringing us down; making a difficult situation even worse. Then one day Emory turns to me and says, 'Love, today we start something new. Instead of lamenting what we haven't done let's talk about what we have done; the places we have been; the friends we've known. Let's celebrate our life together.' It was a turning point for us. We'd had a wonderful life. Sure there were things we wished we'd done but we began looking at all we had done together. It made our remaining time together so much richer."

While she continued Frank retook his place on the sofa. "Your cup of life isn't full. Keep pouring in new memories. Chase your dream. If Simone is your dream, chase Simone. Then someday you won't be caught thinking about all the things you wished you'd done. Instead you, or maybe you and Simone, will be celebrating all the things you did. Do you see; do you see what I mean?"

Later that night Frank had a hard time getting to sleep in room 207 at the Holiday Inn.

"Dad, Dad, are you here?" said Anita, as she let herself into Frank's darkened condominium. She had dropped by unannounced to deliver two chicken casseroles she'd prepared for his freezer. Cooking was not her most renowned skill but, on the occasion that she prepared a noteworthy dish, she would make up extra servings, pack them in small plastic containers with cooking instructions taped to the outside and deliver them to her father. He seemed to appreciate her efforts and would return her plastic containers with rave compliments on little notes taped to the lids.

She dropped her purse near the door, flipping on the kitchen light on her way to the refrigerator. Removing the two containers from a plastic bag, she tucked them into the well organized, half empty top freezer. I'd better leave him a note, she thought, as she moved to the small phone desk at the end of the counter, searching for pen and paper.

Instead she found something else of interest. Lying there, on top of his recent mail was a beautifully handwritten letter from Simone. Anita's mind quickly processed the situation. Now, I am not a snoop, she told herself. I have never opened a single letter from Simone though I know exactly where they are stacked on the back of his desk. But this one is already open. Without even touching it I can see every word. Well, at least every word on the first page. If he left it out like this it can't be that personal. Even his cleaning lady could see this. Oh, if I just glance at it…

Her eyes swept the rooms, burglar-like, before she pulled out the small stool and sat at the desk.

Dearest Frank, *2 May 1996*

It was wonderful to speak with you the other day. I still cannot believe I will be seeing you in less than two months. I am looking forward to that time. There are so many things I want to say to you and share with you that I do not know where to begin. For some reason my memory escapes me when we are on the phone and I hang up frustrated by all the things I wish I had said. Maybe I will do better with my pen in hand, sitting here looking out over my garden that is about to burst into bloom.

You are a very special person. I feel like a new woman since you came back into my life. Though you live far away you have given me a new reason for getting up each morning, for having my hair done up just the way you like it, for buying that new dress that I think you would like; for oh so many things. It is crazy really and I do not know why I am telling you this.

In our lives we have been apart far more than we have been together. I am sure there are experiences that have impacted your life that I know nothing about. I know there are things about me you cannot even imagine. And yet, I feel we know so much about each other. It is strange, no? I think it is.

Your talk of marriage melts the heart of emotional me. But the list of complications always sobers up the rational me. So where does that leave us you ask? Dearest Frank, I do not know.

For now my heart and mind are on the day I board the plane that will carry me to your home and arms. That is enough for me. Beyond that is a hazy cloud of uncertainty.

I had best sign off now. Give my love to Anita. I am looking forward to seeing her again. She has surely stolen the heart of Leon and I have never seen him happier. I hope they are not setting themselves up for disappointment when he returns to Belgium as I believe he someday will.

With all my love,

Simone

Anita sat for a moment with her eyes fixed on the small snapshot of Simone pinned to the oak framed cork board above the small desk; a cork board that once hung over her mother's writing desk. The words, "your talk of marriage melts the heart of emotional me," rolled across her being like a cold shower. And what was it that Francine had said, "Mother is more than a pen pal to your father."

With sweating palms and shaking hands she pushed herself from the stool, tidied up the small desk, examined the area for other signs of her indiscretion and, satisfied with her work, let herself out of his condominium.

Frank would have to discover the presence of the chicken casseroles on his own.

16

Frank cut an impressive figure as he paced outside the exit from airport customs. His new blue polo shirt, a gift from Anita, khaki pants with a razor sharp crease and brown deck shoes gave him a yachtsman's air. Dressing was normally an absent-minded act. Today he'd given it a great deal of thought. Normally he arrived at the airport at the last possible minute. Today he'd arrived an hour early.

Travelers were dribbling out of customs one or two at a time. Each time the door opened Frank came to attention and each time it wasn't Simone a small furl skimmed over his brow. Then she came looking a bit tired, but to Frank, no less beautiful. Her ivory silk blouse and navy slacks appeared to have survived the ten hours of flying without wilting and her pace accelerated as she launched herself into his waiting arms. They babbled forgettable nothings to each other and then, practical sides taking over, retrieved her luggage and his car and settled into the rush hour traffic on the way to Leon's home, where she would be staying while in Seattle.

Anita placed the last of the evening dishes on the counter next to Leon, who was busy loading the dishwasher. It was quiet in the house. When Frank left for home an exhausted Simone had excused herself and gone to bed leaving Anita and Leon with the clean up duties.

"I hope we're not wearing your mother out with all the running around we've been doing," she offered.

"Oh, I don't think so. We gave her Saturday to relax and today's trip to Whidbey Island wasn't too taxing," Leon responded.

"She seemed to enjoy Whidbey. I tend to forget that neither of you ever spent much time near salt water."

"Oh, she did enjoy herself," Leon replied. "On the ferry back she said she could now understand why I love the area so much."

Anita wandered back into the dining room, gave the table a quick wipe with a damp cloth and turned on some soft music before returning to the kitchen where Leon was washing the final pan.

"How would you describe Simone's relationship with Dad?"

"How would I describe what?" he replied, turning toward her with a quizzical look.

"Oh, I don't know. Would you say they're friends or, I don't know; how would you describe them?"

He dried his hands on the dish towel and hung it carefully on the oven door handle. Turning he grasped her lightly by the shoulders. "How would you describe us, Ms. Chase?"

She smiled and embraced him, laying her head on his wide chest. "Lovers. Yes, lovers for sure."

"Maybe they are lovers too."

She released him and stepped away. "I'm serious Leon."

"So am I. Why couldn't they be lovers? They are certainly more than just friends. Mother has lots of friends and I can tell you she is much different around Frank than she is around them. They seem to have a very indefinable special relationship. Did you not see them on the beach today?"

"But lovers? Really Leon. They're both seventy and widowed and they live in different parts of the world. Special friends I can see but lovers? I just have trouble with that, at least the way I think of lovers," she said, embracing him again.

"Whatever you say dear."

Frank, Simone and Lenore Rushing walked slowly toward his car, parked in front of Lenore's Portland condominium. He helped Simone with her door and then turned to Lenore before walking to the drivers side. "Thanks so much for having us down for lunch. It was delicious, as usual."

"The pleasure was all mine and I'm so glad I met Simone," she said as she reached up and gave him a friendly kiss on the cheek. "Now go find a castle," she whispered before stepping back, offering him a sly wink.

Smiling and shaking his head in subtle disbelief he walked to the driver's side and was soon pulling away with Lenore waving to them from her porch.

The mid-afternoon traffic swept them north toward Seattle on the sun drenched freeway. With the clear skies Frank was able to point out Mt. St. Helens volcano ravaged cone in the distance.

"Lenore is a delightful woman," Simone offered after a period of silence. "It was nice of her to have us down. Is she my competition?"

"Your what!"

"You know; the other woman in your life."

Finally "getting it" he smiled and squeezed her knee, where his hand had been resting. "My dear woman, at my age I have enough trouble handling just one woman. I'm not sure I would be up for two."

"What a diplomat you are," she replied, tilting the seat back slightly and settling into the plush leather. "What a busy few days. The public market, the art museum, dinners with the kids and now lunch with your friend. And here it is Wednesday already. Where has the time gone?"

Frank kept his focus on the driving as she continued.

"You do live in beautiful country. It reminds me a little of the hill country near Bastogne but there is just so much more of it. This is a big place. And sun all the time. I can see why, in addition to the presence of Anita, Leon has fallen in love with this area."

"Don't be fooled by the sun. I always tell people there's a reason everything is so green and it isn't the sun. And as for Leon, he's been good for Anita." He adjusted the music volume and continued. "Simone, sometime we need to talk about us."

"I know. I know we do but not now. Let us just enjoy the next few days together and see what happens, OK?"

He smiled and gave the knee another squeeze. He knew he would do whatever she wanted.

It was Saturday, the first day of a long 4th of July weekend. Frank and Simone were sitting on Leon's sunny patio when he and Anita returned from the airport with Francine, fresh from her Alaska cruise.

"Well, how have they been treating you Mother?" she said sweeping onto the patio and giving them each a welcome kiss. "As a tour director I am always concerned about my guests' welfare."

"I am not one of your guests, dear, but I have had a wonderful time. Between Frank and those two kids," she said, nodding toward Anita and Leon, "I have been well toured. It will take me weeks to rest up from this so called vacation. Now tell us about your week."

"Not much to tell. It was a good group and I put the same number on the plane today that I arrived with a week ago. That is always good! Charles, the dear, is my acting tour director for the long flight home but, now that they are on the plane there is not much he needs to do. I wish he could have joined us here but business called."

"I don't want to rush you dear sister but dinner tonight is at the Space Needle. We need to leave in about an hour," said Leon. "We can plan the rest of your stay later."

"That's a good place to start your tour Francine," offered Frank. "I can point out the highlights of our fair city from the top of the Needle and then you can decide what you want to see from the ground."

The hour flew by and soon Frank, with Simone in his car, and Leon, with the others, were winding their way across town to dinner. Leaving their cars with the valet they joined a family from Omaha in the compact Space Needle elevator and were rocketed skyward entertained by the canned tourist banter of the operator. They exited at the restaurant level knowing how fast they had traveled, how high they were, when the Needle was built and a plethora of other forgettable facts.

Their dinner was presented as the revolving restaurant made its hourly transit around all points of the compass. They were well into their second revolution when the waiter arrived with a chilled bottle of Champagne and five sparkling glasses.

"Well, what's the special occasion?" said Frank as he looked across the table at a beaming Anita. "Or are we just welcoming the Challon clan to beautiful Seattle."

"I don't need a special occasion," said Francine, as the waiter filled their glasses. "Charles has taught me that Champagne is good anytime."

"Well, it is a special occasion," said Leon. "I am pleased to announce that Anita has agreed to marry this itinerant lawyer from Belgium."

Frank, who had been holding Simone's hand beneath the table, felt her hand squeeze hard, quiver slightly and then release its grip. Glancing her way he was struck by the painted-on quality of the smile she offered the newly engaged couple.

"This, this is wonderful; it's a wonderful reason for a little bubbly," said Frank, recovering from his initial surprise. Raising his glass he continued, "Welcome to the family Leon and here's to many years of happiness."

"To happiness," came the reply from all as glasses were raised in celebration.

Francine seemed the most excited of all. She bubbled with questions for the couple, most of which defied early answer. Where did he ask her? When? When are they getting married? Where? Where would they live?

"Whoa, sister dear. Not so fast. We are still trying to figure this out ourselves. Give us a break."

Under the watchful eye of a subdued Simone the happy chatter continued while they finished the Champagne, Leon paid the bill and they descended with the same fact filled elevator operator.

The sun was settling toward the horizon as they waited for the valet to recover their cars at the base of the Needle. "Well Mother, do you want to ride with us and save Frank a few miles," said Leon.

"Thank you dear but I need to pick up something at Frank's. That is, if you do not mind," she said, turning to him.

"Not at all," Frank replied, as he helped Simone into his car, the first to arrive. "Don't worry Leon. I'll have her in at a respectable time."

Everyone laughed with Frank; everyone but Simone.

Frank and Simone walked silently into his darkened condo. She moved nervously to the dining room table, set her purse and coat on a chair and helped herself to a brandy from the nearby liquor cabinet. Frank looked on in surprise since she rarely drank hard liquor. But it wasn't a total surprise. She'd been distant since Leon's marriage announcement and strangely silent on the ride home. And now this. He helped himself to a glass of Yukon Jack, straight up, and joined her at the window overlooking the bay.

It was a clear summer Seattle evening with the sparkling ferries tracing predictable routes across the water as if riding on hidden rails. They stood quietly until she broke the spell. "Frank, we need to talk. We really need to talk."

"Let's sit down," he said as he led her to the sofa.

She set her drink on the coffee table and nervously wrung her hands. Her mind was processing but the words were not coming forth. Finally her thoughts took form and she began. "There is something I need to share with you; something you need to know." She paused and seemed to be carefully selecting her words. "When we met again last fall, after all these years, I thought of telling you but I just could not do it. Then again, as we have grown closer...Oh Frank, I do love you deeply. As we have grown closer I have struggled with telling you and the words have just not come out. But now, with Anita and Leon, I need to tell you. I need your help to understand what to do. Do you understand?"

"I'm not sure but I'm listening." He put his drink on the table and took her shaking hands in his.

"Frank, Francine is your daughter."

Francine is your daughter. The words tumbled and twisted through the room; through his mind. Francine is your daughter. His eyes met hers but now it was Frank who could find no words to match his thoughts. Francine is your daughter.

"I'm sorry to tell you like this but..., are you O.K.?"

"Yes I'm fine. I'm fine. It's just that, well, I don't know what to say.

"Say you love me. Please say that," she said as she fell sobbing into his arms.

Frank's emotions twisted and turned flying high, plummeting and then soaring again as he tried to grasp what he had just heard. Joy, guilt, compassion and a succession of high and low emotions competed with his orderly mind for control. Those wonderful days in that little hunting lodge had produced a beautiful daughter. He knew Francine. She was a daughter to be proud of. But the challenges and shame Simone must have gone through to give birth and raise this child must have been excruciating. There were so many questions he wanted to ask; so many questions he feared to ask. But now, with the exquisite Simone in his arms, all those could wait. She had laid her heart in his lap and he would be gentle with it.

"Simone, Simone, Simone; I have never loved you more. Never....

Sunrise found Frank sitting on his sofa, looking out at the same view he and Simone had shared just a few short hours before. Her unfinished drink was still on the coffee table with its telltale lipstick mark on the rim. He picked it up, examined the lipstick and swished the remaining drink around the glass before setting it down in its old water ring.

He thought about her, perhaps still in bed at Leon's. He wished she was with him. There were so many questions coursing through his mind since last night's revelation. But instead of speaking they had just held each other until they felt the kids would be concerned by their absence. He thought it would have been wonderful if she could have stayed the night but, that was not to be.

He'd slept poorly, tossing and turning all night. His mind had been jammed with "what ifs."

What if I had known she was pregnant?

What if she'd received my letters?

What if she'd moved to the states?

What if he hadn't gone to the reunion?

What if Anita had not met Francine?

What if. . . .?

As dawn approached the "what ifs" had been replaced by "what nows." Should the secret remain with them or should they tell the kids? If so,when? What would be gained by telling; what was the risk?

One thing was certain. They needed time alone; time to talk. The plan for the day was to give Francine a tour of Seattle. Anita and Leon could handle that. He would just have to find a polite way to send them on their way so he and Simone could be alone. Then they could decide; together decide what to do.

And he could spend the day with Simone.

Francine answered Leon's front door with a steaming cup of coffee in her hand, greeting Frank with a kiss on each cheek. She was clad in a loose fitting dressing gown and her hair had a recently climbed out of bed tousled look.

Francine had welcomed Frank in the same manner before, both in Belgium and Switzerland. It was different this time. His blood was coursing through her veins. He was being greeted by his daughter and she was greeting her father. He knew right then that she must be told, for his sake if not hers. She was his daughter and he wanted to love her like a daughter. Too many years had already been lost.

"You Seattle people are early risers. You will find Leon in the kitchen and mother is on the patio with her coffee. I assume you know your way around this place."

"I do indeed. Did you sleep well without your husband at your side and the hum of the ship to lull you?"

"I slept very well, thank you. I would still be out cold if the neighbors had not decided to have an argument beneath my window this morning. But, I needed to get up anyway. So, if you will excuse me I will take my coffee and retire to my chambers," she said with a smile.

Frank watched as she turned and proceeded up the narrow staircase. Simone was right. Francine did have hints of Larson in her makeup. He'd never noticed it before. She had a hint of his jaw and his mother's eyes. And her hair color, if it was her color he was seeing, was closer to the Larson clan than the color of her mother's family. He shook his head as if mystified and proceeded to the kitchen.

"Frank. Our first guest! Make yourself at home. The coffee is over there and mother has a plate of biscotti out on the patio. I cannot join you," Leon said as he tended the sausage in the frying pan, "but the paper is out with her and the sun makes the patio very comfortable this early. If it gets too warm you can put up the umbrella."

"The coffee sounds good," he replied, as he filled a nearby mug. "Say, Leon, I can't tell you how pleased I am with the engagement announcement. I really am. Anita is all I have and I can't think of anyone I'd rather have her run off with. I hope you'll have many wonderful years together. You're getting a fantastic girl."

"Thank you," he responded, bear hugging Frank and nearly spilling the newly filled mug. "Your blessing is very important to Anita and me. Trust me. I plan to take good care of her."

"I'm sure you will. Now maybe I'll wander out and interrupt your mother's solitude."

Frank stepped outside and found Simone seated comfortably in the sun, gazing absentmindedly at the garden with her reading glasses resting on the unread newspaper in her lap. Undetected he approached her, bent over gingerly and kissed her on the neck relishing her familiar fragrance. "I love you," he whispered.

"Gracious, you startled me," she exclaimed as she reached her hand back and pressed it against his cheek. "I am so glad to see you. We have so much to think about and I much prefer doing my thinking with you close by. I hope you do not think that is silly."

He placed his coffee on the table and sat down, facing her. She was dressed in a loose fitting top with khaki cotton pants and her hair was perfect. But there was a tiredness to her look; the look of someone who had slept poorly. He leaned forward, taking her hands in his. "How are you this morning?"

"I fear I am a bit groggy. I did not sleep well I am afraid. How about you?"

"The same. Too much to think about I guess. But I have thought about last night. You were right to tell me. I'm glad you told me. If you have any doubts about that, squelch them."

"Thank you. I wasn't sure how you would take the news. You are such a lovely man I should have assumed you would want to know but…I did not want to burden you and risk…risk whatever we have."

They sat quietly for a while, each lost in their own thoughts but comforted by the presence of the other. The serenity was finally broken when Frank lost a soggy biscotti in his coffee cup as he lingered too long while dipping. Leon joined them as the laughter was beginning to subside.

"What are you two up to out here," he asked as he approached with the coffee pot to refill their mugs. "Oh, I see you have a little problem Frank. Do you want a clean mug?"

"No. This one will be fine. The floating biscotti will be a constant reminder of my culinary ineptitude. Just top off this one. Are you going to tear yourself away from the galley and join us?"

"Why not. Let me grab a mug and I will be right back."

When Leon returned he positioned the large table umbrella to keep the sun from his mother's eyes and then settled into a nearby patio chair.

"What are your plans for the day?" asked Simone.

"Anita and I thought we could all give Francine a grand tour of Seattle; the Pike Place Market, the waterfront, the Seattle Center…."

"That sounds like a wonderful idea. But I think Frank and I will take the day off and relax somewhere. You young people can cover more ground without us along and I have seen much of the city. We are going to have a quiet day, lunch on the waterfront, and just generally take it easy. Then we can meet someplace for dinner."

Frank gave Simone a surprised look. She caught the look and gave him a subtle wink, waiting for Leon's reaction.

"If you two do not feel abandoned I guess that works. You see Francine all the time anyway. If you two have an idea where you will be we will just meet you at dinner time. I can leave you a key if you want to hang out here."

"Why don't you assume we will be at my place," said Frank. "If we change our plans I will leave a message on the recorder for you. But I suspect we will make it back there so we can put our feet up and rest from a busy day."

Frank smiled at Simone, thinking they made quite a planning team.

Frank and Simone did not have lunch at the waterfront. Instead they spent the warm summer day alone at his condo. After a lazy lunch on his sunny deck, watching the boats scurry across the busy harbor below, they sat together talking and planning for the discussion they would be having in just a few hours. And then the kids returned.

"Well, don't you two look comfortable?" announced Anita as she joined them on the deck. "Have you been back long?"

"Not long; not too long," Frank replied, refilling their glasses. "We have lemonade out here. Bring a glass or help yourself to something in the refrigerator."

Soon Leon, Francine and Anita joined them on the deck.

Frank caught himself looking at Anita and Francine in a new light. My girls, he thought to himself.

"What a wonderful view," offered Francine, standing at the railing. "This is a beautiful setting for your city. And I think these two have shown me most of it in a scant six hours."

"So the tour leader was taken on a tour," said Frank. "The tables were turned on you huh?"

"Francine, would you mind joining us over here for a moment?" said Simone in a voice too serious for the occasion. "Frank and I would like to share something with you all,"

Leon pulled a chair out for Francine and quipped, "Do I need Champagne for this discussion?"

Simone gave him a polite smile but didn't respond. When the others were seated Frank began. "Simone and I have been talking and feel there is something we need to share with you." He paused, turning to Simone, "Do you want me to go on?"

"Please."

"Well, of course you all know that your mother and I knew each other many years ago. But more than that, we loved each other very much." He paused, as if gathering his thoughts. "I feel strange discussing this with all of you but..."

"Let me," said Simone, gripping his hand. "As we have told you, Frank returned to us the summer of 1945, for just a short time. When he departed he left me...; he left me with a child. Francine, Frank Larson is your father."

The words dropped to the patio like a stone. Frank and Simone, squeezing each others hand to the point of pain, looked from face to face for a reaction.

Leon, the first to react, was concealed behind a grin the width of a saucer. It seemed he had instantly processed the idea and was delighted.

Then, eyes welling with tears and an "Oh Mother" on her lips Francine lunged forward embracing her mother. Her body heaved with partially repressed sobs.

Anita sat in stunned silence. Her eyes darted in rapid succession from Simone to Frank and back again. Leon turned to her, "Isn't this wonderful Anita? Our families are bound together in so many ways."

She nodded in acknowledgement with her lower lip quivering. Then, she released his hand and rose, passing quickly through the sliding door into the living room.

Leon pulled to the curb in front of Anita's condominium. "Please let me come up; just for a few minutes."

Head down; eyes staring at an unseen lap Anita shook her head with an emphatic no.

"I have never seen you like this. What happened; what was said...?" Leon continued, reaching for her hand.

She caught his hand in mid-flight and set it on the gear shift knob. "No, please. I just need...I just need some time to think; that's all. Please try to understand."

"But...?

"Please? With us and now Dad, Simone and Francine I'm a bit overwhelmed, that's all. I just need time to...time to think."

"May I come by later?"

"Call me in the morning. Let me sleep on it for now."

Anita slipped from the car and scampered up the walk to the lobby entrance. She stepped into the waiting elevator, paused before selecting a floor and pressed the button for the floor below hers. When the door slid open she stepped out, walked slowly down the hall and knocked on Liz's door.

"Anita, what a surprise," exclaimed Liz as she swung the door wide. "Come in; come in. To what do I owe this evening visit?"

"Oh, I'm so glad you're home. I really need a glass of wine and a good listener."

"God, you look like you've had a long day. Have you been crying?"

"Only on the inside," Anita responded, wiping her eyes self consciously.

"Well have a seat. I can surely supply the wine and you can decide if I turn out to be a good listener."

Liz joined Anita with a bottle and two glasses and was soon hearing all the news that had been generated in the last 24 hours.

"When did you learn about Francine?"

"Within the hour. I just came from Dad's."

"You mean you just heard the news and then took off?"

"Sort of; I'm still in shock. I told them I wasn't feeling well and Leon brought me home."

"How did the others react?" Liz asked, refilling Anita's glass.

"Better than me I suspect. Leon seemed delighted and Francine broke into tears but I think they were more from joy than sadness. But she must be a bit taken aback by it all as well. I mean, after all, she finds out who her father is after fifty years."

"Wow," Liz said when Anita paused to sip her wine. "So, I'm confused; this all sounds like exciting news. You're engaged; Frank and Simone are reunited after all these years and Francine is your half sister."

"You're confused! I'm the one that's confused. First the man I love turns out to be my half brother…."

"Not really."

"Well, that's what it feels like. And my dad has a love child living in another country that he doesn't even know about. It's all so unfair, particularly to my mother."

"To your mother?"

"Sure; don't you see? It's like Dad was living a lie all those years they were together. It's just—oh I don't know—it's just so unfair somehow. What if Mother knew?"

"But she didn't. Neither did he."

Close to tears Anita rose and paced nervously. "I just need time to think. Things are happening too fast. I need time to sort things out. Maybe I need to get away for a few days….to think."

"Maybe you just need a good night's sleep. That could do you wonders."

Anita paused and turned to her friend. "You're right; that would do me good. Maybe my mind will be clearer tomorrow. Thanks for the wine. And Liz…"

"Yes."

"You are a good listener too. Thanks."

Simone laid her dressing gown on the narrow bench at the foot of her bed, adjusted the flowered curtains to allow the breeze a better course across the stuffy room and climbed into bed with her book and reading glasses. Leaning against the pillow cushioned headboard with her legs lightly covered by a sheet she found herself staring at the pictures on the far wall, distracted by a replay of the weekend events.

Leon had laughed when he first showed Simone to this bedroom. He had rented the furnished house from a family that was out of the country on a work assignment. Simone's room, apparently belonging to a teen age girl, was decorated in pinks and posters depicting movie stars or singers that were unfamiliar to Simone. But the bed was good and the decorations, except for the leather clad fellow on the poster by the closet, were acceptable.

A hum of nighttime city noises provided background distraction in the otherwise quiet house. Her fifty year old secret was out. How would it change things for everyone? When they had time to digest the news would her children feel and think differently about her; about themselves? Frank thought he had one daughter. Now he had two. Francine thought one man was her father. Now she knew that, in addition to the father she loved for fifty years, she had a second one she barely knew.

Her reverie was interrupted by a faint knock on her unlatched door. "Mother, are you still awake?" Seeing Simone upright and very much awake Francine eased into the room looking much like a little girl with her hair clipped back and her long legs exposed below a light cotton nightgown. She moved to the head of the bed and sat down resting her head on Simone's chest; the safe place she had often visited as a child on stormy winter nights.

Simone held her lightly until she heard Francine's muffled voice say, "Mother, will you forgive me. I reacted badly at Frank's. This secret must have been a terrible burden all these years and then I go a little crazy when you finally tell me. But there are so many questions; so many things I don't understand."

"Well dear, this is the day for answering questions so why don't you climb up here on the bed and let's have a little mother-daughter talk."

Francine scooted onto the foot of the bed, assuming a position facing her mother, far enough away to give her a clear view of Simone while close enough to hold hands from time to time. Simone reached to the bedside table, retrieved a box of tissue and placed it between them on the bed. "Just in case," she said, with a slight smile. "Now, where would you like to begin?"

"With father; I mean Jules. Oh, I don't know what to call anybody anymore."

Simone paused for a moment and then said, "For now, please call Jules 'Father.' He adopted you, he raised you and he loved you very much. It's true; Frank is your biological father but, for now, why don't we keep calling him Frank."

Francine nodded her understanding and continued. "Well, long ago I figured out that you were married after I was born. That was easy. But I just assumed you and father had, well, you know."

"And that was fine with him. He never knew who the real father was and, bless his heart, he never pressed for an answer so I never had to lie. He only knew that I had an infant with me when I moved back from Wiltz to Bastogne. Unfortunately there were lots of young girls in my situation after the war. So, while it was viewed badly by many, it was tolerated after a fashion. Then I met Jules at the clinic, we grew to love each other and, well you can fill in the rest."

"So he adopted me?"

"Without hesitation. And then sister and brother came along and our little family was formed."

"But the gossip; I mean talk and speculation? Growing up it seemed that everyone in town knew everything about everybody else."

Simone paused for a moment, distracted by a refreshing puff of air that billowed the curtain and gave a promise of cooling. Looking back to Francine she continued. "Do you recall hearing the name Jan Reuss?"

"No," she nodded, moving to a cross legged position on the bed.

"Jan and I had been friends growing up. Now people would say we appeared to be 'going together' but we were just friends. Jan suffered badly in the war. He and his older brother were conscripted by the Germans and sent to Russia. His brother was killed and he was wounded, which in hindsight probably saved his life. Then, during the siege of Bastogne his parents were killed. Jan returned to Bastogne the summer of 1945 in terrible condition. He had escaped from a German hospital and lived like a fugitive for months before making it back home. Anyway, I saw him several times that summer when I came to visit my folks. He was staying with an aunt at the time. Having lost everything he cared for he had become an angry young man with a love of cheap wine. But, since people had seen us together the rumors suggested that he was the father of my child. It was a convenient rumor so I just let it go."

"Did he go along with the rumor?"

"He didn't need to. In a drunken stupor poor Jan was killed by a truck one fall evening."

"Oh mother, I'm so sorry."

"You needn't be. He was just another casualty of the war. Another in a long list of casualties of that war."

Simone sat silently studying her daughter, Frank's daughter, at the foot of her bed. There was so much of Frank in her, she thought. The hair, the chin, the smile.... In a way a part of Frank had been with her all these years. Even her name was a silent tribute to him. And he never knew.

Francine took a tissue and began methodically tearing it into thin strips at her feet. "What did people think when you got pregnant. I mean, surely they noticed."

"Dear, a person you would never suspect came to my aid. In fact, until yesterday he was the only person in the world who knew Frank was your father. My cousin Mark proved to be my savior."

"Mark Gelsi?"

She nodded. "I had to share my condition with someone. He was my closest friend and someone I could trust. And the trust was well placed. To my knowledge no one, absolutely no one, ever heard the truth."

"How could he really help you?"

"I was OK for the first five months or so. I was putting on weight but then, with better food everyone was. So I could hide my pregnancy. Then he found me a room with a widow lady in Diekirch. She was a dear woman who actually helped deliver you in the end. That was not the plan but then, my life was not going according to any plan.

"Mark also covered for me. People in Wiltz thought I was in Bastogne. Those in Bastogne thought I was in Wiltz. And Mark made up wonderful stories to maintain the little charade."

"But, at some point you returned to Bastogne?"

"Yes. That wasn't a pleasant experience. Father was silent but loving. Mother was absolutely beside herself. I think she spent the next month in church in an attempt to save my tarnished soul. But she could not resist you. After all, no matter how you were conceived you were her granddaughter and she loved you with all her heart. So there were a few very difficult weeks but then, well, then life went on. The gossips did what gossips do, I went to work at the clinic, she took care of you, I met Jules and, well..."

Francine eased off the bed and moved forward to hug Simone. "Oh mother, I feel the wraps have been taken from my life's story. I will need to think about it all and I'm sure there will be more and more questions but, well I do not know what to say other than you are the most wonderful mother a girl could ever have."

"And I am a lucky one too. Now let me get my beauty sleep? At my age every minute counts."

"Oh mother," she said, leaning back and pressing her hand gently against Simone's cheek, "I cannot imagine you more beautiful than you are right now."

Francine dropped from the bed and, gathering her tissue scraps from the sheet, walked toward the door. "Mother," she said, turning back to Simone, "what about you and Frank. I mean what...?"

"I have no idea dear. Perhaps tomorrow you could give me some advice on that question. But for now, good night."

17

Frank sat on his balcony looking out over boats of all sizes scurrying across Elliot Bay, brilliantly lit by the morning sun. With many downtown businesses closed for the long Fourth of July weekend the city sounds from the street below were subdued for a Monday morning. This has been quite a holiday weekend, he thought with a smile; one that changed so many things in his life. Anita was going to be married and Francine was his daughter. Both revelations were still hard to grasp but gave him a warm feeling none-the-less.

Doris would be pleased with Anita's choice. Had Doris been living when Anita divorced she would have been terribly worried about Anita's welfare as a single woman. Who will take care of her, she would have asked. Doris was that way. She would have fretted about leaving Anita unattached even though Anita had shown herself to be quite capable of living on her own. So Anita's mother would be pleased with the prospect of marriage to a fine man like Leon.

As Frank topped off his coffee mug his thoughts turned to Francine. That would have been more difficult for Doris to accept; yes, more difficult indeed. He shook his head at the thought of explaining Simone to Doris and then gave a silent thanks that he never had to face such an uncomfortable situation. He recalled a 1950's movie about a GI who fathered a daughter in Italy during the war. Feeling an obligation the father chose to send money to the girl, much to the chagrin of his American wife. What was the name of that movie; oh yes, "The Man in the Gray Flannel Suit." Well, Doris empathized with the poor wife at that time. Yes, it was better that he didn't have to face that kind of discussion with Doris, God rest her soul.

His reflection was interrupted by the phones persistent ring. "Good morning," he answered after reaching the kitchen.

"Good morning Frank," came Leon's familiar accented voice. "Sorry to disturb you so early but is Anita with you by chance?"

"Nope. Haven't spoken with her since she left last night. Isn't she at her place?"

"No. I am at her place. I tried to call her last night and again this morning with no luck and now I find both Anita and her car are gone. I just hoped she might be with you or something."

A look of concern slipped over Frank's face as he sat at the small phone desk. "Was she OK last night? I mean she wasn't her normal cheery self when she left."

"She was tired and upset when I left her. The Francine announcement was a bit of a shock for her and she said she needed time to think or time to digest the news or something like that. She wanted to be alone but said not to worry. So I came back to your place."

"Wanted time to think, huh," said Frank, doodling on a small pad with a short, number two yellow pencil. He pondered for a moment and then continued. "I have an idea where she might have gone. Let me make a few calls and get back to you. Better yet, why don't we meet back over at your place where we can talk? I'll see you there in a few minutes."

Leon was standing on his front porch when Frank came to a stop at the curb. He dropped from the porch and greeted Frank as he stepped from the car. "I spoke to my neighbor at Whidbey. She's at our cabin, Leon, and I'm sure she's fine. Now let's go inside and see the ladies."

Frank was escorted to the patio where Francine and Simone were settled, protected from the already warm sun by the large umbrella which hung over the area suspended from a heavy curved metal arm. They listened intently as he explained his Anita discovery concluding, "So when Leon said she wanted to think I thought of Whidbey. She has often called it her 'thinking' place."

"If you don't mind," said Leon rising from his chair, "I'd like to get going."

"Get going where?" asked Francine.

"To Whidbey; to Anita," he replied.

"Now don't rush off so fast. Maybe we should all go. Or maybe just Frank. Or maybe just me," said Francine.

"What! She is going to marry me. I need to go."

"What are you thinking?" asked Simone, looking at Francine.

"I've been thinking about what Frank and Leon have said about Anita and about what happened last night. She was fine until she learned I was her sister. I can see her being surprised but it seemed like more than that. And there was no sign of any problem until that announcement was made. She'd been full of fun all day. I think it may have been the sister thing that upset her so."

"She has a point," offered Simone.

"This won't be easy for you. I know you like to jump in and fix things. But this time you need to trust your sister's intuition. I think I should go...alone," said Francine.

"But you do not know the way," protested Leon.

The discussion and protests continued until Leon succumbed to the combined weight of Francine and Simone's arguments. "Better give in," said Frank who had been silent during the family debate. "You're outnumbered and they may be right. I think this might be a time for the guys to take a back seat."

"Back seat?"

"Just an expression. Just an old American expression."

After a few more rounds of discussion a compromise was reached. Maps were drawn and driving directions written down and reviewed by a nervous Leon. He did insist on escorting Francine as far as the ferry dock. Soon the small convoy, with Francine in Leon's old Jeep and Leon in his Audi, left on the first stage of Francine's Whidbey Island adventure.

Barefoot, with hair still tousled from a restless night's sleep, Anita sat in the morning sun, nursing her second mug of coffee. Confused thoughts continued to course through her troubled mind and, each time her resolve began to firm, a new idea would knock the support from beneath her latest plan. Dad and Simone; Dad and Mom; her and Leon; her and Francine....

Her reverie was interrupted by the sound of a car, crunching its way down the gravel drive. Good God, she thought. I'm not ready to meet anyone. She rose, looked at her reflected image in the window and took a stab at making her hair presentable. In a way fearing it was Leon, she was relieved to see Francine step from Leon's Jeep. Anita stood silent and expressionless as Francine approached.

"Hi Sis," Francine said with a tentative smile.

"Oh Francine," Anita finally said, as she stepped forward and threw her arms around her. Like old friends, they embraced warmly before Anita released her and stepped back, tears streaking her cheeks. Taking hold of Francine's hands she said, "I'm so glad you came. Ignore the tears. I am pleased to see you."

Anita led Francine around to the deck and pulled a second chair near hers in the sun. An anxious Anita asked about the others and about the trip up the island. Then she ran inside and filled a coffee mug for Francine. Finally the sisters sat down, facing one another, separated by a small plastic table and fifty years of life.

"Leon is, how do you say, worried sick about you. I almost had to tie him down to keep him from coming but I thought that, maybe, you and I needed some time to talk," Francine began. "How are you doing?"

Anita gazed out over the water, watching two seagulls float upward on a hidden air current. "I'm really sorry about Leon. I'm sorry about everyone. I didn't mean to upset things but, I don't know; I just needed some time to take it all in. Do you know what I mean?"

Francine smiled and nodded.

"How are you feeling about all this?" Anita continued. "I mean, you have a new sister and the news about my father, your father.... That must have been a shock. How are you doing?"

"I was in a bit of a daze at first. I really was. The questions began tumbling through my mind like a whirlwind but then, last night, mother and I had a long talk. And we had more time together this morning when Leon was wandering around the city trying to find you. Oh, I wish you could have heard her. She and Frank were so much in love. They were together, they lost track of each other after the war and now they are together again. I mean it is such a wonderful story; like a fairy tale," she said, dabbing at her eyes with a napkin.

"So you're OK with it?"

"I am not entirely sure. I love the idea of having you as my sister. I mean that is really special. In a way it is sad we haven't known each other for fifty years but we know each other now. And you are going to be my sister and my sister-in-law. Think about that," Francine said.

"You make it sound so normal. But now I feel funny even thinking about marrying Leon when his mother was my father's lover and his sister is my sister. It's just too weird. I'm not sure I can handle it?"

"But you two are made for each other. You are thinking about it too much. We are the only ones that know I am your sister and it can stay in the family. There is no need to tell the world."

Anita rose and leaned forward, resting her elbows on the railing, as if in deep thought. She paused and then turned to Francine, frightening the birds from the nearby feeder. "What about your father; I mean the man who raised you? Wasn't his name Jan or..."

"Jules. His name was Jules. What do you mean, what about him? He was a wonderful man. I loved him very much."

"But it doesn't seem fair to him. Your mother loved someone else. You weren't his child."

"He knew I was not his child. But he loved me unconditionally. And mother loved him dearly. They were good together."

"But I thought you said she loved my father, Frank."

"She did, but he was lost to her forever, or so she thought. Do you not believe you can love more than one person in your life?"

"Oh Francine, I don't know what I believe."

"Did you love your husband when you were married?" Francine persisted.

"Yes, I did, or thought I did."

"And now you love Leon. It does not mean you loved your first husband less or that you have used up some of your love supply so you cannot love Leon now."

"I just don't know," replied Anita, turning to conceal the tears, gripping the railing with both hands. "It seems so unfair to my mother. She thought he loved her and all the time there was another woman and a child in another part of the world. And she had no idea."

"And neither did Frank. When were your parents married?"

"After the war. They met in school."

"Anita, Anita, Anita, do you not see?" Francine said, putting her arm around her shoulder and handing her a napkin for her eyes. "Frank and Simone were another time and another world. He lost Simone and found your mother. Simone lost him and found Jules. It was not Frank and Simone's time. Maybe now is. But do not believe your father did not love your mother just because he and Simone shared something special together. You cannot do that. It would break his heart."

"Oh Francine," Anita said, turning to embrace her, "It's all so confusing. It's all so very confusing."

The two sisters spent the day talking, wandering and sorting out their feelings. They talked in the kitchen while Anita prepared a light lunch. They talked on the beach while Anita taught Francine how to skip flat rocks. They talked on the deck, while a family on the beach got a head start on the holiday by firing off a collection of noisy fireworks. As the afternoon wound down Anita broke out cheese, crackers and wine and they settled on the deck to enjoy each other and the view.

"Now can we put all this 'I can't marry Leon' talk to rest?" asked Francine. "I may be your sister but he is not your brother. I suspect the term 'lover' better describes your relationship."

Anita studied the late afternoon view over the rim of her glass before responding. "I guess I've been a little melodramatic about the whole thing but…."

"There is a lot going on in your life right now. Everyone understands how you might want some time to digest all this news."

"I hope so. I don't want Leon or your mother to think that I'm some sort of an emotional wreck."

Francine reached across and took Anita's hand. "No one thinks any such thing. Now, if you'll still have my brother's hand in marriage we should really call and tell him you have not been kidnapped by gypsies or anything. He is probably beside himself. Do you have a phone?"

"No, but I can run next door. Kelly is a great guy and he wouldn't mind us using the phone. But I'm not ready to face everyone just yet. I need a little time to absorb all that we've talked about. I'm not ready to go home; maybe tomorrow. You could stay too, if you liked."

"I'd like that very much. From the looks of the refrigerator in there we won't starve. Go call Leon and tell him to take a cold shower and that we'll see him tomorrow. Us girls need our space," she said with a glint in her eye.

"Well, that is a relief," said Leon, rejoining Frank and Simone on the patio after speaking with Anita. "I don't fully understand what's going on but she said something about marrying her brother and you two being faithful to your spouses. It didn't make a lot of sense. She was borrowing a phone and it was apparently awkward to talk but everything is alright and she says she loves me. How about that?"

"Oh dear, being faithful to our spouses. I wonder what that's all about?" asked Simone.

"Don't worry about it. She is over it now. At least I hope she is," said Leon, kissing his mother on the cheek.

"When will they be returning?" asked Frank.

"They are spending the night up there. Something about sisters bonding, whatever that means."

"It means that Francine has fallen under the spell of our little island paradise," said Frank, rising from his chair. "And it means that I need to stretch and get a little exercise. I've been sitting and eating too much today. Anyone interested in a walk?"

"Why don't you two boys go? It would do you good. And I will see what magic I can do with that chicken I saw in your refrigerator, Leon. Now move along, both of you."

Agreeing to her suggestion, the two men were soon ambling down the street in the warm evening air, heading for the nearby yacht club, where Frank moored his boat. After recovering a book from his on-board library Frank suggested they stay a little longer and enjoy the view from the aft cockpit with a drink in their hands. "This way we will stay out of your mother's way and she will think we've been getting our exercise. It's a win all around."

It was quiet at the yacht club; most of the boats were away for the holiday weekend. But a stream of small boats and kayaks provided a constantly changing scene. After sitting silently for a time Leon surprised Frank by asking, "Are you and mother planning to marry?"

"Are we planning what?" said Frank, nearly choking on a mouthful of salted peanuts.

"Oh, I'm sorry. I do not mean to pry but I was just wondering if the two of you had any plans to..."

Regaining his composure Frank sipped his drink. "Does she want to get married?"

"Oh, I have no idea. I just thought, well, you two seem to enjoy each other so much that, well, I just thought the topic might have come up."

"What would you think of the idea?"

"I think it would be wonderful for mother; and I hope for you. She seems so happy when she is with you. But I am not trying to play cupid here or anything. I am just a verbally clumsy son."

"I don't believe that. I think you're a pretty good son and Simone is fortunate to have you. It's just that you pose an interesting question; one that I have asked her and myself on many occasions."

"And what conclusion have the two of you reached."

"We seem to come up with lots of good reasons why it is not a very good idea. Too far, too old, too stuck in our ways, too much family in too many places....You could probably add a couple ideas to the list too."

Leon smiled, watching Frank carefully. "That sounds like a 'why not' list. How about the 'why get married' list."

"It's short. We seem to love each other. That's all that's on it," he said with a little laugh.

"Hell Frank. Anita and I had the same lists to work with. But we gave the 'we love each other' more weight than the 'why not' list and are going to figure the rest out as we go." Leaning forward Leon looked hard at Frank and continued. "If you love each other do not let the 'why not' questions drag you down. You both deserve to be happy again."

The two men finished on the boat and retraced their steps to the house. Pausing before going up the front stairs Leon turned to Frank and said, "Forgive me if I was too bold on the boat. I am not trying to be a matchmaker or anything."

"No forgiveness is needed. You've given me some things to think about, and I thank you for that. Now let's see what your mother has done with that old chicken."

The morning sun was warm against his back as Frank, wearing his neatly pressed walking shorts for the first time that summer, climbed Leon's front steps. He was carrying a small bag of scones from his favorite coffee house in the market. It was a particular treat since the shop was one of the few businesses open on this holiday, the Fourth of July. Despite being a bit self conscious about his knobby white legs the forecast of unusually hot weather had been enough to encourage Frank to expose the world to the hairy view.

Following a light breakfast of scones and coffee Leon excused himself and left on a flower buying mission. "I want to fill her place with flowers," he said as he left.

Following Leon's departure Frank and Simone moved to the shade of the umbrella with their newly filled coffee mugs and settled down to talk.

And they talked until nearly noon, when Francine arrived home.

"Don't you two look comfortable?" Francine said as she swept onto the patio, giving each of them a warm embrace.

"Where's that...that other daughter of mine?" asked Frank.

"Anita? She escorted me here, so I wouldn't get lost, and then headed on to her place."

"I hope she doesn't miss Leon," said Simone, with a laugh. "He was headed over to her home with a bundle of flowers with which to secure the maiden's hand."

"I am sure she will appreciate it though I think the hand is already secure!"

Francine went on to tell them about the Whidbey Island discussions she had with Anita concluding with, "So I think she is just fine now. In a way I am glad we had the time together. Maybe we both needed that. And Frank, you and I haven't really spoken since you two broke the news and, I don't know how to say this but, I am so pleased you two found each other again. And I am glad you decided to share your story with me; with us."

Frank, with moist eyes, leaned to Francine, took her hands to his lips and kissed them lightly. "We've got a lot of time to make up now don't we?"

She nodded silently.

Anita fumbled with her keys before discovering her front door was unlocked. Great, she thought. I left in such a hurry I didn't even lock the damn door.

She pushed it open and gasped in shocked delight, "Oh my God Leon; you scared the whatever out of me."

Standing at the end of the short hall his beaming face was nearly hidden by a bouquet of red roses. "Welcome home," he said, through the blooms.

"Oh you dear, dear man," she cried, dropping her bag and running down the hall. Dodging the bouquet she threw her arms around his neck, nearly knocking him off balance. "I'm so glad you're here; there is so much I want to tell you."

Later, with the fresh flowers resting in a nearby crystal vase, they sat on the sofa facing one another like Victorian suitors while Anita told him of her time with Francine. "So, here I am," she concluded, "feeling a bit foolish about the way I reacted. Can you forgive me?"

"Well, I don't know," he answered with a sly grin. "Perhaps I should insist on penance."

"Oh, you're awful," she exclaimed, slapping him on the chest with both hands. "No penance but perhaps I will come up with a special treat for you."

"Now?" he asked, brightening.

"No, not now you lusty creature. You can just wait. Then you'll appreciate it more," she said, kissing him on the cheek before bounding from the sofa. "Now I need to find Dad. He's probably worried sick about his runaway daughter."

"I am sorry to tell you that I saw him this morning and he did not seem worried about you at all," he said, following her into the kitchen. "In fact he and Mother seemed quite content when I left them."

"Really? Well I'm worried about him. I'm afraid he's in for a big let down when she leaves. And this revelation about Francine must be upsetting."

"Sorry again; he doesn't seem upset about that either. Pleased might be a better way to describe him. In fact we had a nice talk yesterday on his boat and he seems to be taking everything very well. But I did sense he is in a little turmoil over what to do with Mother."

"What to do with her?" she echoed, boosting herself up on the counter to face Leon.

"Whether he should marry her, for instance."

"You two talked about Dad marrying Simone?"

"In a way," he replied, helping himself to a glass of orange juice from the refrigerator. "But he did not seem to reach any conclusion.

"You two must have had quite a talk. Well, I can't see my dad getting married. He's too stuck in his ways. I could see him doing a lot of traveling to Belgium but marriage…not likely."

"Perhaps you are right. After all, you know him much better than me. But he did not say no."

"But I suspect he thought 'no' whether he said it or not." Hopping down from the counter she continued, "Why don't I change and then we can go see the others."

"You are sure I cannot have my 'special treat' before we go?" he asked with a smile.

"Quite sure Romeo. Have some more juice. I'll only be a minute,"

"Fabulous dinner Frank. Really fabulous," said Leon as he carried the last of the dinner dishes into Frank's compact kitchen.

Anita looked up from the dishwasher. "Be careful with him Leon. You'll give him a big head. All he did was barbecue the steaks. Your mother did all the hard work."

"Why don't you forget the rest of these, Anita?" said Frank. "We don't get sunsets like this very often and, besides, I have a little surprise I want to bring out before the fireworks display begins."

Anita, acceding to her father's request, dried her hands and joined Francine, Simone and Leon on the balcony. "This is a wonderful place to watch the fireworks. They fire them off of that barge over there; we have the best view in Seattle."

The conversation was interrupted by the tinkle of champagne glasses on a silver tray. "A little bubbly for a special occasion," said Frank, setting the tray on the table.

"Is the Fourth of July the occasion?" asked Francine.

"No, it's more than that. It's, well...should I go on Simone?"

She gave Frank an embarrassed smile and silently mouthed "yes."

"I'm not sure what international protocol calls for so I'll just wing it," he went on, shuffling nervously from one leg to the other. "Well, Francine and Leon, I would like to ask for your mother's hand in marriage. I figure it would legitimize Francine and...."

"Oh Frank, stop that," said Simone, rising and putting her arm around his waist.

The three children bounded to their feet as one.

Anita stepped forward, laughing through a brief eruption of tears, and hugged them both while panting, "this is wonderful, oh so wonderful I just don't know what to say…."

Francine and Leon turned and high fived each other as if a bet had been won and then joined in a buoyant series of group hugs.

"This calls for a celebration," said Leon, reaching for the champagne and tearing at the foil.

As if on cue, the night sky erupted in a booming frenzy of red, white and blue fireworks that lit up the sky and masked the joyous cries from the little party on the twelfth floor balcony.

"I take your reaction as approval of our intentions," said Frank, as Leon filled the glasses.

"Absolutely," shouted Francine, over the din of the display. "If mother will have you, welcome to the family and may you have many happy years together."

"But where will you live; will you keep two homes? And what about your boat?" pondered Anita as Leon filled her glass.

Frank smiled, still standing with Simone. "Those are all 'why not' questions. We'll deal with them later."

"What's a 'why not' question?" she asked, brow furled.

"Ask your fiancé," he replied, with his voice nearly drowned out by a spectacular explosion of color and sound. "Ask Leon…."

THE END

Reading Group Questions and Topics for Discussion

1. What themes did the author emphasize throughout the novel? What do you believe the author was trying to get across to the reader?

2. Did the characters seem real and believable? Can you relate to their predicaments? Do they remind you of someone you know and, if so, in what ways?

3. How do the characters views evolve throughout the course of the story? What events trigger the changes?

4. Frank is reluctant to "love again" due to a fear of loss. How does his reaction to "loss" compare with others of his generation you have known?

5. Daughter Anita has trouble accepting that her father, Frank, could love anyone but her mother. How realistic is her reaction to the budding romance with Simone?

6. How does Frank's suppression of his wartime memories compare to veterans of his generation you have known?

7. How does Anita's view of Leon change from being "Francine's brother" to "someone special?"

8. If you were advising Frank or Simone what advice would you give them for managing a transatlantic relationship? Where should they live? How should they divide their time, etc?"

9. What do you believe accounts for the bond between Frank and Emory Rushing, the veteran who encourages him to attend the reunion?

10. If you were the casting director for a movie version of "Simone" who might you cast in Frank and Simone's roles? Why?

11. Which character do you most relate to and why?

Would you like to hear of other work by the same author? Simply send an e-mail to Simonereads@comcast.net

www.ingramcontent.com/pod-product-compliance
Lightning Source LLC
Chambersburg PA
CBHW020048180626
46812CB00006B/2237

* 9 7 8 0 6 1 5 4 4 0 7 7 4 *